KELLIE HAILES declared at the age of fi̶Ꞌꜟ̶Ꞌꜟ̶Ꞌꜟ̶Ꞌꜟ write books when she grew up. It took a w̶Ꞌꜟ̶Ꞌꜟ̶ ꞌꜟr her to get there, with a career as a radio copywriter, freelance copywriter and web writer filling the dream-hole, until now. Kellie lives on an island-that's-not-really-an-island in New Zealand with her patient husband, funny little human and neurotic cat. When the characters in her head aren't dictating their story to her, she can be found taking short walks, eating good cheese and jonesing for her next coffee fix.

Also by Kellie Hailes

The Cosy Coffee Shop of Promises
The Big Little Festival
Christmas at the Second Chance Chocolate Shop

The Little Unicorn Gift Shop

KELLIE HAILES

ONE PLACE. MANY STORIES

HQ
An imprint of HarperCollins*Publishers* Ltd
1 London Bridge Street
London SE1 9GF

This paperback edition 2018

First published in Great Britain by
HQ, an imprint of HarperCollins*Publishers* Ltd 2018

ISBN: 9780008310073

MIX
Paper from
responsible sources
FSC
www.fsc.org
FSC C007454

This book is produced from independently certified FSC™ paper
to ensure responsible forest management.

For more information visit: www.harpercollins.co.uk/green

Typeset by Palimpsest Book Production Ltd, Falkirk, Stirlingshire
Printed and bound in Great Britain by
CPI Group (UK) Ltd, Croydon, CR0 4YY

For 'The Manor Girls'.
Friends, forever.

Chapter 1

An ear-piercing trilling ripped Ben from the soundest sleep he'd had in weeks. His hand blindly scrambled round his bedside table, searching for his phone. Who could be calling at this time of night? He'd collapsed into bed just after midnight, so he knew it had to be late. He peeled open one eye. It was nowhere-near-dawn kind of late if the pitch-blackness in his room was anything to go by. Finding the phone, he squinted against the glare of the screen to see who would be so rude as to ring at such an ungodly hour.

His heart, already thumping from the shock of being yanked out of his sleep, ratcheted up to a worrying state.

Poppy.

Apprehension settled heavy in his stomach. If she was calling at this time of night it couldn't be for any good reason.

He peered at the screen. Not a phone call, a video call. Well, that ruled out her being in prison, at least. He was pretty sure they still only allowed voice calls.

He glanced at the time. Just gone three. Which made it the afternoon, maybe, if she was still in New Zealand. Though knowing Poppy, she could have tired of the place and moved on to South America, where no doubt she'd be in a jungle

1

hugging a tree in protest of it and its foliage-filled friends being cut down.

He swiped across and watched the internet decide whether it was going to connect him to her or not. A creased forehead and impatient stare gave him his answer.

'Ben? You there? Ben? Can you hear me?'

Ben clicked the sound down and reminded himself to mute his phone before he went to sleep from now on. 'I hear you, Poppy.' He stifled a yawn. 'Where are you? Are you okay? Are you in trouble? Do you need bail money?'

'Of course I'm okay.' Poppy rolled her eyes. 'I'm not a teenager, Ben. You don't have to keep me from getting into trouble anymore. Not that you could've if you wanted to. And bail money? Really? I've never been in that kind of trouble. God, dramatic much?'

'Fair enough. Sorry, Pops, but when I get a call in the middle of the night I fear the worst.' Ben folded his pillow in half and elbowed his way into a half-sitting position.

'Fine. Whatever. And turn on your light. It's weird talking to the black hole of Ben.'

'Sorry. Forgot you couldn't see me.' Ben switched the phone to his other hand, then leaned over and flicked on the bedside lamp. Its golden glow illuminated the small space around him.

'Geez, Ben, what've you been doing?' Poppy's hand covered her eyes, her fingers splitting apart to peek through at him. 'Do you even work these days? Or do you spend all your waking hours at the gym?'

'Huh?' Ben peered at the square on the phone to see what Poppy was seeing. 'Oh, God, sorry, Pops.' He pulled the sheet up to his armpits. 'There, all decent.'

Poppy's hand fell down, a wide grin lifting her cheekbones high as strands of her black hair blew in front of her face. 'Ugh, blimmin' wind. It's so cold I'm amazed my lips haven't frozen together. I'll be glad to come home to a bit of warmth.'

Ben straightened up in bed. Had he heard what he thought he'd heard? 'Come home? What are you on about?'

'Well, I've been travelling for over a decade now. It's time I returned. I mean, look at this place. It's freezing. My plane ticket's all booked.' She switched the phone's camera around and moved it slowly, showing him a snow-covered mountain range that sloped down to a tumultuous grey-green sea, its waves crashing onto a beach smothered in time-smoothed stones.

'It's beautiful,' Ben observed. 'And it gets freezing here too, remember?'

The camera switched back to Poppy. 'Yeah, but here is not home, and it's time.'

'And why are you telling me this, Poppy?' Ben yawned, not bothering to hide his tiredness. He had a busy day at the office ahead of him tying up loose ends, and he had to make sure his finances were in order for when he viewed the shop he hoped to lease in three days' time. 'More importantly, can you make it quick? It's beyond the middle of the night and I've got to get some sleep if I'm going to function like a human being tomorrow.'

'Fine, fine, Mr Busy Pants.' Poppy grinned. 'I just need you to do me a favour and pick me up from Heathrow. I'll send you through the details.' She flapped a hand in his direction. 'Now go back to sleep. Get some rest. I'll see you soon.' She blew a kiss and wiggled her fingers in goodbye, before signing off, leaving Ben staring at a Poppy-less screen.

Poppy Taylor was coming home.

An email alert popped up on his screen. He opened it and scanned the contents.

Not only was Poppy Taylor coming home, she was having him pick her up on the day he was meeting with his potential landlord. He worked out the time it would take to drive from Heathrow to Muswell Hill. He could do it. Just. Assuming traffic wasn't awful.

You could just say no…

He untucked his pillow and settled back into bed. As if no was an option. No was never an option where Poppy was concerned. Even after all these years.

Chapter 2

'Excuse me.' Poppy dodged and ducked her way through the throng of people squealing, hugging and, sometimes, crying into each other's arms as family, friends and lovers arrived from their various destinations. Every few seconds she went on tiptoe to search the crowd waiting at arrivals for a familiar face. Not just a familiar face, a friendly one. 'Where is he?' she wondered aloud, as she hefted her bulging backpack a little higher to stop the waist belt further cutting into her hips.

'Poppy?'

She spun round and found herself gazing into warm brown eyes. The very same pair that had greeted her when she'd poked her head through the hedge that had bordered their properties when they were four years old.

'Ben.' She wrapped her arms around him and pulled him into a hug. The muscles she'd briefly viewed during their video call were no figment of her imagination. Ben was *toned*. 'Now tell me…' She pulled back and squeezed his biceps. 'Where did these come from?'

Ben shrugged, a faint glow rising on his cheeks. 'I swim at the gym every morning. Then do weights if I feel like it.'

'All that on top of being a fancy pants lawyer?' Poppy threaded

5

her arm through Ben's and let him lead her through the crowds. 'Do you ever sleep?'

'I do. When I'm not being woken in the middle of the night.' He nudged her with his elbow. 'Now can we up the pace? I've got a business meeting I have to get to.'

'All work and no play makes Ben a—'

'Makes Ben a late boy. And I can't be. I'm opening a business. Well, I'm planning to. But I need to secure the premises first, and I think I've found the perfect spot.'

Poppy quickened her step as Ben pulled her through the busy airport, ducking out of the way of the dawdling travellers. 'Business? What kind of business? And how do you plan on running a business when you've a day job and apparently one hot bod to maintain?'

Ben's cheeks lost their blush as he propelled her to the carpark and towards a sleek, black Audi. 'This is me.' He opened the door for her, then strode to his side of the car and got in. 'And I won't be doing both jobs. I'm leaving law.'

'You say that like it's the end of the world.' Poppy ran her hands over the seat's buttery leather. Ben was leaving a job that had bought him *this* to set up a shop? And it sounded as though the thought of it was making him sick. Or perhaps it was the risk? Taking risks wasn't Ben's way. He'd always been the solid, dependable one. The one who made his parents proud... Ah. The green tinge to his skin suddenly made sense. Ben's father was a lawyer. Ben had done as expected and followed his father into law. Leaving it couldn't have been easy on Ben. And she'd have bet all of the worldly goods she owned, all that were tucked into the backpack Ben had placed into the boot of the car, that his father wouldn't be making his defection easy on him.

'Buckled up?' Ben started the engine and focused on the backup mirror's camera as he reversed out of the park.

Poppy relaxed into the seat and took a moment to inspect her old friend. Twelve years had changed him, and yet he was the same. Fine lines framing the outer corners of his eyes crinkled as he focused on the road. Time had seen the soft curves of his jawline and cheeks evaporate into sharp lengths. Yet, as always, his chin and cheeks were bare of stubble. Still, there was no denying Ben's boyish good looks were there, albeit more… manly. Stronger. Defined. The kind that probably had women's knees going a little – or a lot – wobbly when he walked past. Poppy patted her knees. Solid as two knobbly rocks. Ben may have been good to look at – better than good – but he was the serious, settling down type. And she wasn't. Which made her interest in Ben strictly platonic.

'Could you stop staring?' The corners of his lips lifted up into a smile. 'I feel like a bug under a microscope.'

Ben's eyes flicked in her direction, then refocused on the road. Yep, between that smile and those eyes, and the rest of the Ben-shaped package, Poppy suspected Ben had more than his share of admirers.

'Sorry, Ben the Bug, can't help it. It's been *ages*.' Poppy stretched her legs, and circled her neck backwards then forwards to release the tension of being cooped up in a metal bird for so many hours. 'You don't do social media so I can't stalk photos of you, and you haven't picked up a video call from me in longer than I can remember, so I feel like I'm seeing you for the first time in *forever*.'

'I didn't pick up your calls because you call during work hours.'

'I figured that, eventually. That's why I called in the middle of the night. I knew you'd have to answer.' Poppy unzipped her carry-on bag, found a tube of lip balm and applied it, smacking her lips together in satisfaction. She may have had years away from Ben, with minimal contact, but that didn't mean she didn't know him.

'I could have had my phone turned off. Or on silent.'

Poppy grinned at his churlish tone. 'Not the Ben I know. He's far too responsible. If your parents needed you, or if work was to have some kind of emergency, I knew you'd need to be on hand to deal with it.'

'Wow, you make me sound boring… and in need of a life.' A frown sent lines sprawling across Ben's forehead.

'Don't get all upset about it, Ben. I'm not saying you're boring, or in need of a life. I just knew you'd answer, that's all.' Poppy crossed her arms over her chest and tucked her hands into her armpits. Since when had Ben become so touchy?

'No, it's not you. It's the time. It's later than I thought. And this driver in front of me is going at a snail's pace.' The car surged forward as Ben stepped on the accelerator and manoeuvred into the next lane.

Poppy released her hands and gripped onto the edges of the seat. 'Steady on, Ben. No need to speed.'

'I'm not.' He flapped his hand at the speedometer. 'There's no way I'm going to get pulled over and make myself even later.' He ran his hand through his short, sandy brown hair. The same cut he'd always had. Shorter on the sides, with a little length up top. 'No, it'll be fine. It has to be.'

'Do you want me to call the landlord for you? Explain you'll be late?' Poppy held out her hand. 'My phone's dead. Give me yours.'

'No, not a good idea. That'll make me look like I'm unreliable. He might think I'll be late with payments. I was hoping to have time to pop home and grab a fresh shirt, but I'll just have to make do with the one I keep spare in the back. It's not the exact right shade to go with the tie or jacket, but it'll do. It'll have to.'

Poppy bit a laugh back, sensing that giggling at Ben's super-serious suit dilemma when he was this stressed would only inflame the situation.

'And you'll have to wait in the car before I drop you… wait, where am I dropping you?' Ben's eyebrow cocked as he glanced at her. 'You never said. Are you staying at your mum's house?'

Poppy's stomach shrivelled. She took a deep breath as the

unappetising meal of frittata and fruit salad they'd been served on the plane threatened to deboard. Stay with her mother? Not if she could help it. The plan was to keep her distance as long as possible. Why invite pain back into her life when she'd spent twelve years trying to keep it out? She waved the suggestion away. 'No, not Mum's. I've found a studio in Muswell Hill. And waiting is fine. I've nowhere to be. I'll just work on my plans while you have your meeting.'

'Plans? Since when has Poppy Taylor planned anything? You didn't even plan leaving to head off overseas. You just took off.'

There was no missing the bitter edge to Ben's words, but no way was Poppy going to explain why she left. Not to Ben of all people. The events that had led to her leaving were best left well alone.

'I'm not eighteen anymore, Ben. Believe it or not, I've become rather good at planning and organising. You have to when you're travelling. When you move around a lot. The thing is, you're not the only one who's planning on starting a business. I've one in mind, too. A gift shop, featuring all things unicorn. And I think Muswell Hill may well be the perfect place to set up shop.'

Ben's lips quirked, then mashed together, then quirked up again.

'What? You think I'm not serious? You don't think I can?' Poppy re-folded her arms, more to stop herself from punching Ben in the arm than to shield herself from his amused disbelief.

Ben's chest rose and fell, his lips straightened out. 'It's not that I don't think you can, I just didn't expect you to say that. I mean a business is a lot of work. You can't just flit in and out. You have to think ahead. You have to be serious. And, well, just how serious is a unicorn gift shop?'

'It's very serious. You wouldn't know. You've spent your working life with your head in textbooks and papers and whatnot. Your lack of online presence alone tells me you've no idea about the explosion of unicorn everything. People love them. Not just kids either. Teens. People in their twenties. Thirties. *Everyone*. There are webpages dedicated to them. My social media feeds are dotted with random snaps of them. They're huge. Which means my unicorn gift shop is going to draw crowds from all around, you'll see.' Poppy gave a definitive nod. Ben's reaction only added fuel to her plans. He thought she was the same old flighty, fun Poppy? Well, he was going to find out otherwise. 'Anyway, you never told me what business you were planning to open?' Poppy gazed out at the window, her heart picking up pace as she took in the streets whizzing past. As familiar to her as the back of her hand, these were streets she'd roamed day and night, her mother giving her more freedom than any child should ever have. Freedom, when what she'd really wanted was love. To feel loved. To feel wanted. The only person who'd made her feel that way sat opposite her. But that was a long time ago. Things had changed. *She* had changed.

'A gourmet tea shop.' Ben expertly parallel parked outside a row of houses around the corner from the shops. 'High-end teas sourced from around the globe. Delicious cakes. Slices. Biscuits.'

'And who'll be making these cakes and slices? You?' Poppy released her seatbelt and got out of the car. She lifted her arms in a long stretch, breathed in the sun-warmed air, and allowed herself a small smile as she took in the terraced homes, many fronted by perfectly clipped hedges perched atop matching brick fences. So different to the wooden one-storeyed Sixties-style bungalows and Eighties-built style-free square boxes that had lined the street she'd flatted in last.

The slam of the car door brought her attention back to Ben, who was expertly knotting his tie.

'Yes, me.' He scooped up a suit jacket and shrugged it on, then buttoned it up. 'I'll be doing the baking.'

'Really?' Poppy released the stretch, then leaned against the car. 'I know you were the king of Home Economics at school but baking at school is one thing – baking for business is another.'

'And you'd know this how?' Ben locked his car and started up the street.

'Am I coming with you?' Poppy trailed after him. 'I thought I was to stay with the car.'

'You can come for the walk if you want. I'd have thought you'd be tired of being stuck inside. Or you can stay here. Do what you want. I don't care.'

He could say he didn't care, but the squaring of his shoulders and the frostiness in his voice told her otherwise. *Stupid, Poppy.* She'd just pooh-poohed his business idea. Pooh-poohed him. It was one thing to listen to her horrid inner critic that always tried to make her second-guess her abilities, her worth, but she had no right to project that inner critic onto Ben. Not when she knew how determined and disciplined Ben could be. He could have taken night classes. Watched online tutorials. Done any number of things to learn how to bake for the masses, and she wouldn't know. Their steady stream of communication when she'd first left had turned into a trickle over the years as Ben had become busier. His emails shorter. To the point. And, eventually, she'd got the point, Ben didn't have time for her. Yet she'd still emailed on occasion, whenever she moved, just so someone at home knew where she was in case anything went wrong.

Poppy jogged a few steps to catch up with Ben. 'Sorry, I didn't mean to offend you. I'm an idiot. I should know better. Whenever you put your mind to something you make it work. More than that, you succeed. You always have. I bet you could enter a baking competition on the telly and win. Easily.'

'I bet I could too. And it's not like I stopped baking once I left school. It's been my stress relief for as long as I can remember. It also made me very popular at work when I brought in the previous night's goods.' Ben turned onto a bustling side street, dotted with shops that hadn't been there when she left. A generic chain-store coffee shop, a designer clothing store, a store selling cutesy baby gear. She spotted the charity store where she'd got

11

most of her wardrobe from as a youngster. Got? More like stolen. Hunching in the doorway in the middle of the night, rifling through bags left at the door, praying she wouldn't be caught, not wanting to admit to anyone that her mother was too busy with her art and friends and gregarious lifestyle to be bothered to think her daughter might need clothes. To be bothered to think, or care, about her daughter at all.

Give big anonymous donation to store. Poppy added the thought to the top of her mental 'to-do' list.

Next to the charity store stood an empty shop, a 'for lease' sign hanging in its window. Was the sign a sign? Was that the shop she could set up her business in? Lightness infused her heart, dispersing the dread she hadn't realised had been sitting dark and heavy. She'd take note of the number and call the shop's owner once she was settled in her new place.

Ben crossed the street then stopped in front of the shop. *Her* shop. No, surely not. He wasn't stealing her shop from underneath her, was he? Not that he knew it was her shop, but it had to be. She felt it deep down. The same way she'd known deep down that it was time to come home.

'How do I look?' He straightened his shoulders, ran his hand over his perfect-as-always hair and flashed her a winning smile.

'Perfect. Is the shop around the corner? On the main road?'

'No. It's this one, right here.' He angled his head towards the space. 'It suits my budget, and the street's busy, and close enough to the main street that people won't be put off making a small detour to visit.'

'You've thought it all out.' Of course he had. That's what Ben did. His life had been mapped out since he was young. He didn't do anything without careful thought. The opposite of herself. She'd figured she'd come home, find a flat, nab herself a space, place an order for a bunch of cute unicorn product and watch the customers and money roll in. She'd not even thought about budgets, other than to have enough money in the bank to start the business.

The squeak of the front door snapped her out of her darkening mood. 'Mr Evans? You're on time. Excellent. I like that. You didn't mention anything about bringing someone? No matter though. There's not much to see, just the main space, the kitchen behind, and there's a small office. But it's always good to have a second opinion. Come in. Come in. Lovely to meet you, dear, I'm Monty Gilbert. Call me Monty.'

'Actually, she was going to stay out—' Ben went to correct the bespectacled gentleman who'd greeted him, but stopped as he was hustled inside.

Poppy gave him a 'what can you do' shrug, trailed inside and then stepped to the right, giving Ben some space to chat to the landlord and giving herself a moment to view the shop that would have been hers if Ben hadn't seen it first.

It was beautiful. Perfect. Polished wooden floors gleamed under subtle downlights. One end of the shop was lined in redbrick, the other plastered and painted a barely-there cream. She could imagine white-painted shelves pushed up against it, filled with unicorn stationery – holographic pens, unicorn stickers, writing sets. Mugs from bombastic and brilliant to sweet and subtle. Stuffed unicorn toys could take pride of place in the corner, and a range of unicorn-printed clothing could hang from a rack by the far wall.

She glanced over at Ben and saw his eyes brighten as he took in the brick wall. She knew what he was seeing. She could see it too. Wooden shelving stained the colour of long-steeped black tea would be perfect against that red and would look marvellous holding tea-sets and tins of tea. And the ornate timber counter could easily be stained the same colour and would provide a striking centrepiece for the shop. It was the perfect space for his venture.

'I must apologise, I was a little misleading in my advertisement.' Monty shoved his hands in his brown corduroy pant pockets and rocked back and forth on his feet. 'You see my son told me I was asking too little rent for this space. I haven't had to rent it out in years, you see. The only reason I'm renting it now is because the previous tenant passed, may she rest in peace, and I thought a little hike in the lease was fine. Turns out I was going to be doing myself no favours…'

'Oh.' Ben's face stilled. His eyes narrowed. Was that panic flashing through them? Or had Poppy imagined it? 'What kind of rent are you looking for?'

Monty paused, then uttered a number.

The colour drained from Ben's face. 'That's twice what you were asking in the advertisement.'

'I know, and I'm sorry if I've wasted your time.' Monty looked up as the door opened and two gangly teens walked in. A boy and a girl, both the same height, with hair the identical shade of auburn.

Fraternal twins, Poppy guessed.

'Sophie, Joseph. Didn't I tell you to wait outside if you saw I was with people?' Monty folded his arms and fixed the twins with an irritated stare.

'Sorry, Grandad. Forgot.' The girl, Sophie, shrugged, then held up her hand and began inspecting her nails.

Monty's chest rose and fell as a huff of irritation filled the room. 'I'm so sorry for the intrusion, Mr Evans. Would you mind giving me a minute while I sort these two out, then send them on their way?' His palms flipped up in a silent apology, before turning his attention to the twins. 'So, how did the job search go?' Monty's pitch heightened with hope.

'Nowhere.' Sophie leaned against the counter, her petite nose wrinkling. 'The job search went nowhere, right, Joe?'

Her brother nodded, his eyes fixed on the floorboards. 'Nobody wants us.'

'And we tried, Grandad, we really did.' Sophie pulled out her phone and buried her nose in it.

Poppy grinned. Sure they'd tried. That explained the splodge of what looked like chocolate ice cream on Joseph's shirt. And the leaf attached to the bottom of Sophie's shoe. Grabbing ice cream and going for a walk through Queen's Wood was hardly what she'd call a job search.

'Well, you'll have to try again tomorrow.' Monty shook his head. 'I can't have you two underfoot all holidays. And I promised your parents we'd keep you busy, keep you out of mischief, until you decided what you wanted to do with your lives.'

An idea swirled in the back of Poppy's mind. She may have found a way to launch both businesses, while getting onside of the landlord, who – if the look of despair on his face was anything to go by – had two charges on his hands that were going to drive him crazy if they weren't kept busy.

'How much did you say the rent was again?' She made her way to stand beside Ben, hoping he'd go along with her idea. Provide a united front.

Monty repeated the price.

'Would you consider shaving ten per cent off that, in exchange for hiring these two?' She nodded at Sophie and Joe, whose mouths formed identical o's, their aquamarine eyes widening in horror. Poppy suppressed a smile. 'Because we're going to need some help, Ben and I, if we're going to open our shops in this space in couple of weeks' time.'

'Our shops?' Ben shot Poppy a quizzical look.

'Sparkle & Steep. That's the name we agreed on, right?' She raised her eyebrows, praying that Ben wouldn't work against her.

'Sparkle & Steep. Yes, that's right.' Ben nodded, his face free from emotion.

A bit shell-shocked, Poppy guessed. 'You see, Monty, we are going to open a gourmet tea shop, and London's most fabulous unicorn gift shop.' She turned to her new employees. 'Now, Sophie, Joe, I may as well be upfront about this. We can't afford to pay

15

much, I'm sorry, but being new and all there's just not the money there for more than the living wage.'

'That's fine,' Monty interrupted. 'These two need work, and you're offering it. It'll keep them out of my hair, and keep them out of trouble. I've got the papers all drawn up out back. Take a look at them, and if all is in order, the shop's yours. But the sooner you decide the better, I've another interested party keen to take a look. They should be here any minute, actually.' Not waiting for an answer Monty turned and made his way through the door to the back room, leaving the two teens to huddle up in a murmur of mutters.

Ben pulled Poppy to the furthest corner. 'What are you doing?' he hissed. 'Opening a store with me? That wasn't the plan. And why'd you go and throw the twins into the deal? They clearly don't want to work.'

'First of all, you had your budget and this was out of it. I, too, have a budget.' Poppy crossed her fingers behind her back. 'And our budgets combined will make this work. Also, you'll need help. And I'll need help. And it's clear to me that Monty is being driven round the bend by those two being under his feet. It all makes sense. I'd go so far as to say it's meant to be.' Poppy flashed Ben a thumbs up, along with an encouraging nod.

Monty returned in a rustle of paper and a hustle of feet. 'Here you go. Here are the papers. Look over them. It's all above board, but I want you to be happy.'

Poppy thrust her hand in Monty's direction, and ignored Ben's choke-cough. 'No need for that. I trust you. We trust you. Consider us your new tenants.'

Chapter 3

Ben ran his eyes over the documents before him. Poppy may have been willing to sign away her life without checking things out first, but there was no way he was about to. Still, they looked fine to his professional eye. Everything was in order as Monty had said. But what was not in order, in fact what was highly *out* of order, was Poppy springing this on him without even considering his thoughts, his feelings.

Sharing a space with her? Not just a space, but a business space? This wasn't like sharing a fake rock-pet as they had when they were young and neither set of parents had allowed them to own a puppy or kitten. This was their lives. Their livelihoods. And if the fate of the rock-pet was anything to go by, going into business with Poppy was not a good idea. She'd lost the darn thing between school and home three days into their deal to share it.

'Didn't see that coming, did ya?' The girl – Sophie – nudged him with her elbow. 'I've never seen someone look so green in my life. Do you need a bucket?'

'Sophie, don't be rude. That's our boss you're talking to.' Her brother pulled Sophie away and gave Ben some breathing space.

Breathing space? He'd need more than the air in the shop to

breathe after everything Poppy had just flung at him. He'd need a small country's worth of air. Speaking of Poppy, where had she gone? 'Poppy?'

'I'm out the back. With you in a sec.'

The light tip-tap of excitable feet greeted him, followed by Poppy, her green eyes sparkling with excitement.

'This place is perfect. The kitchen's great. You'll love it. The office is a little small, but I'm sure we can take turns in there to have our cups of tea when we're on break, or eat our lunch, or whatever. Or we could squeeze in together if you don't mind getting cuddly with me. The toilet could do with a scrub, but I think we can get Joe or Sophie to do that. Whoever's annoying us most at any given time.'

'We heard that,' Sophie sniped over her shoulder, before turning back to her brother, who had his eyes glued on his phone, his fingers tapping away furiously.

'You were meant to.' Poppy's smile didn't falter. 'It's my not-so-subtle way of telling you not to annoy us. And to do that you need to do as you're told, when you're told, and to not walk around with that grimace on your face. You'll scare off the customers.' Ignoring the grunt from Sophie's direction, Poppy focused on Ben. 'So, Ben, have you signed the papers? Does it look good? Are you happy with everything? Do you think we could have this place up and running in a week or two?'

Ben set the papers down, closed his eyes and took a breath. This was too much, too fast. This was pure Poppy. All go, no slow. 'Poppy.' He opened his eyes and took her by the shoulders. 'I'm not sure about this. You and me, running a business in the same room? It's a recipe for disaster.'

'Piffle.' Poppy shook her head, sending her signature black braid swinging. 'We used to make a great team. Aced all the school projects we did together. And sure, we got into a little trouble here and there...'

'Because of you,' Ben asserted, hoping to remind her that her past follies hadn't been forgotten. Even if they had quickly been forgiven.

'Yes, well, I was younger. Now I'm not. Look, I've got the money.' She pulled out her phone and began swiping furiously. 'I have an app that I can show you. I've been saving every penny I can for a couple of years now.' She went to lift her phone, but Ben held up his hand, stopping her.

'It's not that I don't think you have the money. You could get the money in a second, even if you didn't. Your mother, your family, isn't exactly poor…'

Poppy's smile disappeared, the line of her jaw sharpened. Ben inwardly cursed himself. Poppy's mother may have been a successful artist, and the family she came from may have been well off, but that didn't mean Poppy was a pampered princess who was given everything her heart desired. His home had shared a wall with Poppy's, and he'd heard the raised voices when she and her mother had argued, followed by the door slamming.

What had gone on at the Taylor household to cause so much friction, he had no idea; Poppy and her often red-rimmed eyes had refused to speak of it, but he knew enough to know that the relationship she had with her mother wasn't the kind where you asked for money. Or, come to think of it, where you'd turn up on the doorstep after twelve years away expecting your old room back.

And maybe that meant he needed to put his misgivings on pause, to trust Poppy. For all her youthful transgressions she'd come home with a plan, with money to execute that plan, and she'd been the one to find a way to reduce the rent on the space, while hiring two helping hands who she had managed to wrangle into submission with just a few words and the lightest of warnings.

'The thing is, Poppy, what do you know about running a business? It's a big ask to expect me to just leap into this with you. There's a lot of risk involved…'

19

'And I know how much you hate taking risks, which is why I'm not making you take any. Like I said, I have the money. And while I've never owned a business I've worked in plenty. I've even been put in charge of a couple. Look, Ben. I'm offering a solution. The rent's lower. We've got two people over there who, despite their surly and disinterested demeanours, I think could actually be quite helpful. More importantly, we've got each other. We can make anything work.' Poppy took his hands in hers and gave them a shake. 'Come on. Trust me. But trust me quick. Look outside.'

Ben twisted round to see a couple hanging around the shop's front window, their noses all but pressed to the window.

'Monty said it was ours, but if they're willing to pay the full amount...' Poppy let the sentence hang, her eyebrows raised.

Damn it. She was right. And he wanted this place. Had done since he saw the advertisement. The exposed bricks, the polished floorboards, the simple but chic décor. It was perfect for a gourmet tea shop. 'Fine. Pass me the pen.' He took in a deep breath as he scrawled his name, and prayed he wasn't making a mistake.

'Fantastic.' Poppy scooped the papers up from under him. 'Monty. We're all signed up.' She passed the papers to their new landlord then half-danced, half-skipped her way to the front door, opened it and flapped her hands at the would-be tenants. 'Sorry, shop's gone. Good luck with your search. Have a fab day.' She twisted round and rubbed her hands together. 'Right. What are we waiting for? We've got two shops to open. Sophie? Joe? Consider this your last day of freedom. Be here tomorrow morning at nine sharp.' Poppy turned her attention back to Ben. 'As for you and I, let's get the keys and you can take me to my new abode, and we'll nut things out there over a bottle of something yummy. My treat.'

***

20

'Well, this wasn't what I expected.' Ben did a slow three-sixty as he took in Poppy's new home, tucked away on the top floor of a terraced house that had been converted into flats. The open-plan living and dining area was on the small side, with just enough room for the two-seater couch, coffee table and dining suite. Through an open door he spotted a bed, and another door, which presumably led to the en-suite. Despite its cosiness, it was surprisingly elegant, with white-washed wooden floors throughout, walls painted in a soft grey, and the architraves and skirtings in a fresh white. 'It must be a relief that you were able to rent it furnished.' Ben ran his hand over the cream knotted throw that lay over the soft chestnut-coloured leather couch.

'Yeah, well, I knew I wanted to hit the ground running when I arrived, so it just made sense to find a place that was all set up for me.' Poppy grabbed the bottle of sauvignon blanc she'd picked up on their way home and cracked the lid. 'Screw tops. How did we ever live without them?'

'My father calls them the work of the devil.' Ben rolled his eyes towards the ceiling and shook his head.

Poppy's laughter filled the space, light and free. 'Why does that not surprise me?' She sloshed the wine into two glasses and passed one to Ben. 'So, what made you do such a U-turn? Upping and leaving a safe, secure job in order to start your own business venture? That's not the Ben I grew up with. And, how *is* your father taking it?'

Ben swirled the wine round, creating a miniature maelstrom. He inwardly grimaced; it was the perfect symbol for the current state of his life. 'He's taking it as well as you'd expect. Dad can't get his head around me wanting something other than what he wants for me, if that makes sense. All these years and we've shared the law. Bonded over it. Now… I'm doing what makes me happy. Pursuing a career that fills me with joy in here…' He tapped his heart. 'A career that excites me. I think Dad sees that as a betrayal. Hell, I know he does.' He took a sip of wine, hoping to wash away the grief that had created a knot in his throat. 'We're not really talking right now. Mum's trying to mediate, but…'

'She's wasting her time?' Poppy moved to the small dining table and pushed aside the curtains, allowing the late afternoon light to spill into the room.

'Something like that.' Ben pulled out the chair opposite Poppy, sat down and closed his eyes against the sun, glad for the moment to rest, relax… and try and figure out what the hell he'd just gotten himself into.

'"Why did I agree to this?" That's what you're thinking, isn't it?'

Ben opened his eyes to see the tip of Poppy's tongue peeking out between her lips, a teasing smile lifting her lips.

'I'm not going to screw this up, Ben. I promise. Sparkle & Steep is going to be amazing.' Poppy took a sip of her wine and set the glass down. 'It'll be as brilliant as this view. Look at the view, Ben. Isn't it brilliant?'

Ben turned to the window and saw a length of London sprawling before him, the cityscape rising tall and proud into a bright blue sky. 'You're right, it's brilliant. God, I can't believe you managed to find this place while living on the other side of the world.'

'I'm lucky like that.' Poppy grinned, her fingers rhythmically drumming on the table. 'I'm also lucky to have you. You could have said no to me coming into the shop with you. You could have told me to stay in the car back there. You could have flat out refused to entertain the idea of going into business with me. But you didn't. So, thank you.'

'You're not going to make me regret it, are you?' Ben laid his hand over Poppy's, stopping the incessant drumming.

'No. I'm not. We're going to prove your father wrong. More than that, we're going to make him proud.' Poppy lifted her glass. 'To us. To Sparkle & Steep.'

Ben raised his glass to meet hers, then took a sip as was tradition. Making his father proud. Poppy made it seem so easy. So simple. But how did you make a man proud when you'd walked away from a profession that, for the men in his family, being part of was every bit a tradition as sipping your drink after proposing a toast?

'Stop stewing, Ben.' Poppy sprung up, crossed the room to where she'd dumped her backpack, then unclipped and rifled through it, sending a tattered lump of greyness, with a faded rainbow mane, falling to the floor.

Mr Flumpkins? Surely not? Had Poppy really carried the unicorn she'd found in Alexandra Park and – after being unable to find its owner – decided to adopt, around the world with her? She must've had him for twenty odd years by now.

'Am I seeing things? Is that… Mr Flumpkins?'

Poppy hugged the soft toy to her chest. 'It is. In the cosy, cuddly fluffy-ish flesh.'

Ben held his hand out, and Poppy passed the toy to him. 'I can't believe he's still in one piece.'

'Barely.' Poppy continued rummaging through her bag. 'He nearly lost his ear in an airport escalator a couple of years back. Fell out of my backpack, nearly got chomped, poor wee soul. Luckily a young girl snatched him up and gave him back before it was too late.'

'I'm surprised she didn't keep him for herself.'

'Hardly. She told me I needed to chuck him and get myself a newer, prettier one. She liked the ice cream I bought her to say thanks well enough though. Ah, here's what I'm looking for.' She pulled out a shining, shimmering notebook, a pen threaded through its ringed spine. 'We need to plan how we're going to do this thing.'

Ben placed Mr Flumpkins on the windowsill and straightened up. Yes, a plan was needed. Big time. With a plan in place he'd feel less like he'd been shoved into a whirlwind and spat out again.

'So…' Poppy slid into the chair, opened the notebook and wrote the name she'd proposed at the top of a blank page. 'I was thinking we could have multi-coloured chairs scattered around multi-coloured tables. Industrial style metal ones. They'll look amazing. Also, unicorn-headed teaspoons. Oh, and I could get some of those cushions that are covered in sequins that can be brushed two ways to create different patterns so that the chairs are nice and comfy for those who want to sit and natter.' She reached over and grabbed her mobile from its spot on the kitchen bench. 'Find out where to get reversible sequin cushions,' she said aloud as she typed the reminder into her phone. She set the phone down with a satisfied nod. 'I'd sell them as well, of course. They're fabulous.'

Ben blinked, trying to comprehend what he was hearing. So much for being spat out of the whirlwind. What was Poppy on about? Multi-coloured this and that? Sparkly cushions? That wasn't the plan. That wasn't gourmet. It sounded like… a unicorn had eaten too many sweets and thrown up all over the place.

'Nooooo. No. Uh-uh. This won't do. This isn't going to work.' He pushed the chair back, and began to pace the width of the room, trying to get his thoughts in order.

'What do you mean it won't work? It has to. We've signed the lease. We've committed.' Poppy tapped the end of the pen on the notebook. 'I've seen some unicorn-themed clothing that I was planning to sell, but maybe we could find tea lovers' apparel too? Cake lovers' apparel? There must be some out there we could import, or we could create our own?'

Ben's stomach swirled. Tea and cake-loving apparel? Where was the sophistication? The class? This wasn't what he had in mind, not by a long shot. It was like Poppy thought that by sharing a space with him they were joining forces, going into business together. An inseparable team. Just like the old days. But this wasn't the old days. They'd been separated for years now. Gone down different paths. And, if he were one hundred per cent

24

honest with himself, while it was one thing to share a lease, he didn't want to share his shop. Not with someone who could so easily pack up and pick up in the middle of the night without saying a word.

Fear froze his frenetic pacing. And what if she did that anyway? Even if their shops were separate, he'd be left with one surly teen, one disengaged one, and half a shop's worth of lease.

Ben swallowed hard, pushing the lump that was threatening to choke him, to drown his dreams, out of the way. 'Poppy. Ground rules. We need to set some.'

'Ground rules?' Poppy's head angled, her brows drawing together. 'What kind?'

'First of all. You are not to leave in the middle of the night without warning.'

Poppy huffed and rolled her eyes. 'I did it once. Years ago. I'm a grown woman, I'm not going to do that again. I wouldn't do it to you. There's too much riding on this. I get that.'

'Which leads me to the next rule. We have to keep our businesses separate. We can share a space, share the lease, but under no circumstances is any of your… paraphernalia to enter my side of the shop. "Steep" is not to look like a fairy chundered in it. There will be no glitter. No sparkle. No tackiness. No unicorns. My side of the shop—' he placed his hand on his chest to emphasise the point '—is to be a place of refinement. Where people who appreciate good tea will come and discover new flavours and broaden their tea horizons, all while enjoying delicious morsels.'

Poppy rolled her eyes. 'How did you and I ever end up friends? You're such a stick in the mud. And who says "morsels" anymore? Food, Ben. They'll be coming to eat your food.' Poppy placed her hands on her hips. 'Honestly, I can't believe you're so anti-unicorn. I knew I should've set up a cat-themed shop instead. Cat cafes are big business. I went to one in New Zealand and there was something so centring about having a cat purring on your lap

25

while you were sipping a flat white. Although when one decided my braid was a plaything that wasn't so fun. Who knew getting a kitten out of your hair could be so difficult?' Poppy's braid swayed as she shook her head. 'We could do it, you know. Adopt some cats and kittens. A gourmet tea shop with kittens running amuck sounds pretty fab.'

Ben forced himself not to rise to the bait. Poppy had always known how to press his buttons – had been amused by how he toed the line compared to her freedom-loving ways. She, more than anyone, knew he wouldn't have time for the frivolity of kittens and cats skittering through a store, let alone time for cleaning up after them and maintaining their health.

'What? You're not going to tell me I'm being ridiculous?' Poppy laughed, the sound brightening the room, as it had always done. 'I was expecting you to give me that look of derision that I bet had people quailing in court.'

'I wasn't in court, Poppy. You know I worked in property law.' Ben sat back down and took a long drink of his wine.

'Well, you could have been. You could have changed directions, for all I knew. It's not like you've bothered replying to the emails I've sent in the past year or so. Not with any news of substance. "I'm fine" does not an email make.' Poppy crossed her arms and tucked her hands in her armpits.

Guilt swarmed in Ben's gut. That was Poppy's signature move when she was hurt, sad, upset or wanting to shut someone out. And he'd been the cause of it. 'I'm sorry I didn't reply all that much, or all that well. Life got busy. You know how things are. Or maybe you don't… I don't know.'

'Of course you don't know. You didn't ask. Even when we were emailing on a sort-of regular basis you never asked questions about my life.' Poppy sunk her top teeth into her bottom lip, then released them. 'You probably thought my life was one great adventure. Swanning from country to country. Chasing summer. Sunbathing. Swimming. Being frivolous and free while you spent hours poring over papers and whatnot. The thing is, I worked, Ben. The whole time. Yes, I saw sights. Yes, I had a good time. But I also worked my arse off. It wasn't one long holiday.' Poppy's jaw jutted out, just as it always did when she was holding back – trying to keep her emotions in check, trying to be brave. 'Just because I choose to smile instead of scowl, choose to laugh instead of lift my lip and sneer at the world, it doesn't mean I don't have a serious bone in my body. It doesn't mean that I don't *care*.' Poppy untucked her arms, lifted her chin, and took a deep breath in. 'Whatever. It doesn't matter. I'm being an idiot. So, back to business…' She picked up her pen, lowered her gaze to the page so he couldn't see how she was feeling, and scrawled two short sentences.

'No combining space. No combining anything.'

Poppy set the pen down on the paper with a slap. And just like that, Ben was a boy again, and the urge to make Poppy feel better was there. The need to reach out and run his hand down her braided rope of ebony hair. To hold her close. To tell her she was wonderful. She was enough. That despite whatever complicated things were happening in her life, in her head, that they could deal with it together. If she just let him in.

Except she wouldn't. He was an idiot to think her time away travelling would have changed that. Changed *her*.

'I know you didn't just sunbathe your way round the world. Sorry. I didn't mean to upset you.'

Poppy waved his apology away. 'I'm fine. Really.' She looked up, a smile fixed on her face. One that didn't chase away the shadows in her eyes. 'If anything, I'm kicking myself. I should have expected this to happen. You've always been so paint by numbers. Knowing what you wanted, why you wanted it, and how you were going to get there. You're the most organised person I know. Heck, I bet even your underwear drawer is colour-coded. Light to dark, from left to right. Or is it alphabetised by brand? Or arranged by occasion? Your day-to-day underwear would be at the top, followed by church underwear, because you'd be too respectful to wear anything threadbare or holey to church.'

'I haven't been to church since I moved out of home. I just went because it made Mum happy.'

'But I bet you still go to St James' every Christmas and Easter.' Poppy raised an eyebrow, daring him to deny it.

'I do. With Mum.' Ben nodded, not seeing any point in lying. 'But I don't have special church underwear.'

'But I bet you've got dating underwear. The good stuff. Fits perfectly. Manly colours. Navy blue. Black. No tacky patterns. Although I did see some unicorn boxers that I could order for you if you wanted to shake things up...'

Ben waved Poppy's suggestion away. 'Not in a million years will I wear unicorn boxers. Or unicorn anything. And frankly, Poppy, I'm starting to think you're far too interested in the contents of my underwear.' Ben bit down on his tongue. What had he just said? He surely didn't say 'contents of my under-wear'.

He glanced at Poppy who was doubled over, elbows on knees, her shoulders shaking as airy gasps filled the space between them.

'I mean... not my underwear... my contents... er, I mean my drawers. I know you wouldn't be interested in the contents of my...' *Shut up, Ben.* God, what was going on with him? Usually he was calm, collected, in control of what came out of his mouth. But being in the same room as Poppy meant the words flew off his tongue as quickly as they came into his head. It was the Poppy-effect in full flight. Her presence had always left him a little unsteady. Off kilter. Hell, he never put a foot wrong when he was left to his own devices, but whenever she entered his sphere, since the day they met, he'd found himself in all sorts of harmless trouble. Nipping over to his neighbour's house to relieve their tree of apples. Getting tipsy on cider Poppy had stolen from her mother's fridge when they were fifteen. He'd been so ill the next day his parents had taken pity on him and decided the hangover was punishment enough. Life with Poppy was more interesting, but it also meant there was a huge chance things could go askew.

She could promise things were going to go smoothly all she wanted, but he only had the past to go by, and that made him nervous.

'Oh God, you're hilarious. You and your rules.' Poppy straightened up and smoothed back the tendrils of hair that that had come loose from her braid to frame her face. 'You were always one for them, but gosh, look at you now. So serious. So earnest. So much more… rule-y. What happened, Ben? You used to know how to have a bit of fun, but now…' Poppy's gaze started at his perfectly shone shoes, before she worked her way up to his suit pants, his suit jacket, lingered on the tie, then finished on his cut-just-that-day hair. 'Now you're all about looking perfect, and making everything perfect, and *being* perfect. What's wrong with a little sparkle and shimmer and shine? What's wrong with unicorns? They make people happy. They make people smile. Do you not want to be happy and smiley, Ben?'

Did he not want to be happy? Of course he did. But right now he had too much riding on the success of Steep. If he didn't do well, if leaving his practice had been a mistake, he'd have to deal with the disapproval of his father for… well, probably ever. 'Look, Poppy, I just want to make sure my business succeeds. And for that to happen "Steep" needs to be taken seriously, and unicorns don't exactly project that mentality. It's one thing to go halves in this space, but there needs to be separation. No sharing, no boundary crossing, you understand? "Sparkle" can shimmer and shine all it likes, but "Steep" needs to be as solid and dependable as a good cup of tea.'

Poppy rolled her eyes so hard Ben feared they were going to pop out of their sockets. 'Fine. I understand. I'll stick to your stupid rule, but I've got one rule you need to abide by.'

'Really?' Ben mashed his lips together to stop a smirk appearing.

Poppy, the ultimate disregarder of rules, was going to set one? 'What's your rule?'

'My rule is this – if you so much as look at one of my customers like they're mad for loving unicorns, if you so much as make a snide remark, if I see a hint of side-eye when a man comes in and buys the unicorn underpants I plan on selling, then I'm out. I'll give you plenty of time to find a person to take over my side of the space. Or enough time for you to see your bank manager, or whoever, and sort out your expanding into my side of the shop, but I won't stick around. You take Steep seriously? Well, I take Sparkle every bit as seriously. My life savings are going into this, and I don't have assets I can sell or people I can ask to help me should things falter. Which, they won't.'

Ben nodded. 'You're right, they won't. Because as much as I'm sure I could fill the space or figure out some alternative arrangement, I have neither the time nor the inclination. So, I guess that means I agree to your ridiculous rule.'

'Good.' Poppy held out her hand for Ben to shake and caught the edge of her wine glass, knocking it over, which saw it domino into his wine glass, sending a stream of wine over the table and onto the floor.

Please don't be a sign. Ben shook his head in despair. *Please don't let it mean that 'Sparkle & Steep' is destined to become 'Debacle & Weep'.*

Chapter 4

Poppy clapped her hands, the sound bouncing off the bare walls. 'Righto, you lot. Welcome to the first day of the rest of your lives. A grand day no less. A day that will go down in history as being the start of two of the most fabulous businesses London has ever seen.' Poppy paused, and waited for a cheer of encouragement, or at the very least a grunt to show that she'd been heard. None came.

She'd successfully managed as a nanny to six-year-old triplets, you'd think she could hold the attention of two eighteen-year-olds, but no. Sophie was inspecting her nails. Joe had his eyes on that damn phone of his. And her business partner was clomp-clomp-clomping back and forth in the kitchen, muttering into his phone. Pausing every now and then to flick her the thumbs up. Why? She had no idea. But if it meant things were moving forward at a rapid pace she was happy for him to leave the teen wrangling to her.

'Joe? Are you listening to anything that's coming out of my mouth?'

No answer came. Right, then. Drastic measures were called for.

Stomping over to where he stood, Poppy plucked the phone

out from his palm and marched it to the kitchen. Turning on the tap she threatened to douse it in water. 'Don't think I won't,' she warned. 'We're not paying you to spend hours looking at mindless gaming videos, or… half-naked women… or whatever it is that has so captured your imagination.'

'Unicorns.' Joe folded his arms across his chest and popped his hip out. 'I was looking up unicorn suppliers with quick delivery times. I get the feeling you want things up and running soon as possible.'

Poppy glanced at the screen to see a wall of unicorn giftware. 'Oh, I see. And how long do these sites you've found take?' Poppy returned the phone to Joe. 'And what's the pricing like?'

Sophie shook her head. A disgusted puff of air escaping her lips. 'Are you telling us you haven't even sorted that out yet? Have you thought about storage? And getting things through customs?'

'I'm not daft, you know. Of course I've got that worked out.' *Kind of.* Poppy had known she'd have to figure that stuff out, she just hadn't expected for things to race ahead at breakneck speed – but there was no way she was letting Sophie know that. If they got a hint she was flying by the seat of her pants, they'd try and take advantage. 'But, it's good to have fresh stock, different stock, and I really appreciate that you've taken an interest in my business, Joe. Nice work.' She slapped Joe on the back, then motioned to Ben to hang up the phone as soon as he could. 'Speaking of space. We need to decide who gets what.'

With a quick goodbye Ben shoved his phone in the back pocket of his navy pants and leaned against the door. 'I was hoping…'

'To have the side with the bricks? I agree. It will suit your vision.' Poppy fisted her hands and placed them on her hips. 'I'm happy with the other side. It's lighter, brighter. And I was thinking I'd get some holographic tinsel and drape it down the windows on my side of the shop.'

'Coooooooool,' breathed Joe.

'Oh, God. No.' Sophie gagged.

'I'm with Sophie.' Ben shook his head so quickly Poppy wondered if he would sprain his neck.

'What's wrong with that? It's my side of the shop, isn't it? I can do what I want, can't I?' Poppy tucked her tongue into her cheek.

'Poppy. No. I forbid it.' Ben placed his hands on his hips, mirroring hers, his face growing pink. Then red. Then almost purple. 'It will look beyond tacky. What will people think of the shop? Of my shop?'

'They'll think it's a fun place to visit. That *our* shop is a warm, welcoming, engaging, and just a little bit magical, place to spend time in.' Poppy reached for her braid and stroked it.

'She's having you on,' Sophie said flatly. 'Honestly, Ben, can't you see that? You'd think you'd know when your girlfriend was having you on.'

Ben's eyes went from Poppy's straight face, to her hand on her braid. 'Damn it, you're right. Her hand is on her braid. That's what she does when she's telling a white lie. And she's not my girlfriend.'

'Really?' Sophie's bottom lip slackened with surprise. 'I totally thought you were. You're kind of cute together. Like an old married couple.'

The colour in Ben's face had beaten a retreat from its purple shade, but still held a blush. 'Well, we're not. We've just known each other forever. Right, Poppy?'

'Right.' Poppy dragged her hand away from her braid. 'Just friends. That's all. And since you outed my joke, Sophie, you can work for Ben. I get the feeling you two will get along well. Joe, are you cool to work for me?'

'Cool.' Joe shoved his hands in his jean pockets with a nod. 'Do I get a staff discount?'

'Sure do. More than that, you can have whatever takes your fancy at cost.'

'Awesome.' Joe nodded his approval, then picked up the bucket of cleaning supplies Poppy had brought with her. 'In that case, I'll get onto it.'

Poppy flashed him a thumbs up, then turned to Ben. 'That means Sophie's yours.'

'Good.' Sophie nodded her approval. 'I like tea. I can bake a bit. And I'm all class.'

'And all ego,' Joe muttered as he walked past them towards the kitchen.

'Whatever.' Sophie elbowed her brother.

'Well, now that's sorted…' Ben took in the space that was to be his. 'I'm going to stain that counter a dark brown and find shelving that can go up against the brick wall and stain it the same colour. How are you with a paint brush, Sophie?'

Sophie held her hands up, showing off her intricately designed nail polish. 'Steadiest hands you've ever met.'

'Excellent.' Ben held his hand up for a high-five, which Sophie ignored with a shrivel of her nose.

'Here, I've got you.' Poppy's palm met Ben's. She tried not to show her surprise as something zippy and zappy ran its way up her arm and danced its way to her heart. *Must've slapped his hand too hard*. She shook her head and ignored the tingles warming her skin. 'We've got this, Ben. And I promise no holographic tinsel in the windows, but fair warning, there will be holographic other things, glitter and gold, not to mention fluff and fur.'

'What you're saying is that if it'll make a five-year-old girl squeal in delight, you'll be buying it.' Sophie lifted her lip in a sneer that matched Ben's perfectly.

Poppy bit back a laugh. Those two were peas in a pod. Sophie was like Ben had been at that age. Serious. Sure of himself. Not one to suffer fools.

Then again, Ben had suffered Poppy their whole childhood. Putting up with her whimsical ideas and devil-may-care attitude.

The part of her that expected rejection from those closest to her – that had *learnt* to expect it thanks to the way she was shunned by her mother – had led Poppy to wonder why Ben had stuck with her through thick and thin… then the moment the answer had revealed itself, she'd upped and left London. Left Ben.

One heart-stopping moment with Ben. One heart-wrenching argument with her mother. And her life had changed course…

Poppy put on her imaginary blinkers. There was no point thinking about that night. The past was the past. This shop was her future.

She just had to hope that history didn't repeat itself.

**

Ben heaved the last of the flatpack shelving into the shop, shut the door, then leaned against it, resting his tired muscles. 'All those hours spent working out, you'd think unloading shelving would be a breeze. I might even be able to skip my morning workout.'

'Don't you dare.' Poppy glanced up from the floor, where she'd been spreading out the takeaways she'd ordered for dinner. 'If you mess with those muscles you'll lose your female customers. Maybe even some of the gentlemen customers too.'

'I don't have any customers.' Ben sank down and began piling rice onto a paper plate, topping it with chicken tikka masala.

'Not yet. But you will. I can feel it in my bones. By the way, thanks for sourcing the shelving. It's perfect. The white shelves will look utterly gorgeous on my side, and that wooden shelving will be lush once it's stained. I found a company who'll put it all together for us, so we can concentrate on getting the stock sorted.'

'You mean you're not going to force Joe and Sophie to put it together?' Ben forked a spoonful of curry into his mouth and closed his eyes in appreciation. Rich, aromatic… and, most importantly, filling. They hadn't stopped all day. Cleaning, sourcing products, nailing down the days and times that Joe and

Sophie would be working, not to mention what their duties would be. It was tiring work. And there was still so much to do.

Poppy piled her plate high with prawn biryani. 'There's no way I'm letting them loose on the shelving. I want it to stand the test of time. And I don't want to be forking out extra because they've not read the instructions properly and screwed it all together the wrong way round and not realised it until it's too late. Those shelves aren't the rescrewable type.'

Ben set his plate and fork down and took in the woman before him. The Poppy who'd left would've done exactly what she didn't want Joe and Sophie to do. This Poppy though? She'd been full steam ahead all day, but there was a structure to her ways. And apart from when she'd suggested he make candy-floss cupcakes with little unicorn icing creatures sprinkled on top for any kids who came into the tea shop, he'd been on board with all her suggestions. Any lingering worries he had about opening his shop side-by-side with hers were beginning to evaporate.

Poppy crossed her legs and let out a sigh, her shoulders inching down. 'God, it's good to relax, finally. It's been go-go-go all day. Heck, it's been go-go-go since I decided to come home. We haven't even had a proper catch up. We need to remedy that. So, Ben, tell me about your life. Is there anyone special who's currently resenting you for spending all your spare hours with me at the shop? Has a pearl-clutcher finally scooped you up? Are you keeping her from me in case the Poppy-curse sees another potential wife bite the dust?'

'You give yourself too much credit.' Ben tore off a piece of naan and ran it through the gravy. 'And what on earth is a pearl-clutcher?'

'Really? You don't know? A pearl-clutcher is your ideal woman. A woman who likes things to be done the correct way. Who can't bare the idea of messing with tradition, of breaking the rules.' Poppy's hand flew to her throat. Her eyes widened in horror. 'You'd never believe what I saw the other day. It was shocking, I tell you, shocking. Meredith from down the road put her milk bottle in the rubbish bin. *Not* the recycling bin. Can you believe it? Terrible. Has she no heart?'

'Who's Meredith?' Ben reached for the bottle of red wine Poppy had placed on the floor along with two plastic cups and poured them each a half-glass. Enough to be enjoyed, but not enough to render them useless at work the next day. 'And why do you care so much about what she does with rubbish?'

'Meredith is your ideal woman. A bona fide pearl-clutcher. She is prim. She is proper. She is easily outraged. She would always recycle anything that could be recycled, and anyone who doesn't is an ingrate, in Meredith's opinion.'

'Well, it's nice that she cares so much.' Ben took a sip, then set the glass down. 'Do you recycle all that can be recycled, Poppy?'

'Of course I do.' Poppy shovelled a forkful of food into her mouth.

'And would you be outraged if you saw someone flout your recycling rules?' Ben covered his mouth with his hand so Poppy wouldn't see the amusement that was threatening to make its way onto his lips.

Poppy nodded. Then shook her head. Then hastily swallowed. 'Oh no you don't, Ben. I will not have you insinuating that I'm a pearl-clutcher. No way. Not going to happen. The difference between me and a pearl-clutcher is that I wouldn't get all vocal about seeing someone do something I consider outrageous.'

'Really? I'd have thought you'd march up to them and give them a lecture about saving the environment one recyclable at a time. Kind of like you did to my mum when you were hell-bent on joining Greenpeace and doing everything you could to ensure the… how did you put it?'

Poppy shut her eyes and groaned. '"The health and safety of the earth and all its residents". Are you ever going to let me forget that? And you can drop your hand, I know you're laughing at me.'

Ben did as he was told, holding back a snort-laugh when Poppy flicked him the two-fingered salute. 'Well you went through our rubbish and separated everything out and made Mum solemnly swear that she'd never let a recyclable into the bin again. It was the funniest thing. I think she fell a bit in love with you that day.'

That made two of us. Ben pushed the thought away. There was no point in entertaining feelings from the past. They'd gotten him nowhere then, they weren't going to get him anywhere now. He had to get his brain off this thought track, and the best way to do that was to change the subject. 'Interesting bracelet, Poppy. Where'd you get it?'

'This old thing?' Poppy held up a bronze chain filled with charms.

Amongst the collection, Ben spotted a koala, a rugby ball, a tiny pizza slice, a water buffalo. A random assortment, yet somehow on Poppy it worked.

'It's just how I keep track of where I've been. A charm for every town or country I've visited. And don't try and distract me from our conversation, Ben. Let's get back to you.' Her bracelet jangled as she pointed in his direction. 'Now, tell me, why isn't there a Meredith in your life? To be honest I was surprised you and Milly didn't get back together after I left. She was a Meredith all the way.'

'Milly was a bit of a Meredith. Although she sounds like she's loosened up.' Ben folded the gravy through the rice.

'"Sounds"? Are you two still in contact?' Poppy picked up a napkin and wiped at a splodge of red gravy that had nestled in the groove of her mouth. 'All gone?'

'Not quite.' Ben took the napkin and patted away another splodge that had landed on her chin, then passed the napkin back to Poppy. 'You still eat like a starving animal.'

'Habit of a lifetime.' Poppy's lips turned down in what looked like a frown, but in a blink of an eye it was gone, a smile in its place. 'Anyway, back to Milly. I didn't know you two still talked.'

'It's a recent thing. She called. Said she was going to be in the area. We've texted each other a bit.' Ben gave a non-committal shrug. 'Anyway, maybe I'm just not in the market for a pearl-clutching Meredith type of woman. Maybe I'd prefer a woman with a bit of fire in her belly. Someone fun, funny, not afraid to take a chance. Someone with a good heart. I don't suppose you know anyone who fits that description?'

Poppy leaned forward, a gleam in her eyes. 'Not off the top of my head, but maybe I could help you find her. We could load up some dating apps onto your phone. Go through the prospects together. It'd be great fun!' Poppy looked around the shop. 'Where's your phone? Let's put together a profile and get you out there.' She leaned over to snatch up the phone lying at his side, groaning as Ben whipped it up before she could get her hands on it.

'Let's not, Poppy.' Ben tucked the phone in his back pocket, well out of reach of Poppy's grabby hands. 'I know you'll think me boring. Too traditional. But I like the idea of meeting a girl the old-fashioned way. Like, at a bar, or at the shops, or when I'm jogging in the park.'

'You mean you want a romantic movie type meeting?' Poppy stroked her chin and gazed into the distance. 'Maybe I could go places with you and you could point out women that you like the look of and I could maybe throw you in front of them and make it looked like you tripped?'

Air-sucking frustration built in Ben's chest. He had to shut this down. The last person he wanted to talk about love with was the only woman he'd ever fallen for. The one woman he'd had to work hard to get over. 'You know, I could ask the same of you, Pops. You haven't mentioned anyone, so I'm guessing there's no man in your life?'

'God, no.' Poppy gagged. 'No boyfriend. I don't do boyfriends. At least, I don't do the serious ones.' Poppy visibly shuddered. 'I'm always honest with any man who shows interest. I tell them

I am in it for a fun time, not a long time. I tell them if I see a hint of their wanting more then I'm out.'

'But why? What have you got against relationships?' Ben set his fork down. Something was wrong. Off. He couldn't believe that Poppy with her big, kind heart didn't do relationships.

'It's quite simple. I don't believe in them because I don't believe in that kind of love.' Poppy took a sip of her wine and set it down with a nonchalant shrug. 'Stop looking so freaked out, it's no big deal.'

'No big deal? But you were just trying to get me dating. Marry me off. How can someone who doesn't believe in love do that?'

'I was just trying to inject some fun in your life, Ben. Not love. Besides, you're the marrying type. The type who'd make it work even once what you thought was love died out. People do it all the time. They stay together for financial reasons. Or because they know no better. Or out of stubbornness. Not for love. Love is really just a bunch of hormones racing around your body that make you hook up with someone so that babies can be made and the human race gets to continue. Love's really just a giant myth as far as I'm concerned. A fairy tale to keep you warm at night.'

Ben pushed his plate away, his appetite as existent as Poppy's belief in happy-ever-afters. 'How can you say it's a myth? My mother and father have stuck it out through thick and thin for over thirty-five years. They're proof that love exists.'

'But that's the thing. You just said it yourself. They've "stuck it out". If love was real you wouldn't have to stick it out. And it's not like my parents are the best example. My father left before I was born. And my mother…' Poppy paused as colour flooded her cheeks, and her eyes drifted to the window. The look in her juniper-green eyes was as dark as the night sky. 'Well, she wasn't the best role model.'

Ben wanted to ask why, but Poppy's taut jaw told him she wasn't about to elaborate. He checked the time on his watch.

Nearly eleven. He had to be up in a few hours to get his morning swim and workout in. Needed that time to plan out his day. To figure out what had to be done, and the best way to do it. But he didn't want to leave Poppy like this. All twisted and tortured by some aspect of her past that she clung to. That haunted her. He had to go, but before he did he wanted to see the sadness in Poppy's eyes recede, to see them brighten once more.

'You know, Pops, you may not believe in love, but I know you believe in friendship. And I probably should have said this when we decided... well, when we were kind of forced into business together. But I'm glad you're back, Poppy. Really glad.' Ben raised his cup. 'To the rekindling of a beautiful relationship.'

Poppy's jaw relaxed as she raised her cup. 'To a beautiful friendship. One where I won't have to worry about you going all lovey-dovey on me. The best kind.' The shine returned to her eyes, as her ever-present inner light beat off the dark. 'The only kind.'

'Indeed. The only kind.' Ben clinked his cup against Poppy's and ignored the stab her words had brought to his gut. Indigestion. That was all it was. All it could possibly be.

Chapter 5

The sight of towering boxes, threatening to topple over, sent an army of ants marching through Poppy's stomach.

There was so much to unpack. So much to set up. And such little time to do it.

Although the way the tower was teetering, there was a chance one floor-shuddering step would see her die under a box avalanche.

Death by unicorn.

How ironic would it be if her demise was caused by that which was meant to be the start of the rest of her life?

'What was I thinking getting myself into this? I must be mad.'

Poppy's lips quirked in amusement at Ben's self-chastisement. He mustn't have heard her arrive minutes before.

Connect automatic door chime.

Another thing to do on a list that seemed to get longer the closer they got to opening their joint venture.

'I heard that,' she called in a sing-song lilt. Her quirked lips spread into a cheek-stretching smile as a curse met her ears.

The sound of brisk footsteps on wooden floorboards told her Ben was on his way to apologise.

Bless his cotton socks. He'd always been too nice for his own good.

'Sorry, Poppy. Didn't hear you come in.'

Poppy turned to see Ben leaning against the doorway that led to the kitchen, his hands shoved deep into rust-red chinos that were as perfectly pressed as his blue and white checked short-sleeved collared shirt. Poppy glanced down at his brown leather loafers. Not a scuff in sight. Her tummy did a little flip-flop. Ben looked good. Better than good. The way he was dressed, the way his hair was just so, he could've come straight from a fashion shoot.

'I didn't know you were here.' His cheeks pinked up, no doubt embarrassed to have been caught saying something that could potentially hurt someone's feelings.

Such a Ben thing to do. He'd always cared. About everything. And everyone. Too much, as far as Poppy was concerned. He'd taken his only-child status seriously. Studying hard. Using his manners. Pleasing his parents in every way possible.

They were total opposites. Perhaps that's why their friendship had worked. Perhaps that's why even now after all these years – despite Ben's apparent misgivings – they still worked.

Poppy grabbed a box cutter from her counter that had been put together then painted a soft lavender two days previously, and ran it along the taped lines of the box closest to her. One of about fifty. The contents within each needed to be unpacked and placed on the shelves in an eye-catching matter.

Not that the eye-catching part would be hard. The holographic, iridescent and glittery materials that made up so much of the stock would certainly draw people's attention. But would it see them buy what she had to sell?

Yes. It would. It had to. She'd sunk the majority of the money she'd saved while travelling the world into this venture, and there was no way she was returning to her mother's house, sparkly unicorn cap in hand, asking for a hot meal – or worse, for a bed to crash in until she got herself sorted out. Give her mother another chance to ignore her? To remind Poppy exactly how little her presence on this earth meant to her? Give her a chance to shut the door in her face as she had every time Poppy had come to her bedroom as a child, seeking comfort after a nightmare? That wasn't going to happen.

'You're not going to give me grief for having a moment of second thought?' Ben took a cautious step into the room. Then another. Until he was within swatting distance. Then sank down beside her, his eyes filled with caution.

Poppy shook her head. ''Course not. It's normal to have freak-outs. I'm having about ten an hour. But every freak-out makes me more determined to make this work.' She pulled out a tissue-covered package and carefully unwrapped it, revealing a crystal figurine: a unicorn, rearing up, its mane tossing in unseen wind, its horn sparkling with gold and silver glitter.

'That is the ugliest thing I've ever seen in my entire life.' Ben's voice held equal awe and disgust.

Poppy set the figurine down, then punched Ben lightly on the arm. 'Now *that* you have to apologise for. How can you say such a thing? That is the epitome of class and sophistication. Every person in Muswell Hill – no, in London – no, I mean England. No.' She shook her head. 'Every person in the *world* needs a crystal unicorn in their life. They could keep it on their car's dashboard for luck. They could have it by their bedside to keep the nightmares away. They could sit it on their windowsill so the light refracts through it, creating a smile-inducing rainbow.' Poppy ran her thumb over the gravelly surface of the glittering horn. She smiled as a fragment flaked onto her thumb. 'Okay, it's a little bit ugly. But there's a market for it. Little girls will adore it.'

Ben shook his head, reached into the box, unwrapped another figurine and passed it to Poppy to set on the shelf. 'Frankly I can't believe there's a market for any of it.'

Poppy snorted. 'Well, at least one of us is going to be happy working next to the other. Not only will I get to be surrounded by the spirit-lifting goodness that are unicorns, I'll also be able to help myself to a cup of matcha, or Lapsang Souchong, or plain old garden variety breakfast tea with a splash of milk, any time I feel like one. I'm going to be living the dream.'

'Well at least one of us will be.' Ben nudged her with his hip, then passed her another box to open. 'At least I won't have to go far to buy you a birthday present I know you'll love.'

'Oh, shush.' Poppy lifted her finger to his lips. 'You know I don't do birthdays.'

Ben grinned, then took her finger in his hand. 'We'll see about that. Now, less talking, more unpacking.'

Poppy wiggled her finger free, grabbed the box cutter and sliced into another box, and pulled out a smaller box. Printed on the side of the plain brown packaging was an image of the unicorn mug held inside. The tail forming the mug's handle, a swirled golden unicorn horn poked out opposite the handle, and painted on either side of the mug were big black eyes complete with lush, long glitter-dusted lashes.

She pulled up the box's lid and lifted the mug out. 'Where should we put this? It would look great next to those fancy double-walled glass teacups of yours…'

Ben held his hands up, as if warding her off. Her, or her unicorn mug. 'No. No way. We have a deal, remember? Under no circumstances will I be allowing any of that… that uncouth frippery into my side of the business.'

'Frippery?' A giggle tumbled out of Poppy's mouth. 'Well that's a new word to me. I like it. And, fine. I won't put my mugs alongside your precious glassware. I was just testing the waters. Testing the boundaries. You know how I am.'

'Indeed, I do.' Ben sighed. 'So, how do you feel about a tea tasting? Sophie and Joe should be here any minute, and I was going to hold a tasting for them since it's important they know what they're talking about.'

'Hold on. Hold up. What? Joe's doing the tasting? He's my helper. Not yours.' Poppy wagged her finger. 'I will not have you seducing him with your aromatic ways.'

'Plonker.' Ben picked up the crystal unicorn, turned it over in his hands, then held it up to Poppy. 'If Joe's sick, and you're unwell, who do you think will look after your shop?'

Understanding dawned on Poppy. 'I would say you, but we both know you'd sooner take a dip in the boating lake at Ally Pally in the middle of winter.'

'Exactly. We need to have Sophie and Joe up to speed on both sides of the shop.'

Ben turned and made his way to the kitchen, Poppy followed in his wake and took in the set-up he'd put together.

Five glass teapots sitting atop warmers, were placed on the bench. Each pot held a strainer, in which different teas were releasing tantalising aromas into the surrounding air. While various colours – grassy greens, vibrant pinks, and mahogany browns – softened as they blended out into the hot water.

The squeak of the door alerted them to the arrival of Sophie and Joe.

Attach door chimes and fix the squeak, Poppy reminded herself, trying to ignore the stepping up of her pulse as another item was added to her list.

'We're here,' Joe announced. 'On time, too. Look at us being responsible workers. Must mean we're due a pay rise?' He winked as Sophie closed her eyes, shaking her head in a long-suffering manner, just the way Poppy had seen Ben do all the time when they were younger.

'Convince your grandfather to lower the rent by another fifteen per cent and it's a deal,' Poppy shot back. 'In lieu of more money you can have free tea. Look at this spread Ben's put on for us.'

'Is it meant to smell like that?' Joe's nose wrinkled. 'I mean, there's fruity whiffs from that one.' He pointed to the tea that was blossoming a pinky-red. 'But that green one's… weird.'

'That green one is Japanese green tea. *Sencha*, to be precise.' Ben lifted the pot and poured a little into three cups, then passed a cup to each of them. 'Try it.'

Poppy tried not to laugh as Joe's face screwed up when he lifted the cup to his lips and sipped. 'It's…'

'Really something,' Sophie piped up, then took another sip, smacking her lips together. 'Fresh. Almost zesty.'

Poppy sipped the tea. 'Kind of grassy, but not in a gross way. And almost… seaweed-ish? Or am I imagining that?'

'No, you're not imagining it.' Ben nodded his approval. 'It's all that. And the reason it's a nice kind of grassy is because it's quality.' He rounded up their empty glasses and rinsed them out. 'Now try this.' He poured the pinky concoction. 'This is a fruit tea, also known as a tisane. Tell me what you taste.'

Joe took a sip. 'Too easy. Strawberry. It's yum.'

'And?' Ben raised an eyebrow.

'There's more?' Sophie set her cup down and tapped her finger on her chin.

'Apple.' Poppy grinned. 'Definitely apple.'

'You really do have a good nose.' Ben's eyes widened. 'Maybe you should be working on my side of the shop.'

'Don't know about my nose, but my eyes can see bits of apple drifting about in the infuser.' Poppy set her cup down and ducked out of the way as Ben went to give her a friendly flick. 'It is creamy though.'

'That's because it's a strawberry and cream tisane. Or did you see the tin it came from?' Ben went about rinsing the glasses fresh for the next tasting.

'No. Just tasted it. Turns out my tongue's quite talented.' Heat rushed to Poppy's cheeks that had nothing to do with the warmth of the tea. Beside her Joe and Sophie snorted into their closed fists, their faces matching the colour of the strawberry tea. Meanwhile Ben began to cough, his eyes filling with tears.

'Omigod, I'm so sorry. That sounded…'

'Filthy.' Joe filled in the blank.

'And hilarious,' Sophie added. 'Keep that up and I might enjoy working here.'

Poppy went to remind Sophie she was lucky to be here, that she and Ben were the only people willing to take her and Joe on, but held her tongue as the door squeaked, announcing a visitor to the store.

'Hello?' A voice as smooth as Ben's tisane floated through the air to greet them. 'Anyone there?'

'Are you expecting another delivery?' Ben asked as he straightened up and wiped his eyes.

'No. I've got all I need. You?'

Ben shook his head as he put on a welcoming smile and marched into the main shop. 'Welcome to Sparkle & Steep, what can we help you with today?'

Poppy trailed after him, and lounged against the doorway, curious to see who the visitor was.

The unexpected visitor turned to face Ben, a bright smile on her face. 'Oh, this place is divine. A high-end tea shop? Genius. I love it. You've done a marvellous job, Ben. Now I hope you don't mind my popping in unexpectedly, but my mother saw your mother and mentioned your shop was close to opening, so I simply had to come by, say hello, and have a sneak peek.' The woman laid her perfectly manicured hand on his forearm and gave it a squeeze.

There was something familiar about her, but Poppy couldn't quite put her finger on it. She clearly knew Ben, felt comfortable striking up a conversation with him, but she was dressed too… well, too much like Poppy to be someone he knew. Denim cut-off shorts, frayed at the bottom, were embroidered with multi-coloured flowers around the pockets. Her cream camisole was loose and billowy, yet sheer enough you could see her turquoise bra underneath.

Her hair was the perfect blonde. Not too white, not too yellow. Princess golden… just like…

'Oh my God.' Poppy took a step forward, her eyes wide, hand covering her mouth. 'Milly? Is that you?'

Ben squinted in an effort to see what Poppy was seeing. Milly? *His* Milly? No. Surely not…

Oh hell. It was Milly. But the carefully curled blonde locks she'd sported when they were younger were now effortlessly beachy and tumbling down her back and over her bare shoulders. The formerly nude lips were now a bright red pout. And the smile was bright-white and straight. Milly Smith, his teenage girlfriend, had gotten her teeth straightened, possibly whitened, and had grown into a woman.

A beautiful one at that.

Bloody hell.

'In the flesh.' Milly grinned and did a quick shimmy.

Milly shimmied? When did Milly shimmy? She was a wallflower when they were young. Her idea of revealing clothing had been a skirt that sat on her knee. Or a boatneck top as opposed to a turtle neck.

Milly took another step into the shop, picked up the unicorn ornament and held it up to the light, sending a skittering of rainbows across the floor. 'Interesting.' She set it back down, her distaste obvious.

'Shooting for a younger target market than you with that, I'm afraid.' Poppy crossed the floor, swept up the ornament and placed it on a shelf. 'Everything will be out by tomorrow when we open. Maybe you should pop back then and have a look?'

'Oh, tomorrow's out for me. Wall-to-wall meetings, I'm afraid.' Milly turned her back on Poppy and focused on Ben. 'That's why I thought I'd come by today, say hello and wish you good luck.'

'Oh, well, hello.' Ben shifted from foot to foot, unnerved by the way Milly was looking at him, her smile spreading wider by the second, showing off those gleaming, straight teeth. Was this how a mouse felt when cornered by a cat? 'Have you been visiting your mum just now?'

'No, not today. Remember when I said I'd be round these parts? What I meant was that I've bought a place here. I was just over there while the movers dropped off my furniture. It's so nice to settle down, lay some roots, have a place to call my own. Life can't be all cocktails and dancing 'til dawn…' Milly glanced over at Poppy, her upper lip curling in disdain.

Ben mashed his lips together as Poppy ripped into a box with her bare hands, her eyes murderous. He didn't want to believe that Milly was taking a pot shot at Poppy's lifestyle, but the two had never seen eye-to-eye when they were younger. Milly believed Poppy was a bad influence on Ben, whereas Poppy thought Milly far too boring to spend time on. Yet that hadn't stopped Poppy from urging him to go out with Milly in the first place. Something he'd never quite figured out. One of the many Poppy mysteries he'd yet to uncover.

'Oh, I absolutely know what you mean, Milly.' Poppy's tone was light enough, but Ben caught the taut, tense edge to it. 'After seeing so many wonderful parts of the world, experiencing all the amazing things different countries and cultures have to offer, I've found it a real joy to come home and know that I'll be waking up in the same bed, seeing the same sights, building a future for myself. One based on a solid foundation of knowing who I am, what I can do, and what my strengths are.'

A muted snort-cough caught Ben's attention. Sophie and Joe were all but hanging off the doorframe, their eyes wide with glee as they watched the two women verbally spar.

This wouldn't do, he decided. Not one bit. They had a lot to get done and they were due to open in less than fifteen hours. 'Well, I'm glad you popped by, Milly. It's been lovely to see you. I hate to cut your visit short, but as I'm sure you understand, we've a lot to get done before we flick that sign on the door there from "shut" to "open" tomorrow morning.' Ben went to the door and opened it for Milly.

'Absolutely, I understand. I know you've a lot on at the moment, Ben, but we should definitely catch up.' Milly's fingers curled around his bicep. 'It's been so long. I'd love to hear more about what you've been up to. There's only so much that can be talked about, *conveyed*, over the phone. That job of yours must have been positively thrilling, far more exciting than my work as an editor-in-chief at a fashion magazine…'

Another snort-cough filled the air. This one from Poppy's direction.

'Er, I don't know about thrilling, but I did meet some characters along the way.' Ben glanced at the ruby-red talons that showed no sign of leaving his arm. When had Milly become so… un-Milly?

'Well then, I'd love to hear about them. I'll swing by in a few days' time, once you're all settled and up and running, and we'll make a date, shall we?' Milly stretched up and settled her lips on his cheek. He caught a whiff of some dark, exotic perfume. So different to the apple shampoo that had been her ever-present scent as a teenager.

'Okay. Great. Well, have a good day, Milly.' Ben waved her off and shut the door to a mixture of wolf whistles and kissy sounds.

'Ben's got a giiiiirlfriiiiiiend,' Sophie and Joe sang in unison.

Ben touched his arm where Milly's hand had been. Breathed in the potent perfume that still hung in the air. He looked over to Poppy to gauge her opinion. Her back was turned, hunched over, as she tore into another box, sending the polystyrene pieces within flying.

He tried to ignore the gnawing in his stomach that told him his life was about to get complicated. Complicated? Try downright problematic. With the opening of his business, the juggling of staff, and the rift between him and his father that if their lack of communication was anything to go by showed no signs of abating, the last thing he needed was Poppy vs Milly, round two.

Chapter 6

Ben closed his eyes. Opened them again. Blinked hard. The bowl of creamy vanilla icing he had tucked under his arm threatened to tip over and spill its contents on their freshly cleaned floor.

Poppy mashed her lips together; she knew what was coming but couldn't stop herself. Couldn't? More like didn't want to. His face began to turn a violent shade of purple. Eruption coming in three… two… one…

'You can't seriously be wearing that on our first day of business. It's completely ridiculous. Totally over the top. What will people think?' Ben shoved the icing-covered spoon he was holding in the bowl and placed it on the counter.

Joe glanced down at his outfit. A snow-white fluffy onesie with a pink oval 'belly' front and centre. 'What? You don't like my uniform?' He spun round, sending the golden tail attached to the onesie's rear flying.

'Uniform?' Ben shook his head so hard Poppy half-worried that his brain would come flying out of his ears. 'It's not a uniform. That looks like the kind of pyjamas a three-year-old would wear.'

Poppy moved to stand beside Joe and pointed downwards.

'Not true. Kids onesies tend to have feet as part of the pyjamas. Joe's feet are bare.'

'His feet are not bare. I can see with my own two eyes that he has unicorn scuffs on his feet. The slipper variety. He's not ready to go to work. He's ready to go to bed.'

'You don't like his slippers? But they're so pretty.'

Joe raised his leg and angled his foot back and forth, displaying the purple fluffy scuffs threaded through with silver, a horn made from shiny golden material protruded from the centre of each slipper. 'I'm with Poppy, they're pretty. Pretty awesome.'

Ben's nostrils flared as he huffed. 'It's not about whether I like them or not...'

'You don't. I can see it from the fuchsia colour of your face.' Poppy grabbed hold of Joe's tail and twirled the tail, burlesque style. 'I'd go as far as to say they're making you angry.'

'They don't make me angry. They're slippers. It takes more than fairy tale footwear to irritate me. No, it's just that I don't think that *uniform* is appropriate for a business such as this. People will be coming to our shop expecting a certain sense of decorum... and, well...' Ben's lips mashed together. 'More important than what others think... what if Joe gets too hot and passes out?'

Poppy crossed her arms over her chest and shifted from foot to foot, setting off a disco of lights embedded in her sunshine-yellow sneakers. 'Nice tactic, making it all about Joe's health and wellbeing rather than what others might think, but the thing is, Ben, I don't think Joe could get hot enough to pass out, not when you insist on setting the temperature in here to freezing.'

'It really is freezing.' Joe mock-shivered. 'So, actually, I'm almost cosy.'

'And you know, Joe, I'm impressed with your commitment to the job. It's inspiring. In fact, it's got me tempted to wear this...' Poppy strode over to a rack of clothing and pulled out a spaghetti-strapped silk nightgown covered in prancing miniature unicorns.

'Although, if I were to wear this then Ben would have to pop the heating up.'

Ben's mouth opened in a perfect 'o' of horror. 'You wouldn't wear that? It would be—'

'Too fun? Too casual?' Poppy pulled the nightgown off the rack, held it up to her body and shimmied like Milly had the day before. 'Likely to give one of your staid old customers a heart attack?'

'Yes, exactly that. I can't have people keeling over, it would give us bad press. Anyway, the temperature's kept low so my customers can appreciate their tea. They'll wrap their hands around the cups. Feel the heat infuse their bodies, their souls...'

'Who knew Mr Business had a poetic heart?' Poppy placed the nightgown back on the rack. 'It's lovely to know that you care about creating an experience for a bunch of strangers.'

'Not strangers. *Customers*. Also, if it gets too warm in here the tea can go rancid. And I can't afford to be throwing money down the drain.' Ben checked his watch. 'Look, the shop's due to open in twenty minutes, and Sophie and I still have to get the tea-of-the-day steeping on the warmer, and the baking plated up and on the counter. Joe, wear what you want. Poppy, don't you dare wear that tiny scrap of material you call a nightie. You'll freeze to death.'

Poppy's chest began to ache from holding the laughter in. She glanced at Joe, whose face had gone vermillion. One cheek was puffed out, like his tongue was literally pushed into it.

An irritated cluck from Ben sent her over the edge. The giggles she'd kept tamped down erupted, followed by guffaws from Ben's direction.

'Oh, Ben, we're just teasing. Pulling your leg.' Poppy bounded over and kissed his cheek. 'I promise I won't wear the nightgown. It's not really my style anyway. And Joe's onesie will only be coming out on Mondays – we're doing unicorn story time for toddlers. We came up with it last night and posted it on our social media page. Thought it would be a good way for local mums to enjoy your tea and treats while we entertained their little ones.'

Ben's chest deflated, his lips pursing. 'Excellent idea, Poppy, Joe. But do you promise that this look will be for Mondays only?'

'We promise.' Poppy made a cross over her heart. 'Although I'm totally getting one to wear at home.'

'You're incorrigible.' Ben backed away towards the kitchen door. 'Always have been.'

'Yeah well, you'll come to love this onesie. Heck, I bet you'll end up buying one.' Poppy smiled as Ben gave another vigorous head shake. 'Now go finish up that icing and get that tea of yours brewing. It's time to make our fortune.'

***

Poppy slumped onto the small wooden desk that occupied a corner of the tiny storeroom and rested her head on her arm. She rarely dealt with self-doubt – refused to as a means of self-preservation – but the numbers on the calculator, the money on the table, and the receipts from the sales were giving her a head-ache, and making her question how wise she'd been to think running a gift shop would be easy.

Sure, it had seemed simple enough on paper. She'd saved the money up so she'd be going in debt-free. Bought the stock. Made everything look as appealing as possible. She'd posted on Muswell Hill's social media pages that Sparkle & Steep was opening, and within a day it had been shared. And shared. And shared some more. Gone viral, according to Joe. And the people had come.

Boy, had they come. In droves. People whisked in on their way to work or during their lunch break. Mothers with babies wrapped to their chests, and toddlers in hand, popped in, excited to see the latest arrival. Retirees poked their heads in, curious to see what had lain behind the store frontage that had been papered-over for the last two weeks.

The store's chimes had bing-bonged all day long as people came to investigate the newest addition to Muswell Hill. Ben's tea shop had been so busy he'd had to put on a second pot of the day's trial tea within the first hour of opening, and both pots had been emptied and refilled by Sophie numerous times. Meanwhile Sparkle had been filled with squeals of delight and joyful sighs as people discovered her range of unicorn clothing, accessories and homeware. And the story-time session had been a hit, bolstering sales on both sides of the store, and ended with the mothers and fathers who'd brought their little ones along asking if it could be a daily occurrence, much to Ben's chagrin.

Her till had beeped its way through the day, and now she had a bunch of numbers to make sense of. At least she didn't have a store to tidy; Joe had taken care of that, bless his unicorn-shod feet.

A Ben-shaped shadow fell across the floor, followed by the man himself. 'You look like I feel.'

Poppy pushed herself into a sitting position and cupped her chin in her hand. 'I don't think so. You don't even have a hair out of place. I'm pretty sure mine's so frizzy I'd be mistaken for an angel.'

She laughed as Ben's forehead creased in confusion.

'I call it the "black halo".' She indicated to the circumference of her head that had a tendency to boof out when she got all hot and bothered – which she had as the day wore on and she'd darted back and forth showcasing her wares to interested parties. 'So, did your day go as well as I think it did?'

'Better. I'm going to have to come in even earlier tomorrow to get more baking done. And I'll need to call my tea supplier because at this rate I'll be scraping the bottom of the tins by the end of the week.' Ben rubbed his hands together in glee. 'I knew this could work. I knew I wasn't a fool to…' The gleam in Ben's eyes disappeared.

'Someone called you a fool for opening your shop?' Poppy didn't need three guesses to figure out who. 'It's one thing for your father to not approve of your choice to open a shop, but he has no right to call you a fool. No right to try and control you.' She pulled out the chair beside her and patted it.

Ben settled into the chair beside her, clasped his hands behind his head and leaned back, tipping his chin so he was staring at the ceiling. 'I don't think he's trying to control me. I just don't think he can understand why I'd give up a solid career – a career our family has found success in for decades – on what he thinks is a whim.'

'When you put it like that…' Poppy spun the pen in front of her, faster and faster. 'I must admit, I did wonder if you'd been hit on the head or something when you mentioned your plans to open a tea shop. Sure, you could bake as a kid. And the last couple of weeks I've tried enough of your creations to know they're better than all the other baking I've ever tried – and I've tried a lot of baking. But you've never been one to take risks. To strike out on your own.'

Ben laughed, harsh and humourless. 'Well, we can't all be like you now, can we, Poppy? Not all of us are able to just give something a go, or leave someone behind, without thinking of the repercussions.'

Poppy didn't miss the hint of hurt. Ben thought she'd not taken his feelings into consideration when she'd left, but she had. Big time. He was one of two very big reasons that she had to leave. In going she'd saved his heart from hurt and saved herself from hurting him. She'd hoped time and space would heal any wounds, but perhaps she'd been a fool to think that.

'I'm sorry.' She laid a hand on his forearm, her heart growing heavy when Ben flinched. 'I know it was sudden, my leaving and all. But it wasn't like I didn't keep in touch.'

Ben turned his gaze on Poppy. His expression impassive, like he'd stopped caring. Or forced himself to. 'I know. But just because you told me you were okay, that it was going well, it didn't mean I didn't worry. I did. Especially in the early stages of your travels.'

Poppy went to defend herself, to tell Ben she could handle herself – that she *had* handled herself – but Ben held up his hand, stopping her.

'You forget I know how lackadaisical you can be about your safety, and how independent you are. And it killed me that even if something happened to you, you wouldn't reach out, you wouldn't ask for help. In the end I just had to hope for the best. It was the only way to stop worrying.'

'Well, nothing happened to me. So I'm glad you stopped worrying. Eventually.'

The edges of Ben's lips turned down, his eyes darkened in disbelief.

'Truly.' Poppy gave an affirmative nod to emphasise her point. 'But you're right, I wouldn't have asked for help if anything had. I wouldn't have wanted to bother you. Or been a burden like I was when we were younger.'

'What are you on about? You were never a burden. Not once.' Ben leaned forward in the chair, his elbows propped on his knees, his hands clasped so tight Poppy could see the whites of his knuckles. 'We were friends, Poppy. Friends aren't burdens.'

'But I got you in trouble all those times. Like when we got caught bunking so I could stalk the Hilton because I'd heard that pop star I had the hots for was going to be staying there, and we had detention for a week. Or when I was hungry and thought borrowing a bag of crisps from the shops was okay as long as I brought them some money later, and I got caught, and since you were with me we both had a stern talking to from the local bobby. Oh, and how can we forget that your one and only girlfriend dumped you because I got in the way.' Poppy sucked her top lip in to stop herself grinning at the memory of Milly Smith stamping her foot and pointing at Poppy and calling her a 'plague on love'. She'd always thought Milly was as inoffensive as a teddy bear, so seeing her lose control had been refreshing.

Ben's face lit up with the smile Poppy had been trying to hide. 'You're thinking about the "plague on love" thing, aren't you? I still feel bad about that. I had no idea how serious Milly was about me.'

'So you're saying you would have ditched me as a friend if you'd known?' Poppy teased, matching Ben's smile. 'I'd have been left cold and lonely on the kerb in exchange for clammy hand-holding and tongueless kisses?'

'Her hands weren't clammy.' Ben's brows drew together in a mock-frown.

'But the kisses were tongueless. I had to endure the sight of you two sucking face enough to know. God, and the way she was all over you yesterday, it may well be that I get to experience a repeat performance.' Poppy kissed the air three times, then sank back in her chair.

'She was just being nice.' A flush made its way up Ben's neck to his cheeks. 'Old mates are allowed to be friendly. I mean, we're friendly, aren't we?'

'She was never a *mate*, though. She was a girlfriend. And from my perspective she is looking to reinstate herself. Anyway…' Poppy flapped the image out of her head. Seeing Milly fawn all over Ben had irritated her. Why, she wasn't sure. Probably just being possessive of her friend, possessive of his business, and how he used his time. It didn't help that whenever she compared herself to Milly she always came up wanting. Hair not tidy enough. Clothes not fashionable. Her demeanour not perfectly polished… *ugh*. Goose bumps of self-induced irritation crawled up her spine. 'Let's not talk about her. Let's talk about me. Far more interesting a discussion. So, maybe I wasn't a burden, but

I did get you in trouble. And I *am* sorry about that. I promise I won't get you in trouble again. You don't have to look out for me anymore, Ben.'

Ben raised his eyebrows. 'I'm not holding my breath. Anyway, I've got myself in enough trouble by quitting my job and opening this shop.'

'But you're having fun, right? And don't lie to me because I'll know and you know how I get when I think someone's telling fibs…' Poppy reached over and tickled Ben in the ribs, eliciting a high-pitched squawk.

'Stop it! You know how ticklish I am.' He shifted to the far side of his chair.

Poppy tickled him again, laughing as Ben jumped out of his seat, his hands held up in surrender.

'Fine. You're right. I am having fun. And it is amazing how adept I've become in just one day at ignoring your unicorn rabble.' Ben jumped back as Poppy held up her tickling fingers once again. Relief flooded his face when she dropped her hands and tucked them under her thighs.

'What about you, Pops? Are you having fun?' Ben sank back into his seat. 'Because if I'm honest, when I came in here just now you looked like a woman who was about to throw herself under the nearest truck. Or who had plans to smother herself with one of those fluffy unicorn cushions of yours.'

Poppy turned her attention back to the receipts. 'It's these.' She swept her hand over the mind-bending bits of paper. 'Or more to the point, it's all of this. I'm out of my league. I know nothing about running a business. Not the numbers side of it, anyway.'

'Nothing?' Ben scooted forward and looked at the notepad on which Poppy had been trying to keep track of the stock she'd sold that day. 'Is that how you're keeping track of your inventory? Don't you have a computer?'

Poppy bristled with indignation. Did Ben think she was that

useless? 'Yes, I have a computer. How do you think I booked tickets and found accommodation when travelling?'

'Poppy, I don't mean for day-to-day stuff, I mean for business. Surely you've a program that keeps track of incomings and outgoings? How are you planning to present your accounts to your accountant?'

Poppy sank her head into her hands and groaned. 'I don't. There is no system. Nothing. Because I don't know how.'

'What about a business plan? No. Don't answer that. I know the answer because you've gone all pale and sickly looking. You have no plan. Plans have never been your forte. You run on pure enthusiasm.' Ben's tone was filled with reproach, and doubt. 'Poppy, if you don't know how to run the financial side of a business how do you expect to make it a success?'

'Simple. Buy pretty sparkly unicorn things from suppliers. Add some money on top so I make a profit. Sell said stuff.' Poppy peeked from between her fingers to see Ben shaking his head, his eyes wide with horror. 'Then with the money I make, pay the bills and buy more stuff to sell.'

Ben ran a hand through his hair, which, predictably, fell back into perfect place. 'Well, I'm glad I found this out now. We can fix this. Poppy Taylor, I know you don't like to ask for help so I'm not going to get you to ask. I'm giving you a hand whether you like it or not. By the end of this evening we'll have your business plan in place, along with systems to keep track of stock and money.'

Overwhelmed with relief, Poppy dragged a tense-shouldered Ben into a hug that she refused to release until he gave in to it. 'Ben Evans, you are a gem. Now…' She rifled through her candy-pink tote bag and pulled out her laptop, ignoring Ben's groan when he saw the laptop protector was holographic with a black glittery unicorn in the centre. 'Let's sort me out. And I'll cook dinner to say thank you. I've got this unicorn-shaped pasta you'll love.' Poppy laughed, as Ben squeezed his eyes shut and let out a rumble of despair. 'I'm only joking, Ben, I've yet to come across *that* particular unicorn gem. But there's no need to act so disgusted by the thought.'

The tenseness in her tummy had disappeared, and her heart felt the lightest it had in years. She had a business. She had her friend. She had everything she needed.

At least that's what she would keep telling herself.

Chapter 7

Poppy's gaze wandered over to Ben's side of the shop for what felt like the thousandth time since they'd opened an hour ago.

He was chatting with a customer. Bringing an open tin of tea up to their nose and encouraging them to breathe in. His free hand twisted and turned as he explained the tea's origin and benefits. His voice was friendly, engaged, but there was something not right. His perfect posture had given way to hunched shoulders. His smile was too tight. His step not so purposeful – and Poppy had a feeling it had something to do with their conversation last night.

She knew how important his family was to him. How much he looked up to his father, how he'd done everything he could to please him. To have upset his father, to have chosen a path that his father disapproved of? It would be weighing Ben down. And while she couldn't fix his relationship with his father – because what did she know about healthy family relationships? – the least she could do was try and bring happiness into Ben's life.

A glimmer of an idea flickered in the back of Poppy's mind, and her pulse picked up as possibilities began to form. Maybe what Ben needed was to have a little sparkle in his life, and Poppy was just the woman to help him.

She eyed the counter, where a plate of Jammy Dodgers glinted in the downlights. Keeping things casual, she strolled over to the foodie section of her shop where unicorn-head-shaped lollipops sat next to petite boxes of chocolate unicorns, rainbow rock candy and, most importantly, edible glitter. She pocketed a vial of red glitter and sauntered back to the counter, all the while fighting to keep her expression neutral, determined not to let her glee give the plan away before it could be executed.

The chiming of the shop's doorbell proved the perfect foil for her excitement as a cute little girl, hair in pigtails and wearing a sparkly summery dress, walked in with her mother and made a beeline towards her side of the shop.

'Hi, welcome to Sparkle & Steep.' Poppy smiled warmly at the little girl whose hand was snugly tucked in her mother's.

The girl smiled back shyly, then darted over to the soft toy corner. 'Mummy, look at these! Can I have one?' She pulled out a small white unicorn with a silver horn and hugged it to her tiny chest, her shoulders jiggling backwards and forwards as she wiggled with excitement.

Her mother followed her over and ducked down to the little girl's level. 'Will you help me tidy your room?'

'Yes.' The wee dot nodded her head. 'And I'll eat my carrots and peas.'

'Then consider it yours.' Her mother leaned in and kissed her forehead. The small show of affection twisted Poppy's heart. What would a loving kiss from her mother have felt like? What would it have been like to be able to ask for something as simple as a toy without fearing a sharp-tongued retort? She blinked back the tears that threatened as the little girl made her way to the counter, her eyes dancing with joy.

'I would like this unicorn.' The toy was carefully placed on the counter.

'Manners?' the girl's mother gently reminded her.

'Please.' A sweet smile and a thank you followed as Poppy

packed the toy in a bag and handed it to the little girl. Her mother nodded her thanks, took her daughter's hand and headed out the door, anchoring it open for an incoming customer.

The scent of Chanel No. 5 wafted in. Poppy only knew one person who wore it so boldly. And just like that, she was a girl again. Unsure of her place. A little nervous. And desperate to be accepted.

'Mum? I didn't know you were coming in.' Ben circled round the counter and went to meet his mother, kissing her on the cheek, then bringing her in for a quick hug.

'That's because I wanted to surprise you.' Mrs Evans broke the hug then turned on her heel to face Poppy.

'Mrs Evans. Good to see you again.' Poppy nodded, mustered a smile, and hoped it would be returned. She'd never felt on steady ground in the Evans' household. Ben's dad had disapproved of her, thought her a bad influence. Ben's mother had been kind, but on the occasions Poppy had led Ben astray she'd been quick to back Ben's father in restricting the time Ben and Poppy spent together. Though Poppy had always wondered if Mrs Evans had been instrumental in allowing those rules to be relaxed once enough time had passed.

'Poppy, you're thirty now! It really is time you called me Pam.' In two quick steps Pam had reached Poppy's counter and leaned across to kiss her on each cheek. 'It's good to see you, my dear.'

Warmth hit Poppy's cheeks, and her heart. Pam had been everything she imagined a 'real' mother would be, and time and age hadn't changed that. Sure, fine lines may have feathered the outer corner of Pam's eyes, as warm and chestnut-coloured as her son's. Her cheekbones may have sharpened with age, but she was still rocking the heck out of her standard twinset and skirt combination, and her demeanour was still one of caring, kindness, and stability. Pam was the picture of home. The kind of home young Poppy had dreamed of.

Pam turned back to Ben, took his hands in hers and gave them a wee shake. 'I'm so sorry I didn't visit yesterday. Your father had me running all over the place with all sorts of needs and wants. Dry cleaning. A certain champagne for a client. You know how he can be…'

Ben nodded amicably, but Poppy didn't miss the tiny vein that pulsed at his temple. He knew as well as Poppy did that Ben's father had sent Pam on the errands as a way of keeping her away from the shop, a way of punishing his son for abandoning his job.

'Anyway, I'm here now. And would you look at what you've done with this place?' Pam did a slow turn, taking in their hard work. 'It really is beautiful, and I must admit – I didn't think a gourmet tea shop and a unicorn gift shop could work, but there's something rather special about the mix of the two…' She paused, her lips quirking to the side, like she was enjoying a private joke. 'And Poppy, when Ben said you were back and that he was leasing a shop with you… well, I was rather shocked – he was doing so well with the practice – but I wasn't surprised. You and he always got along well together. Had a way of making things happen. Although some of those things I rather wished you'd not bothered with.' She lifted an imaginary bottle to her lips, mimicked drinking the lot, then set the imaginary bottle down with an amused shake of her head. 'You know, he missed you terribly when you left, and while he may not be the most sentimental man in the world – takes after his father like that – despite saying he was "fine" a thousand times a day, he moped for a good month. I've never seen him so dejected.'

Guilt sucker-punched Poppy square in the gut. She'd convinced herself leaving Ben, leaving her home, leaving her life was for the best – for everyone – but it seemed that had been something she'd told herself just to feel better about doing it. She felt for the vial of glitter in her pocket. She couldn't take her actions back, but she could make amends.

'Anyway, you're back now,' Pam continued, oblivious to Poppy's shock or to her son's face, which was going paler by the second. 'And would you look at what the two of you have achieved in such a short space of time? I think good things are going to come of this.'

Poppy abandoned the safety of her counter, which was no longer a barricade but a barrier to the woman she'd admired growing up. Whose approval she'd dreamed of when her own mother's approval was non-existent. She linked her arm through Pam's, guided her to a table and pulled out a chair for her. 'Fancy a cup of tea? There's a very nice green tea on the warmer. It's from Japan. Doesn't taste like dirt the way the rest of them do.'

'I'd love one, thank you, Poppy. Always up for trying something new. I think Ben gets that from me, you know. His cute bum, too.'

'Mum.' Ben visibly cringed as he poured the tea into two cups and pushed them in Poppy's direction. 'Is it your mission to embarrass me no matter how old I am?'

'It's my job, dear.' Pam shot Poppy an amused wink, as Ben turned on his heel with an exasperated shake of his head and strode out to the kitchen mumbling something about getting a cake out of the oven, and maybe sticking his head in it.

A soft 'mmm' of approval escaped her lips as she tried the tea. 'You're right, this tea is nice, but I'll stick to my Rooibos, I think. And my white tea.'

'Mrs Evans!' Poppy laughed as Pam raised her eyebrow in a gentle reminder. 'I mean… Pam. I had you pegged for Earl Grey, or breakfast.'

'Who do you think introduced Ben to this passion of his? A few years back I was getting bored of how exacting my life was, and while poor Robert would have had a heart attack had I changed his life up and started serving exotic dinners, or, God forbid, changed the time I served his dinner, I figured I could have an interest of my own. So I took to trying tea and Ben, bless him, joined me. It became our evening ritual for a bit. We'd choose a tea, then he'd bake something he thought might match. I've always loved his baking.' Pam patted her slight hips. 'Possibly a bit too much.'

'You're tiny.' Poppy batted away Pam's cluck of protest. 'Anyway, you said it was your ritual for a bit? Did something – or someone – get in the way of your ritual?' Poppy leaned over the table and lowered her voice, not wanting Ben to hear her prying into his personal life.

Pam's marionette lines grew deeper as her lips turned down. 'It came to an end when Ben announced he was going to open the shop. Robert made it clear he was unimpressed, and since then Ben's not come around home.' Pam rubbed her cheek, her eyes weary. 'I've never seen them this out of sorts...'

Poppy's heart went out to Pam. 'It must be hard seeing them at odds with each other, but I'm sure they'll work it out.'

'I don't know. Robert's stubborn. Ben can be too. And Robert's not getting any younger. It'd break my heart if anything happened to him and they were still fighting... Ben would never forgive himself.' Pam blinked rapidly, then straightened up. 'Gosh, what am I saying? Of course nothing will happen. I'm being silly.' Pam stood and picked up her purse. 'I've also taken up enough of your time. Now where's that son of mine?'

'Ben?' Poppy called. 'Your mother requires your presence.'

Ben appeared in the doorway, drying his hands on a tea towel. 'Sorry, I had washing up to do. And I didn't think I wanted to hear whatever it was you two were discussing.'

'Nothing of consequence, my boy. Now, it's time you took me for a proper guided tour of this magnificent business of yours.'

Ben brought his mother in for a side-hug, and she wrapped her arm around his waist companionably. 'To the kitchen, dear Mother. I'm just about to whip up a quick batch of vanilla biscuits. Poppy, Sophie's on her lunch break, can you grab me if anyone needs anything?'

'Sure thing.' Poppy watched the two of them walk away, their heads angled towards each other as Ben asked his mother how she'd been and what she'd been up to, the mutual admiration – the love – apparent.

Sadness threatened to swamp her, but she shoved it away. No good had ever come from wondering what it would be like to have experienced that same level of closeness with her own mother, so there was no point dwelling on it. Not when she had a mission to accomplish. She thought back to the conversation they'd had last night, and the chat she'd just had with Pam.

Not one mission. *Two* missions.

Bring some joy into his life *and*, if the opportunity arose, she'd help Ben mend the rift with his father.

Gripping the vial of glitter in her pocket, Poppy tiptoed over to Ben's counter, pulled out the plate of Jammy Dodgers and got to work.

'A little sparkle here, a little sparkle there…' she murmured, as she carefully shook the glitter into each jammy hole. 'And there we have it, magical Jammy Dodgers.'

***

Ben led his mum out to the front of the store. She'd stayed longer than he'd anticipated, which was no bad thing. They'd baked. Chatted about the goings on in her life. She'd shown interest in his work, and not once brought up his father or his father's blatant disapproval of his shop. In fact, it was safe to say they'd steered clear of that subject altogether.

The door chimes had sounded regularly, but neither Poppy nor Sophie had called for him, so he'd assumed his side of the shop had hit a lull. People's curiosity had been sated, and now it was a matter of building relationships and getting repeat business. But that didn't explain why Poppy was standing behind his counter.

'I'll call in again soon.' His mum kissed him on the cheek and brought him in for a brief hug. 'And maybe you and Poppy could come around for dinner? Poppy? Would that work for you?'

Poppy nodded, but Ben didn't miss the hint of a frown. Why wouldn't she want to have dinner with his family? She'd always enjoyed the food his mum served, to the point he sometimes had wondered if it was the only time she had a proper meal.

'Good. I'll call Ben and organise a time that suits you both.' Pam stopped to give Poppy a hug. 'Oh, and text me your number. We can have a girls' lunch.' One more squeeze, then Pam released Poppy and stepped out into the bright sunshine.

'I take it it's been quiet on my side of the shop?' Ben picked up a cloth and wiped down the table his mum and Poppy had been sitting at, then stacked the cups and saucers on top of each other.

'No, you had customers. A fair few, actually. But serving tea and cake is well within my abilities. I did a bit of waitressing in the States. And I had Sophie's help once she came back from lunch. I've just sent her back out to get me a bite to eat. Your baking's amazing, Ben, but it turns out a girl can't live on sweet treats alone.' Poppy moved out from behind his counter and strolled over to her side of the shop, all signs of her previous hesitancy and discomfort gone.

Ben took in the state of his counter. Not a speck of crumb or a spot of spillage was in sight. The tins of tea had been arranged a little differently, a little less colour-coordinated than he preferred, yet the hint of discord appealed, and the counter food was...

He leaned closer. Something still wasn't right. Something was... off.

He glanced up at Poppy who quickly turned away from him and began to rearrange a selection of unicorn-shaped USB drives.

He returned his attention to the counter. The shortbread looked as buttery, crumbly and melt-in-your-mouth as ever. The gingernuts as break-your-teeth-if-you-don't-dunk-them hard as

71

ever. Maybe he was being paranoid. It wasn't that he didn't trust Poppy to stick to the rules they'd established before their shops opened, but she'd always been mischievous, and she was acting really weird. Kept grinning to herself, her shoulders slightly shaking in silent laughter.

The door chimed as a customer entered. He stared for a moment, then gave himself a mental shake. *Eyes up, Ben. You're a gentleman.* 'Milly, good to see you again.'

'And you, Ben.' Milly adjusted the neckline of her navy-blue wrap dress, that hugged every curve, while barely containing two very… orb-like ones. 'Hey, Poppy.'

'Milly.' Poppy nodded, then busied herself unpacking a fresh shipment. Mobile phone cases, from the looks of it, a selection of pink, purple, gold, and silver – each with glitter floating around the insides.

'I thought I'd pop in, as promised, so we could talk about that date…' Milly glided up to his counter, a hint of a smile flirting about her lips. Lips that were moving towards him.

She was going to kiss him? Ben's heart picked up. Was that how they greeted each other in the magazine world? Full-on lip kisses? Her head angled to the side. No, she was expecting a cheek kiss. His heart slipped back into a steady pace. *That* he could do.

He pressed his lips to her soft cheek, then pulled away. He didn't want Milly getting any ideas. Thinking he was *interested*. Not that he wasn't interested. He just wasn't… sure. Milly had morphed into the kind of woman he thought he might be interested in. Bold, enthusiastic, but something in his gut told him to take things slow. Tread carefully. He glanced over at Poppy, her eyes flicking their way every few seconds, a tiny crease etched between her brows. Her expression matched his instinct.

Milly's hand fell across his in a proprietorial manner, forcing him to refocus on her. 'I've also had an idea, Ben. It might be a little out there. A little more showy than you're comfortable with, but…' She peered at the counter, her eyebrows raising. 'But maybe not. It seems you've changed. Maybe showy's your thing now…'

Changed? Showy? What was Milly on about? Ben inspected the cabinet more closely.

No. No way. He was *not* seeing what he thought he was seeing. Except he was.

His Jammy Dodgers were glistening.

What the hell was on there?

Small, square, glittery flecks of red. Glitter. Glitter was sprinkled on the jammy bit of his Dodgers.

Bloody Poppy had broken his rule. Sneakily at that. Did she truly think he wouldn't have seen it? Or did she think he'd see it and come over to her way of thinking? He was going to have to have a very stern chat with Poppy, as soon as Milly left. This was unacceptable behaviour. He'd stuck to his end of the bargain, not once letting her customers know that he didn't get their crazy unicorn obsession. The least he expected was for Poppy to stick to hers.

'Ben, they're gorgeous. Adorable.' He tore his glare away from Poppy who was looking at him like the picture of innocence, and was taken aback to see what looked like admiration in Milly's eyes. 'I'll take one, along with a cup of the Pretty in Peach tisane, please.'

'Absolutely. Coming right up.' Ben nodded, going into business mode.

'Does all your baking come with a unicorn-esque surprise?' Milly asked as she sat herself down onto one of the shop's chairs. 'Or is this Poppy's doing?'

'It's all…'

'Because, I was thinking, I could do a feature on your store. At our core my magazine's all about fashion, but we do like to feature things we view as fashionable. And your shop, Ben, is fashionable. And the fact you've elevated a Jammy Dodger is wonderful. They'll photograph beautifully, and those along with the fit-out, your range of tea and, of course, you, will make this the hottest destination store in London.'

Ben glanced over at Poppy who rolled her eyes at him, then went back to unpacking the phone cases.

'Oh, well. Um, that sounds great.'

'More than great, Ben. This is a coup for you. We may have to tweak your wardrobe a little though…' Milly's gaze turned uncertain as she looked him up and down.

Of all the days, why did he choose today to wear a light cotton waistcoat with his standard short-sleeved shirt and business pants combination? He looked like a bloody accountant. Not that it should matter what he looked like in front of Milly Smith. And yet it did. Just a little. Her being an ex-girlfriend and all that.

He picked up a pair of tongs and placed a Jammy Dodger on a gold-trimmed cream plate and set it down in front of her, then poured her tisane. 'I'm sure I've something more appropriate I can wear.'

'Great. Excellent. Good to hear it. That waistcoat is cute and all, in the right setting, but it's not *you*. You know what I mean, Ben?' Her fingertips caressed his hand. Lingered longer than necessary. 'Anyway, I was thinking we should meet up after work. Have a wine or beer. Chat about the shop, arrange a time for the photographer to come in. But, more importantly, we could catch up on old times.' Milly looked over her shoulder. 'You can come too, Poppy. No doubt you two still do everything together.'

Poppy shook her head. 'No, not so much. We managed to successfully spend over a decade apart, and I think Ben here's rueing the day we decided to go into business together. You two catch up, alone. Ben can fill you in on all things Sparkle & Steep without me.'

Ben didn't miss the emphasis on "Sparkle". No doubt Poppy was annoyed that Milly hadn't mentioned her shop being part of the feature, especially since, though he refused to admit it, her shop was the speciality hook. But if people came to his shop they'd technically also be coming to hers. It was a win for both of them. He'd just have to make sure she saw it that way. Diffuse any tension before it began.

'It's a date then. Shall we meet at the bar around the corner? Just after five?' Milly stood and gathered up her bag, took a bite of the Jammy Dodger and set it back on the plate. 'Mmmm, it's good.' She licked her lips, her eyes not leaving Ben.

'Thank you,' Ben choked out. When had meek and mild Milly become so... forward? 'And just after five's fine. Right. See you then.' Ben waved as Milly strolled out of the shop without a backwards glance.

Ben spun round to face Poppy. Her arms were folded over her chest and her cheekbones were high with unrepressed delight.

'What happened to Milly? She's a man-eater! Did you see the way she looked at you? Girl was hungry.' Poppy raised an eyebrow. 'Hell, her overtness nearly makes up for her rudeness.'

'She wasn't rude, she was just focused. Besides, she wasn't hungry for me, she was hungry for a biscuit. That's why she came in. That and to say hello to *both of* us.'

'Didn't look that way to me. Smart though, inviting me to join you both, great way to see if there was anything or anyone she had to worry about. Making sure I wasn't getting in the way of any chance of a redo of your relationship. Oh, and as for being hungry for a biscuit. Why don't you take a look at that plate?'

Ben glanced down to see the Jammy Dodger intact, apart from a tiny bite. And the tisane hadn't been touched. 'Oh.'

Poppy nodded slowly, the satisfaction she was getting from being right about the encounter far too great. Especially as right now she wasn't meant to be smug, she was meant to be apologising for breaking his rule.

'Oh, enough about Milly. She just wants to talk about the business, that and no doubt she wants to reconnect with friends close to home now that she's moved back here. What we need to be talking about, Miss Poppy Taylor, is the fact that biscuit—' he thrust his forefinger in the direction of the barely eaten treat '—and its friends in the cabinet are glistening.'

'Glistening?' Poppy's eyes widened in a show of innocence. 'With jam?'

Ben stared up at the ceiling, exasperation overtaking annoyance. Why couldn't Poppy make anything easy, just for once? He zeroed back in on she who would glue the world with glitter if she could. 'Don't you act all innocent with me. I've seen those big wide green eyes profess innocence a hundred times. A thousand times. You broke my rule. You crossed the line. No glitter. No sparkle. No unicorns in Steep. You agreed. We had a deal.'

'Ben.' Poppy took a step towards him. 'Ben. Ben. Benny. Ben. Ben.' She shuffled closer with every mention of his name.

Ben took a step back. There was no way he was letting her work that you-love-me-even-though-I've-been-a-bit-naughty magic on him. It may have worked on the local priest when, at the age of ten, she'd dipped into the donations bag, been caught and swore the money wasn't for her, but for the homeless person she'd seen sleeping on a park bench on the way to church.

The priest had given her the benefit of the doubt after she'd pulled those wide eyes on him and summoned a few tears. Then he'd marched her down to the park, and around the park, until they found a homeless person to give the money to. By that time Poppy had confessed that she'd planned to put the money towards rollerblades, and the priest was sure she'd learnt her lesson.

'You're thinking about the church thing again, aren't you? I was a little naughty once. Just the once. And you can't let it go. I've given plenty of money to those in need since then.' Poppy thumped her chest with her thumb. 'My *own* money.'

'Well, it seems your good behaviour has come to an end, because putting glitter on my Jammy Dodgers was an act of war.' Ben swallowed down a laugh as Poppy's wide-eyed innocent act transformed into wide-eyed horror.

'You can't do that, Ben. You can't go to war on me. Or my

customers. These are just people who want to let a little happiness into their lives. To introduce a touch of magic. And look, it worked for you.' She pointed to the biscuit on the table. 'That little bit of glitter made Milly nearly jump through the roof with excitement. She'd come up with that article idea to reel you in, but those biscuits will make the article really pop. She's probably thinking you might actually be more fun now, too. That you might be the kind of man she could have fun with. And I'm telling you now, Ben, that Milly is clearly the kind of woman who wants fun. I can't believe I ever called her a pearl-clutcher. Who knew hiding behind that sensible exterior was a vixen just begging to be released? A tigress even.' Poppy pawed the air and purred loudly.

Ben's irritation seeped away as a laugh burst forth before he could tamp it down.

'Yay!' Poppy danced towards him and pulled him into a hug. 'You're not angry at me anymore.'

'I'm still a bit angry that you told the priest I was party to your thievery back in the day. Walking around in the snow for an hour gave me chilblains.' The stiffness in Ben's shoulders and arms disappeared as Poppy pressed up against him. A 'force-hug' she'd called it when they were younger. Her infallible approach to making Ben less grumpy with her. Apparently, it still worked.

He caught a whiff of her hair. Fresh apples, mixed with what smelled like an apricot-based perfume. A twitch occurred in an area that had no business twitching when his friend was trying to diffuse the tension between them.

It seemed Poppy's force-hugs had gained some serious power over the years.

Ben broke the hug before his nether region had any further ideas and turned his attention to the dishes left by Milly.

Milly, who had become a vibrant and beautiful woman. Milly, who also kind of scared him. Unlike Poppy – who was every bit as vibrant and beautiful, but exuded sunshine, not seduction.

'Sooooo.' Poppy stretched the word out in one big wheedle. 'Can we keep the glitter in the Jammy Dodgers? It's not like it looks tacky. I mean, if I'd used the holographic edible glitter it would have looked out of place, just wrong. But the red glitter?' She kissed the tips of her fingers. 'Perfection.'

Ben sighed. He wasn't going to win this one. But then when it came to Poppy he rarely did. Rarely? More like never. 'Fine. But that's it. No more. I'm serious, got it?'

Poppy nodded. 'Got it. Now would you look at the time? Close to closing.' She took the plate and teacup out of his hands. 'You go freshen up for your big date. I'll tidy up here.'

'It's not a date.' Ben passed the crockery over. 'It's just a quick interview about the shop.'

'Sure, sure. If it helps you cement that belief try and mention my side of the shop. See if it makes it into the article.' Poppy air-quoted the last word, then disappeared into the kitchen. 'And don't do anything I wouldn't do.'

Ben grinned at Poppy's sing-song tone. Don't do anything she wouldn't do? Well, that left everything.

Chapter 8

Poppy yawned into her hand and furtively eyed the front door, searching for signs of her erstwhile business partner. Ben had texted at one in the morning to ask her to open up for him as he'd be a little late.

Little? It had just gone ten and she and Sophie had been run off their feet since the early hours serving takeaway cups of tea to people on their way to work, not to mention plating up biscuits and slices and cup after cup of tea to a local group of mums, all busy shushing and rocking their babies to sleep, or bouncing and cooing at them to keep them awake.

Meanwhile her own shop sat unattended since it was Joe's day off, and those who'd shown interest had walked out when she couldn't get to them in time.

It was like she was being punished for glittering Ben's biscuits yesterday. But was she really? Her plan had worked. Bringing a little sparkle into his shop had brought some sparkle into his life.

In the form of Milly Smith, of all people.

She held the flat of her palm to her tummy, the thought unsettling. It was like history was repeating itself and somehow, again, she'd engineered the two of them to get together. Except the first time it had involved prompting Ben to ask her out, knowing that Milly, who violently blushed whenever Ben glanced her way, would say yes.

It had been an act of self-preservation. She's started to feel things towards Ben. Feelings that kept her awake at night. That saw her wake up sweaty, uncomfortable, and scared. Scared that if she let things continue, if she slipped up and admitted her feelings, she'd face rejection from the one person who had time for her. The one person who cared about her. There was no way she was letting those feelings ruin their friendship, and Milly had seemed like an easy way to disrupt the situation.

And it had worked, for a while. Until Milly could no longer ignore the way Ben's friendship with Poppy meant more to him than his relationship with her, and had begun to see her as a tall, black-haired blockade that stopped Ben from talking about any kind of future.

Poppy had done her best to show Milly that her friendship with Ben had nothing to do with his lack of commitment. Even going so far as to put distance between herself and Ben. Telling him she couldn't join them. Saying she wasn't feeling well. That she had other plans. But every time Ben had attempted to involve Poppy, saying that he missed her, that he felt like he never saw his best friend anymore, Milly had pointed the blame squarely in Poppy's direction.

This time would be different, though. Adult Poppy didn't have *those* kinds of feelings towards Ben, because adult Poppy knew better. She knew love was as real as unicorns. A nice idea, but in the end, never really there. Friendship though? That could stand the test of time. Which was why Ben and Milly could date until the end of time, and if things went wrong it would have nothing to do with her.

Poppy checked her phone's clock again. Quarter past. Ben and Milly must have had a good time. But hopefully not so good a time that this was going to become a regular occurrence, because she had no time to be taking care of Ben's business when she had her own to run.

'What's got your knickers in a knot, Pops? You look ready to wage a mutiny.'

Poppy jumped and spun round to see Ben propping up the door, looking…

'What the hell did she do to you? You look…' Poppy searched for the word but failed to find it. It wasn't like Ben looked a wreck, he didn't. His hair was combed in its usual Hollywood matinee idol style. His olive green linen shorts were as wrinkle free as ever, but in place of a crisp short-sleeved cotton shirt he wore a navy polo. And cool, casual, canvas shoes. Not his usual loafers. Red ones, at that. Which struck her as being very un-Ben-like.

'Poppy could you stop staring at me like I'm something on a slide under a microscope.' Ben picked off an invisible fleck of dust on his polo sleeve, then sauntered into the shop.

Sauntered.

Ben was sauntering.

Ben didn't saunter. Ben strode. Marched. His movements were efficient, not fluid.

He looked like a man who'd just spent a night… Poppy clapped her hand to her mouth. Had Ben slept with Milly? Had he turned into a one-night-stand kind of guy?

Something twisted in the depths of her stomach. Tightened. Like when you were about to have to run to the toilet after eating something dodgy. Except Poppy hadn't eaten anything remotely likely to cause her stomach grief. And it didn't explain the dull ache in her heart.

What the hell was wrong with her? Was she upset that Ben had enjoyed a little between the sheets tango? Was it jealousy because it had been so long since she'd enjoyed the company of a man?

Yeah, that had to be it. Must be. But still, weird.

Poppy rubbed her stomach and commanded it to settle down.

'Are you all right, Poppy? You've gone a little green around the gills.' Ben's forehead creased in worry and he made to move towards her.

Poppy backed away, not wanting to be touched by Ben when he'd just come from another woman's bed.

Again. Weird. What was up with that? What was up with her?

'I'm fine, Ben. Women's problems. You know how it is. Except, you don't. Because you're a man.' *With a penis, apparently. A working one.* Poppy forced herself not to race to her side of the shop and give Ben more reason to be worried about her. 'So you and Milly had a good night then?'

The corners of Ben's lips twitched up. 'We did, actually. Better than expected. She's a lot of fun.'

I bet she is. Poppy pushed the thought away and squashed down the squirming in her tummy that felt uncomfortably like… jealousy. There was no way she was jealous. Just… irritated. Ben shouldn't be focusing on a relationship when he had a new business to run. The business should be his priority, not Milly.

'In fact we're going out again tonight.' Ben poured himself a cup of tea. 'God, I need this. I'm gasping. Milly gave me a run for my money last night. She had me up…'

'No, stop.' Poppy put her hands up, halting Ben mid-sentence. Whatever he and Milly had gotten up to last night was none of her business. The less she knew the more likely she wasn't going to be blamed by Milly if things didn't work out. 'I don't need any more information. I'm good. Anyway, I've got to put an order in for fresh stock and there's so much choice in one of the catalogues Joe sourced that I'm feeling a touch overwhelmed.'

'Well, why don't we go through it together?' Ben strolled over to Poppy's counter where she had her laptop browser open on the distributor's website. 'Show me what you're thinking of buying, and I'll tell you whether I think it's a good idea or not. Oh, and I was meaning to ask – you know that tea tasting I'm holding next week after the shop closes? Would you mind sticking around for it? Some moral support would be good. I'd ask Sophie and Joe, but they'd want to be paid extra for staying late, and I can't afford that. Although maybe after Milly's article goes live we might be able to talk about giving them a pay rise if they stick around and keep doing so well.'

Ben made to nudge her but Poppy inched away before he could. He and Milly had something going, and she didn't want to get in between the two of them the way Milly felt she had last time. It was better she backed off. Left them to it. Besides, if he needed moral support for his tea tasting he could ask Milly.

'Sorry, Ben, I've got something on.' Poppy scrolled through the images on the screen and pretended not to see his face fall. 'As for you helping me with the order, there's no point. You don't get unicorns, remember? You hate them. Think they're the epitome of tacky. You'd only end up convincing me to order nothing and then I'd be out of stock and out of business in a week.'

'Then I'd be out of business. We're in this together, remember, Poppy? And it's not like I've ignored what goes on over this side of the shop. I see what people buy. I see what makes their hands clap, or their voices go all high-pitched and excitable. I'm not completely oblivious, as much as I might like to be…' He pulled up a stool for each of them to sit on. 'Come on, let me help. It's the least I can do since you opened for me.'

Poppy knew enough to know when she was stuck between a rock and hard place. If she said no, Ben would know something was up. If she said yes, Ben's close proximity would force her to deal with the strange and uncomfortable feelings that had arisen. Feelings she'd much rather ignore. But, if she didn't say yes, she'd be here all day and night trying to make a decision. It had been so easy at the beginning. She'd ordered the unicorn paraphernalia she'd seen on her travels and noted down as things she'd loved to sell. But now she was being sent emails showing latest releases, and it wasn't just cute cushions and sparkly pens and stuffed toys and unicorn onesies. The whole world, male and female, young and old, had fallen for the happiness and delight unicorns brought, and now it was her job to ensure they were all catered for. Who knew something so cute could create so much pressure?

'Fine.' She settled on the stool. 'But you're not allowed to mock what you're about to see.'

'Oh, come on. Just a little? To make up for you bedazzling my Jammy Dodgers yesterday?' Ben reached over and tickled her waist, sending giddiness spiralling through her stomach.

Since when was Ben a tickler? And why had that little gesture created a whirling dervish in her gut? More importantly, what the hell had Milly done to him last night to make him the most chilled she'd ever seen him?

That had been *her* plan. Her job. To make Ben relax, add some sparkle into his life. And Milly had stolen it from her. Poppy sucked in her cheeks and bit down on them. She was being childish. Ben wasn't exclusively hers. She had no rights over his heart or his downstairs package. She was only annoyed because they'd just begun to get to know each other again, and she'd enjoyed spending time with him, and if he were back with Milly that would cut their time spent together dramatically.

Except you work in a shop together six days a week for hours at a time.

Poppy sunk her head into her hands and groaned. That stupid voice of reason needed to be smothered by one of her rainbow-coloured fluffy pillows, immediately.

'It's okay, Pops. I promise. We've got this.' Ben laid a hand on her shoulder. She made to shrug it off but stopped herself. It wasn't Ben's fault she was having some sort of mild breakdown over something that wasn't important to her. Or at least wasn't meant to be. Just because her emotions had decided to act like a prat she didn't have to hurt him.

Poppy forced a smile to her face. 'Thanks, Ben. You're one in a million.' She moused to the top of the screen. 'Maybe if we go line by line, I can note down what I think I like. You can mock away – if you really feel the need to – and then I'll make some solid decisions on what I can afford based on that program you set up. Which has come in handy, by the way. Thank you.'

Pink tinged Ben's cheeks as he ducked his head closer to the screen. 'It's my pleasure, Poppy. Anything for a friend.'

A friend. She was just a friend. And she was fine with that. It was what she had always wanted.

Totally, absolutely, completely fine.

Yeah right.

***

Ben stole a glance at Poppy. Something was up with her. He could feel it in his gut. Actually, bugger his gut, he could see it with his own two eyes. They'd been working through the online order form on and off all day, and every time he'd come within an inch of her she'd flinched like he was surrounded by an electric fence and she didn't want to get zapped.

Ben rolled up imaginary sleeves. He was going to get to the bottom of whatever was going on with Poppy if it was the last thing he did that day.

'Right, so what have we got here?' He pulled the sheet of paper that Poppy had used to note down potential items to order closer to the laptop and began to go through the form on the screen. 'First up we have a unicorn alarm clock, with the unicorn standing on top, its tail wagging between the bells to set them off at the allotted time. Ingenious. Who'd have thought to come up with that idea? And what a marvellous way to wake up.'

'You don't mean that.' Poppy perched on the edge of her stool, looking like she was ready to take flight if he so much as breathed on her. 'I bet your alarm clock is your mobile phone. Functional. Plain. With some generic alarm sound.'

'True. It is. But that doesn't mean I can't appreciate the joys of a purple and pink plastic alarm clock with glittery green hands, and sparkly silver numbers.' Ben typed a '5' in the order box. 'That many suit you? You get a discount for ten though.'

'Five is fine. If they fly out the door we'll do a bulk order.' Poppy eased back into her stool, apparently comfortable next to him so long as things were strictly work related.

'Fly out the door.' Ben laughed. 'Nice. Punny.'

Poppy's nose shrivelled, like he'd come out with a rank joke. 'What's so funny about that?'

'You said "fly out the door". You know, like a unicorn does. You made a funny pun joke.'

'Unicorns do not fly. Pegasus flies.' Poppy rubbed the side of her face, drawing attention to the bruises under her eyes. Had she not slept last night? Was she worried about the business… or had she been worried about him? About his seeing Milly? Surely not. It wasn't like it was anything serious. Just a catch up. One that had turned into dinner, then drinks, a bit of dancing. But why should that bother Poppy? He was a grown man. She must know he could take care of himself. Perhaps then it *was* work, and the long hours they'd put in, that had her looking under the weather. Though that didn't explain her need to be at an arm's length all day…

Ben rubbed his chin and was surprised to find it whiskery under his thumb. God, he must look a wreck.

And just like when he blended his own ingredients to create a custom tea, the pieces fell into place.

Poppy wasn't unhappy about the ordering. Or the opening up for him. Poppy had put his unkempt appearance and his late-night text together and decided he'd spent the night with Milly… and the idea of that was upsetting her. Which made no sense.

Poppy *wanted* him to find a girlfriend. Perhaps Poppy was worried Milly's presence would be a distraction. Well, he'd just have to show Poppy their businesses success came first.

'Right, of course. Pegasus flies. Unicorns walk, trot, canter, possibly even gallop.' Ben nodded. 'Got it. So what's next on the list to potentially order?'

'What about this costume?' Poppy pointed to an image he'd passed over as being too ridiculous to even contemplate ordering. 'You climb into it so your back legs are its back legs and there's a rein that you hold so it looks like the unicorn is rearing while you're riding it. Brilliant, isn't it?'

Ben leaned closer to the screen, trying to see what part of what Poppy was seeing was so brilliant. Their shoulders brushed, and for the first time that morning Poppy didn't recoil. A small step towards their being back on even ground, but he'd take it. 'Brilliant. Or just plain barmy. Who'd wear such a thing?'

Poppy turned to him, her lips parted, eyes stricken with shock. 'Who would wear such a thing? Who wouldn't? I can imagine stag do's running around in them. Couples heading to dress-up parties wearing them. I'll order a hundred.'

'Poppy.' Ben laid his hand on hers, stopping her from inputting the order. Again, there was no flinching, and the thunderclouds that had hung about her head had cleared. 'Might I suggest you start with a couple of those costumes. See how they go. But, I do think you should get in those fluffy unicorn pencil cases. I can see the young girls in the area going crazy for them.'

Poppy picked up his hand and placed it on the desk. 'Fine. And you're right about the pencil cases. I'm going to order an extra one for me. Why should the bright young things have all the fun?' She waggled her brows, tapped in the rest of the order and sent it off. 'Thanks, Ben. You've been a great help.'

'And so have you. I do appreciate that you opened up for me today, Poppy. I promise it won't happen again.'

'So your date won't keep you up quite so late tonight?' Poppy shut the laptop, anchored her elbow on the desk and placed her cheek in the palm of her hand.

'We're going to a movie, so we should be home and in bed at a reasonable hour…' Ben cursed inwardly as he saw the brightness in Poppy's eyes snuff out.

God, he'd made it sound like Milly was going to spend the night at his, when that was the last thing he intended to have happen. He'd enjoyed Milly's company, but he wanted to take things slowly; that way if it didn't work out no one would get hurt.

Poppy shut the laptop with a heavy hand. 'Right. Well. That's that for the day. I'd better go. I'm beyond buggered.' Poppy's hand went to her braid.

Ben knew what was coming next. A caress. A sure sign she was about to tell a fib. She'd done it since was a girl. Like she didn't want to tell a lie and patting herself made her feel better about the words coming from her mouth.

'I was binge-watching a TV show last night and got next to no sleep. The bags under my eyes are so big I could carry half my shop in them.' She released her braid, picked up her laptop, thrust it into her stripy rainbow tote and made for the door.

She was going to blame her tiredness on watching too much television? Ben knew better. He was tempted to call her on it, to point out the hand on her braid, but stopped himself. Why antagonise a situation when you could apply a salve to it? And he had something up his sleeve he had a feeling would put a spring in Poppy's step. 'Oh, and Poppy?'

Poppy paused at the door but didn't turn to face him.

'I managed to convince Milly to include your shop in the feature. London's first unicorn gift shop is far more fashion-forward than a gourmet tea shop, after all.'

Poppy nodded. Short. Sharp. Like it didn't mean anything to her, but her shoulders relaxed a little from their perma-slumped state as she started down the road, her bag swinging jauntily.

His mobile alerted him to a text.

'I'll be at the tea tasting.'

His phone pinged again.

'And I can't believe you just said fashion-forward. Omg.'

Ben grinned. Warmth flooded his heart, filling it with happiness. And something more. Something deeper. Something that he'd long felt for Poppy but been forced to repress. To forget.

Because there was no point in having those kinds of feelings for a person who didn't have those kinds of feelings for you.

Chapter 9

Ben clapped his hands, the sharp sound not making the remotest impact on the buzzing crowd who'd turned up for his tea tasting. Poppy could see from the slight sheen on his brow that he'd not expected such a turn out. And she was willing to bet he wasn't used to dealing with a crowd like this.

Lucky for Ben, Poppy was, and she knew how to get people's attention.

She jammed her thumb and index finger into her mouth and blew. The piercing whistle stopped the happy chatterers in their tracks, their heads twisting, searching out the source of the high-pitched and, Poppy had to admit, uncouth noise.

Poppy flicked Ben a thumbs up. 'Go. Your turn,' she mouthed and ducked behind the counter before the whistle could be traced to her.

'Er, hello, I mean, good evening. Thank you so much for attending what I hope will be Steep's first of many tea tastings.' Poppy peeked over the counter to see Ben's hands turned over each other as he shifted from foot to foot. 'I've got some good, I mean, marvellous teas lined up for you to enjoy. And er...'

She surveyed the crowd. Their heads were angling away from Ben. Their eyes wandering to the front window where the evening air still held heat and the sun would be warm on their skin. The absolute opposite of Ben's – and Poppy hated to admit it – cold fish demeanour, combined with the air-conditioned air. Someone had to liven up this event, and Poppy suspected that person wasn't going to be Ben.

Straightening up, squaring her shoulders and calling on the skills she'd learnt during her brief career as an in-home party hostess when she lived in New Zealand's capital city, Wellington – one that saw her wax on enthusiastically about overpriced plastic containers of all things – she made her way round the edges of the crowd to stand beside Ben.

'Ben.' She clasped his hand and gave him a small smile, one she hoped said 'trust me'. 'So sorry I'm so late. I was held up by a unicorn of all things.' She turned to the audience whose reception had thawed a tad. A few even had amused smiles on their faces. 'And apologies to you all as well. I know you've braved our chilly air to be here. And, let's be honest, we'd much rather be out enjoying the last rays of the day, probably in a pub, or a bar, or in the garden at home, sipping on something refreshing. But if we were doing that we'd be missing out on the most refreshing drink of all – tea.'

Out of the corner of her eye Poppy could see Ben's stance loosen up. His feet stopped dancing a jig and his hands ceased their fidgeting.

'I must admit, before I began working with Ben all I knew about tea was that it came in a bag, you poured hot water on it, shoved in a spoonful of sugar and a good drop of milk, and boom – instant hangover cure.' Poppy flapped her hand at the audience's shocked faces. 'Only joking. *Two* spoonfuls of sugar. And more milk. If it even looked a hint the colour of tea I'd chuck the whole lot down the sink and start again.'

Eyes grew wider. Heads shook in dismay. She had them right where she wanted them. 'Lucky for me, Ben here has taken it upon himself to show me the error of my ways. Since working side-by-side with him, I've tried white tea. Which isn't tea with a truckload of milk, I kid you not. I've tried green tea. And it doesn't taste like dried grass. And I've even tried something called a tisane, which was so good I nearly kissed him. And I would have too, but he ducked under the table to avoid me.' Poppy rolled her eyes in mock-disappointment as the crowd laughed.

Poppy turned to a curiously flushed-faced Ben and gave him a small nod. She had the crowd warmed up, it was his turn to light the fire under them. 'So, it is with much pleasure that I introduce you to Ben Evans. Owner of Steep, and Muswell Hill's finest purveyor of tea.' Poppy began to clap and the group followed suit.

Poppy stepped to the side and let Ben take centre stage. 'Thank you, Poppy, for that rousing speech. I must admit, the way you used to drink tea was appalling. I'm glad I had the opportunity to save you from yourself.'

Poppy waited for Ben to say 'again' and was surprised when he left it out. Although maybe after all this time he no longer needed to say it. That had been their dynamic from the moment they met. Ben saved Poppy from getting into too much trouble, and Poppy saved Ben from living the world's most boring life ever. Except for the twelve years when she'd been gone.

A lump formed in her throat. What had Ben done during that time? Just sat around working in a job he hated? Going out with women he deemed appropriate but whose company he didn't enjoy? Meanwhile she'd drifted, from one country to another, town to town, city to city. Convincing herself that it was all one big adventure, when really the adventure of her life had been here all the time. Opening a business with Ben. Starting a life with him.

Poppy backed towards the kitchen door. What the hell was she thinking? She wasn't starting a life with Ben. That was... what married people did. And she didn't do marriage. Or relationships of a 'we're in this for life' nature.

Besides, Ben wasn't interested in her. He was seeing Milly. They'd gone out together a few times now, and if his phone's constant text chirping was any indication of how things were going, they were going very well indeed. Whether she liked it or not. Not that it mattered what she thought. It was Ben's life. How he chose to live it, who he chose to live it with, was none of her business. And the last thing she was going to do was ask how he and Milly were going. Getting involved in any way, shape or form was not an option. She'd been blamed for their demise once, she wasn't going to blamed – or give any reason for her to be blamed – again.

Poppy stepped into the kitchen, made her way into the office where she could hear Ben, but didn't have to see him. Where she could hopefully distract herself from whatever weird, peculiar and utterly unsettling thoughts were tumbling around her mind, setting her stomach spinning like a dryer.

'Now I know Poppy talked to you about her reaction to one of my tisanes, but I'm so sorry, there'll be no kissing me tonight, as the tisanes are being kept for a future tasting. Although once you try this white tea, which I've sourced from Eastern Nepal, you may well feel impassioned.'

Poppy dropped into the chair, then slumped onto the desk, lay her head on her arm and listened to Ben's sales patter. Quick bursts of laughter, then sounds of appreciation wafted their way through the walls. Ben may have been a touch nervous at the start of the evening, but he didn't need saving. He never had. He just needed a pat on the bum to get him going. And she was his bum-patter.

Poppy let out a low moan and buried her mouth into her arm. Bum-patter? What was she thinking. And why had an image of Ben's rear looking considerably rounded and toned, and filling out those casual shorts of his too nicely for words, popped up in her mind's eye?

She squished her eyes shut and gave herself a shake. *Get a grip, girl. This is Ben, your friend. Your friend, Ben. He's no different to the guy you grew up with.*

Maybe that was the problem.

Ben was still Ben. Still kind. Caring. Thoughtful. And now wrapped up in a very cool, very hot, package that was trying very hard to confuse and upend her feelings for him.

A round of applause snapped Poppy out of her thought-addled daze. Ben was finishing up, and since she'd introduced him, it would be weird if she weren't there to thank him.

She bolted out of the room, slowed her steps as she approached the door that led to the shop and placed a warm smile on her face. One she prayed belied the fact that after all these years she still had feelings for her best friend.

Ben greeted her with those warm, brown eyes of his, made even more appealing by the happiness sparkling in them. His smile matched his eyes, and Poppy found herself being drawn into a side-hug. His arm felt warm and strong around her shoulder, his body hard against her softness. What else would be hard against her softness? Heat raced to her cheeks. And somewhere lower.

A firm squeeze of her shoulder brought her back to the room, where the crowd had gone silent. The room heavy with expectation.

Poppy picked up an empty teapot and waved it about. 'Looks like you all enjoyed what was on offer. Ben, face me?'

Poppy brought her thumb and forefinger up to Ben's chin, and inspected his cheeks, looking for signs of kisses from enamoured tea-lovers. No rogue lipstick stained his skin. All she could see was his new designer stubble, which he'd seemed to embrace since he'd started seeing Milly again. The bristles soft, yet spiky. Manly. More than that… they were sexy.

She turned back to the crowd. 'Did you not love the tea as much as I said you would? I expected him to be half-ravaged. Does that mean I'm the only person here who when they discover what good tea is gets a little overly passionate?' She winked as the crowd tittered.

She released Ben's chin and sucked in a lungful of air, only to breathe in his lemon-fresh scent. The aroma grounded her. Same Ben smell. Of course he used the same soap he had used as a boy. Sure, the outside might be butterfly-in-the-belly sexy, but he was still that same kid she met in the hedge, who'd told her off for stealing fruit from neighbours' trees, who'd ensured she'd done her homework every night so she wouldn't get in trouble.

Feeling on steadier ground Poppy turned her attention to the crowd. 'Thank you for coming. Thank you for supporting Steep. Now we won't keep you, and if the strains of guitar I can hear floating down the road are anything to go by it sounds like the Muswell Hill Summer's Night Festival is under way. So, go – enjoy your night. And we look forward to seeing you again soon.'

The crowd clapped once again, less exuberantly and for a shorter period, and in no time at all the shop was empty, and Ben still had her in a half-hug. And it didn't feel like he was about to let her go.

Part of Poppy wished he wouldn't. But most of Poppy knew better. 'That went well from the sounds of it.'

Her words broke the spell that had seen them so companion-ably interlocked.

Ben removed his arm, and Poppy took a step back. Despite the distance, something shimmered between them.

Warmth, friendship, success at a job well done. That was what it was, Poppy attempted to convince herself. That was what it had to be. All it could be.

Ben deserved more. Ben deserved better. Ben deserved a Milly or someone like Milly. Not a Poppy who couldn't love. Who'd never been taught how.

She folded her arms across her chest. A barrier. Not so much against Ben, who she knew would never overstep any boundaries, but against herself. In this moment, despite knowing better, she didn't trust herself. Not when Ben was staring at her with open admiration. His lips kicked up in a smile that told her the event had been a raging success, and that he believed she had a great deal to do with that. It was an enticing combination, an alluring one.

But not one she was prepared to do anything about. Ben wasn't a playmate. He was more than that. He was the kind of man who would want the whole package. Everything she had. More than she could ever give.

She picked up two empty glass teapots. Anything to occupy her hands, which wanted to clasp Ben's cheeks, to bring him closer, so she could...

Kiss his moving lips. Bugger. Ben had been talking and she'd been fantasising. Not fantasising. Thinking. Imagining what not to do.

'Earth to Poppy? You in there?' Ben waved his hand in front of her eyes. 'I was just saying thank you. You were amazing the way you took control at the start. Shook me out of my stupor. Put me in front of a couple of clients and I'm fine. In control. More than a handful of people and my heart starts going like a jackhammer and that causes my brain to stutter and, well, I'm glad you were there to steady me. So, again, thank you.'

Poppy shrugged. 'It's nothing really. Just a business partner helping a business partner.' She took the teapots to the kitchen and began rinsing them out. Footfalls on floorboards told her she was being followed.

***

'Don't make out like what you did wasn't a big deal, Poppy. It meant a lot to me. They could have all gotten bored and left. I was competing with that festival out there. They could've turned on their heels and headed out into the sun, ate some candyfloss, enjoyed a kebab. Instead, because of you, they stayed. And, because of you, I can afford to take us out for a celebration. What do you say?'

Ben took the teapot out of Poppy's hand and set it on the counter. 'Those can wait until tomorrow.' He leaned against the bench, ducked his head a little and tried to catch Poppy's eyes.

When she'd taken over his tasting he'd felt an uncomfortable mix of embarrassment that he was so terrible at hosting and anger that she'd jumped in without warning, but she'd worked her magic on the crowd. Making them laugh. Feel at ease. All the while reminding him that he knew what he was talking about. That they had a reason to stay and listen to him. She'd given him the strength that his father's disapproval, still gnawing in the back of his mind, had threatened to take away.

And with every explanation of the tea people were tasting, with every eye-close and 'mmm' of appreciation, with each sale that he rung up, his belief in himself had grown – to the point that he didn't care what his father thought. He was doing what he wanted to do, and he was going to be every bit as successful in business as he was as a solicitor. More so.

And he wanted to share that feeling with Poppy. To show her just how much he appreciated her.

'Seriously, Pops, the dishes can wait until tomorrow morning. I'll come in extra early and get them done. We're due a celebration. We didn't even properly toast the opening of our store. The most we've done is indulge in a little cheap red wine and eat some curry. Come on.' He took Poppy's hand and gave it a gentle shake. 'We could head out. Have a drink or two. Maybe even three. I read there was a pop-up bar selling cocktails, and it's such a nice night for it.'

'Oh God, don't say that word. Remember when we stole bits of booze from our parents' cabinets and made our own cocktails…'

'How could I forget? We curled up under a tree in Queen's

Wood and fell asleep. I swear I still have a crick in my neck from the root I used as a pillow.' Ben angled his head to the left, then the right, a small click filled the air. 'See? Still there. A permanent reminder of my second hangover. And my first and only very serious grounding.'

Poppy drummed her fingertips on the bench. 'I've not had a cocktail since. Well, not one that has seven different spirits in it…'

'Even a whiff of bourbon makes me feel ill.' Ben shuddered. 'But we were seventeen. We couldn't even handle a sneaky shandy back then. Besides, we can both look after each other. If one looks like they're about to take things too far the other has to drag them home. Come on, Poppy…' Ben brought his hands into a steeple and gave her his best pleading look. 'Let me say thanks. I'll even buy you dinner. What do you say?'

The chirp of his text tone broke the silence.

'That'll be Milly.' Poppy's tone was flat, her face void of expression. 'You should check it.'

Ben pulled out his phone and checked the message.

I hope tonight went well. Celebratory drink later? X

'See…' Poppy tapped the edge of the phone. 'She wants to celebrate with you. You should go. I don't want to be seen to be getting in the way again.' Poppy made to turn away.

'Poppy, first of all, I can't believe you just read that message over my shoulder. Second of all, Milly can wait. Tonight's about us.'

Ben caught Poppy's hand. The heat of her palm burned into his. The sensation felt electric, igniting his veins. Searing his blood. That little bit of his skin on hers enough to make him want to pull her to him, to wrap his arm around her waist, to hold her cheek ever so gently, and touch her lips with his own.

This was what he was missing with Milly. That spark. That tiny flicker of passion that, with a simple touch, could flare into an inferno. Never, not when they were young, nor now that they were older, did he feel like this about Milly. His heart singing for her. His body reaching.

Ben released her hand, then offered his arm. 'Poppy, I don't want to celebrate tonight's success with Milly. I want to celebrate with *you*. And I want you to tell me how you had that crowd eating out of your hand so easily.'

Her eyes went to the crook he'd made. Her brow gnarled up, like she was having second thoughts. Then, so quickly he wondered if he'd imagined the hesitation, her forehead smoothed out and her arm was hooked through his.

'Well, Ben. When I was overseas I was actually a bit of a big deal.' They walked through the shop, Poppy scooping up her bag as they made their way to the front door. 'I was, while I was in New Zealand, one of their biggest DJs on the radio. And, part of that job was to host live gigs. The station director said I was like a fish to water. They offered me crazy money to stay, but, you know…'

'Another country, another experience. And you're a big fat liar, Poppy Taylor.' Ben opened the door and pulled Poppy into the barbecue-scented air. 'That hand on your braid says it all.'

'Damn it.' Poppy yanked her hand from her braid. 'I have spent half my life trying to stop doing that. I even did that rubber band round the wrist ping thing to try and get me to stop. Yet, the moment I'm around you all my bad habits come back to play. Ben, you're a bad influence.' She wagged her finger at him, then broke into a smile. 'Truth be told, I was a party hostess for a company that sells plastic bowls and kitchen stuff. I did well. And they did beg me to stay.'

'But… another country, another experience?' Ben nodded at newly familiar faces, and faces he'd known since he was a child, as they threaded their way down the street towards the festival. Only a few weeks in and he already had a good handful of regulars. He suspected he'd have more after tonight's tasting. And it would never have happened without Poppy. He didn't just owe the success of his shop to her. He owed his happiness.

Poppy halted, dragging him to a stop. 'Wow. Would you get a load of all that bunting? It's rainbowlicious.'

He craned his neck to see what she was seeing. Sure enough, row after row of bunting in bright red, yellow, green, blue, pink, purple and orange fluttered in the evening breeze. Interspersed were strings of golden fairy lights, barely glowing in the mid-evening sun, but when sunset came they'd cover the festival-goers in a romantic golden glow.

Romantic golden glow? He wished. But he'd known Poppy long enough to know that she was about as interested in him like that as he was in allowing her to cover his tea shop in unicorn garb. And if anything were to change, as unlikely as that was, it would have to be on her terms.

A good time, not a long time. That's what she'd want. Something as easy and disposable as the bunting above.

'It's a colourful sight all right. It's like one of your unicorns farted all over the sky.' The dry observation earned him an elbow to the ribcage. 'You should probably be stocking this. It'd be great for kids' parties. Maybe see if you can get glittered bunting.'

'You're right. What would I do without you?' Poppy faced Ben, the edges of her lips turned up in a playful smile.

'You'd pack your bags, head overseas and probably find your-self the star of some daytime soap. You've always had a flair for the dramatic.' Ben ducked back as Poppy unlooped her arm from his and went to swat the backside of his head. 'Soap star or some sort of cage fighter…'

Poppy put her fists up, fighting style, landed a soft punch to his arm then rolled her eyes at him. 'As if. I wouldn't want to ruin this face for television that you think I have.' She stood on her tiptoes and took in the lay of the land. 'I can see the cocktail stand. Come on.'

Poppy's hand clutched his and he found himself dragged into

the laughing, smiling, already slightly tipsy throng. Her fingers interlaced through his, probably only to ensure they wouldn't be broken up by the push and pull of the crowd, but it felt so *right*.

And *so* wrong when she released her grip as they reached the stand.

'Two mojitos, please.' Poppy dove into her bag and pulled out her wallet.

'Put your wallet away, Pops.' Ben grabbed the offending item and dropped it back in her still-open bag. 'My shout, remember?'

'God, I'd hate to see you on a date. I bet you never let whoever you're trying to seduce pay.' Poppy zipped her bag shut and faced the barman, who was muddling the ingredients for the mojito.

'A gentleman has no need to seduce. My fine manners and good looks do all the work for me.' Ben paid the barman and handed Poppy her plastic cup filled to the brim with the aromatic concoction.

'And that wonderful streak of humbleness too, no doubt.' Poppy held her cup up and they thunked their glasses together, twin streams of clear liquid spilling over the top, onto their fingers.

Poppy brought her fingers to her mouth. 'Mmmm. That's good.' Her eyes closed as she sucked off the liquid.

Such an innocent action. But Poppy licking her fingers was the most erotic thing Ben had ever seen. The sheer enjoyment, the way she revelled in the flavours, in the sensation.

God, he wanted to be her fingers. No, what he wanted was to take those fingers and do the job for her.

'Ben.' Poppy's sharp tone shattered his reverie. 'Don't tell me you're one sip in and already in la-la land.'

'Just high on success, Poppy.' Ben jerked his head to the left. 'Look, food trucks. We should get some food in us if we're going to have more of these.'

'And we are so going to have more of these. Lots more. I saw a cider stall across the way. We should try that out too.' Poppy took a long sip of her mojito. 'There, now I won't be trying to get the ground drunk. This mojito is too good to waste.'

They walked shoulder-to-shoulder towards the area where the food stalls and trucks were set up, laughing at the juggling clowns who threatened to upend their drinks with wayward balls; ducking the sticky ovals of candyfloss that dotted the landscape; dinging the odd line of song along with the band that was playing a medley of hits from the Sixties.

If Ben could have imagined a perfect setting for a date, this would have been it. And the person he'd have wanted to have with him was right beside him.

Put your arm around her. See what she does. Dare you.

Ben nearly choked on his mojito. Where had that thought come from? He eyed his drink with suspicion. How much white rum was in here? Sure, he'd put his arm around Poppy before. Hell, he had earlier. And she hadn't pulled away. But this voice wasn't coming from a place of friendship. Or a place of gratefulness. It was coming from a place that was telling him if he didn't at least try to make his feelings known to Poppy he could well one day live to regret it.

Go on. Do it. The voice needled. *What have you got to lose?*

What did he have to lose? His business? No, that he was sure would survive if making a move on Poppy caused her to up and leave. Yes, he'd be scrambling to make things work. To fill the space. To have enough customers coming in that he wouldn't have to sink any more of his personal finances into it. But his business would be okay.

His heart however?

His mother had been truthful when she'd said he'd moped after Poppy had left. Every day had been a black hole without her. The only way he'd filled it was by buckling down at university, studying hard, finding happiness in how proud his parents were of his achievements. Eventually he'd believed he was over her.

Turns out you could believe something until the cows came home, but it didn't make it true.

Not that his feelings mattered. Poppy had made it clear she didn't do relationships. Didn't believe in love. If she caught the merest hint of how he felt she'd be gone. And this time he didn't think she would return. And he didn't think he could handle sinking into the black hole of Poppylessness again. He didn't believe his business would pull him out of it, no matter how well it did.

Still, he hadn't done as well as he had by not trying.

Ben took a deep breath. Another. He exhaled slowly, and as he did he brought his arm up and draped it over Poppy's shoulders as casually as he could. 'Poppy, look over there.' He pointed out a food cart on the other side of the street. 'New York hot dogs. I've always wanted to try one.'

'Bet they're nothing like what you get in New York. But, I guess if you've never had one before, then there's only one way to find out. Don't judge me if I find it lacking and spit it out.' Poppy screwed up her face in preparation for hating the potentially putrid food but allowed Ben to steer her in its direction.

Hope surged in Ben's heart, taming its rapid rhythm. She hadn't shrugged him off. She hadn't given him a 'what the heck are you up to' glare. In fact, he'd go so far as to say she looked happy.

Something warm touched his waist. The warmth spreading around his back. He glanced down. It was a hand. Attached to an arm. That belonged to Poppy.

Was this really happening? This wasn't companionable arm-in-arm walking, like they'd often done. This was a couple walk. Intimate. In sync. The kind of walk which led to languorous kisses, and who knew what else…

'Two dogs, please. With the lot.' Poppy turned to Ben. 'You good with that?'

Ben nodded, too focused on the fullness of her lips, and the idea of kissing those lips, to talk.

103

'Good, then pay the man.' Poppy jerked her head towards the vendor who was waiting patiently for his money.

Ben disengaged himself unwillingly from Poppy to fish his wallet out of his back pocket. He'd been brave enough to put his arm around her once. But to do it twice? She'd know something was up.

'Here you go.' Poppy passed him a hot dog dripping in mustard, sauerkraut and some oniony tomato-sauce type concoction. 'There's a table over there, let's nab it before anyone else does.'

Without waiting for his agreement, she took off into the crowd, made a beeline for the table and dropped into one of the seats surrounding it.

Grinning up at Ben as he joined her, she set her drink down, and promptly sunk her teeth into the hot dog. Like the mojito before she closed her eyes and quietly moaned as she chewed. Did she moan like that when she was taking part in other things she enjoyed? Or was it just food and drink that set her off?

Ben took a bite of his hot dog, his eyes closing just as Poppy's had done as the flavours hit his palate. A tantalising mix of sour, spice and salt exploded in his mouth, and he had to stop himself from moaning as Poppy had done.

He swallowed and opened his eyes to find Poppy halfway through her dog. 'So, does it meet up to your exacting expectations?'

Poppy nodded vigorously, her mouth too full of food to get a word out. She raised her hand and gave him the thumbs up, then grabbed her mojito and took a swig, washing the food down. 'Better than I remember. I could do another.'

Ben jumped up to satisfy her request, but was stopped by Poppy's hand on his, pulling him back into his seat. 'No. I can get it. Or maybe I won't. I probably shouldn't ruin my appetite for some of the other goodies I may discover tonight.' Her lips quirked to one side and her cheekbones lifted high.

Was that a double entendre? Was Poppy suggesting that he

might be a treat? His underwear suddenly felt like it had shrunk a size, and he was glad to have worn his more casual dress shorts that had extra room in the crotch area.

'I mean, there's candyfloss. And dumplings.' Poppy's lips flattened out as her brows drew together.

The flame that had kicked up in Ben's heart and in his nether region sputtered out. Poppy must've realised what she'd said came across as an invitation. And in bringing the conversation back to food she'd taken that possibility off the table.

'You've always loved candyfloss.' Ben took another bite of his hot dog. What had started out as an amazing mouthful now felt dry, stodgy, and he had to work extra hard to chew it enough to be able to swallow it. He set the hot dog down on a paper napkin and inspected it. It looked the same, proving what he suspected. It wasn't the hot dog, it was disappointment that had killed his hunger.

'Yeah, well. It's pink, fluffy, and the sight of it makes you happy. What's not to like?'

'It rots your teeth.' Ben tore off a piece of bun and threw it to an expectant sparrow. 'But then, why am I surprised? Pink and fluffy? Sounds pretty much like half of your shop.'

Poppy finished off her hot dog and wiped her hands on a napkin. 'Yeah, well, I'm a sucker for all things happy-making. If it brings a little extra joy into the world then I'm all for it.'

'Like love. That brings joy into the world.' Ben picked up his hot dog and forced himself to take another bite. He knew this was rocky territory, but he was never going to get anywhere with Poppy if he couldn't show her that love wasn't the load of bollocks she believed it to be.

'Are we really going to discuss this again?' Poppy drained her mojito in one long gulp and set her cup down with an irritable thump. 'You know I don't believe in love. Not the romantic kind. Friendship love, yes. Love of cute furry animals, yes. But flowers and jewellery, long walks on the beach kind of love?' Poppy picked up the discarded napkin and began to rip little tears around the edges. 'As far as I can see, love is a waste of time. People say they love each other, but then go on to treat each other with disdain. To go out of their way to hurt the one they're supposed to love. I mean, look at you and your dad. Look at how he's behaving. Ignoring you. Not supporting you. That's not how you treat someone you love.'

Ooph. Poppy wasn't holding back, which meant he was getting to her. 'Dad's behaviour doesn't mean he doesn't love me. It shows how much he loves me. He cares enough to be angry, to be hurt. And he'll come around. He can't hold this grudge forever. He *won't.*' At least Ben hoped that was the case.

'Then that's another reason to avoid love. I can't be bothered with the drama of having someone angry at me. Of treating me terribly. Who needs that kind of pain?' Poppy pursed her lips and looked into the distance. Her eyes glittered, but with one hard and fast blink any wetness was gone.

Who needs that kind of pain? Not Poppy, apparently. And Ben had a feeling that was because she'd experienced it enough to shun that which had caused it. Love. And in shunning love she believed she was safe from feeling pain ever again.

Ben held down a sigh. He was going about this all wrong. Trying to talk logically to Poppy was never going to win her round to the idea that love existed. That it was every bit as wonderful as the unicorns she loved, and comforting, steadying and 'there' as a good cup of tea. The only way Poppy was going to believe in love was if she felt it at her core. If it infused her soul. And if she believed in her heart the person who loved her was never going to hurt her, was never going to make her feel anything less than the brilliant person she was.

'I don't get it, Pops. I just don't. I can't understand how someone who created a whole shop designed to bring people happiness could refuse to acknowledge love. Refuse to believe in it. Surely you've felt it? Surely you've been in love?' Ben picked up his nearly empty cup and finished off his drink, his eyes not leaving Poppy, who had gone still, like someone had hit pause.

'Once.'

The word came out a whisper, so quiet Ben wondered if he'd misheard her.

'Once, I loved someone.' Poppy crossed her legs. Folded her arms over her chest. To keep the memory in? Or to keep him out? 'But I could see where things were going. Knew if things continued it would never come to anything. We were in different places. And very different people. I would have ruined things for him.' Poppy averted her gaze. Looked unseeingly into the crowds. 'That's why I can't believe in love, because it has the power to rip away all that is good. It has the power to make you hate yourself.'

Ben's gut twisted. With jealousy. With sadness. With defeat.

Poppy had loved once. When she was overseas. And it had gone wrong. Her eyes, glittering in the late evening sun, and her hands firmly fixed to her side – not stroking her braid – told him she was telling the truth. For all her bravado she still carried the scars of that love.

'Oh.' Ben was at a loss for words. What did you say to someone whose experience of love was so painful it was easier to avoid it? To pretend it didn't exist? 'I'm sorry, Poppy. I didn't know…'

Poppy blinked rapidly, and when her eyes met his they were clear, and as hard as the stone they reminded him of. 'No. You didn't know. There was no reason for you to. What I don't get, Ben, is why you're so adamant that romantic, soulmate, life partner, kind of love is the be all and end all? You haven't had a long-term relationship – well, apart from Milly when we were young. But then those feelings you have when you're that young, it's not love really, is it?' Poppy continued feathering the napkin, her eyes not meeting his. Like she was afraid of what she'd see in them if she looked up.

'I know love, Poppy. I know it well. And I've known it for a long time.' Ben let the words hang. She could take from them what she wanted. Or she could ignore them. Or manipulate them to keep herself safe. Either way, in his own way, he'd told her the truth. He knew love, because he'd once loved her. He'd tried to love Milly when they were younger, but he'd never got past liking her. But Poppy? He'd loved her the moment her braided head had popped through their joint hedge and she'd introduced herself and informed Ben that he was to be her new best friend, then took him by the hand and showed him how to make mud pies.

Music filled the air as a new band took the stage. The vibrancy of saxophone and trumpet, playing along with the rat-a-tat-tat of a drum and the tinkle of a piano.

Poppy scooted her chair back and held her hand out to Ben. 'Enough of this talk. You know you're wasting your time trying to convince me to give love a shot. Now, come. Dance with me. I adore a good bit of swing.'

Unable to resist her brilliant smile, or the lure of her hand, Ben allowed Poppy to pull him out of his seat and found himself dragged towards the main stage. The infectious drum beat matched the rhythm of his heart. The brass melody skipped over the rapid rhythms, pulsing and pushing the dancers onto the floor.

Before he knew it, he was being swung round and round, back and forth. He went to tell Poppy he was having a great time, but she shook her head. And she was right. Words would ruin the magic. Break the spell the music was creating. For with every touch of their hands, every step they took, every twirl and swirl that saw their bodies brush against each other, a headiness grew between them, their eyes not once leaving each other as the band switched up the tempo then brought it down again. It was like they were one – able to anticipate the others next move before it was taken.

Without warning, the music slowed into the kind of song

where you'd take your lover and bring them to you. Hand to hand. Hip to hip. Chest to chest. Lip to lip.

Ben paused for a semi-second, unsure what to do, but Poppy made the decision for him and closed the gap.

'I never knew you could move like that.' Poppy's words, light and breathy, tickled his ear, sending a rippling shiver over his skin.

'*I* didn't know I could move like that.' Ben's heart danced against his ribcage as Poppy laid her head on his shoulder. Her body melted into his. 'Worn out?' he teased. Then kicked himself. *Way to get the woman you have feelings for to stop being all melty against your body.* He waited for her to stiffen, to break away.

'No. Just comfy. Relaxed.'

They swayed in silence to the tender lilt, surrounded by couples who mirrored their closeness. Their happiness. But Ben was willing to bet money that none of them were dancing on air like he was.

The song finished to rapturous applause, with the band thanking the crowd and wishing them a good evening. And just like that, the festival was finished.

And, Ben realised with a sinking heart, so was their night.

Chapter 10

What are you doing?

Poppy ignored the hissing voice in the back of her head. The one that had been wailing on her ever since she took Ben's hand and dragged him up to the dancefloor.

This is a bad idea.

If you do what you're thinking of doing you'll screw your business.

One more dance and he's going to think you're interested.

Quit those lingering looks. They won't lead anywhere good.

And yet she hadn't been able to help herself.

Maybe it was the music. Maybe it was the mojito. Maybe it was the way Ben's hair was slightly mussed and his newly discovered stubble erased his earnestness and gave him a devil-may-care edge.

Or maybe it was because Ben kept staring at her like he didn't want to be anywhere else, with anyone else, in the whole wide world.

Now here they were. So close. Still swaying to the music that had stopped playing at least half a minute ago. Neither one willing, or able, to break their hold on each other. It was as if their souls had intertwined and refused to untangle after so many years apart.

'People are going to stare if we keep dancing to imaginary music,' Ben murmured. Yet he didn't back away. Didn't allow distance to separate them.

'They can stare. I like our imaginary music,' Poppy whispered back, unable to speak any louder, her throat so full of emotion it threatened to choke her.

Ben pulled back, just enough that she could see his chestnut eyes glint with good humour. 'Do you think we'd hear our imaginary music if we were sitting down? We could companionably sway together on a seat. It's just... my feet would appreciate it.'

Poppy laughed. 'Now you mention it, same. My feet are screaming at me to lie down.' Heat rushed to her chest and travelled up to her cheeks. Did that sound like an invitation? Would Ben think she was suggesting instead of sitting together they should lie down together?

She glanced up to see Ben's eyes swimming with unshed tears. She felt a vibration through her chest and looked down to see his chest heaving with silent laughter.

'What's so funny?' She stepped back, breaking the hold they had on each other.

'You are.' Ben's laughter rumbled freely. 'The look on your face just now. It was like you thought you'd extended an invitation to me to come back to yours for a mutual lie down.'

Poppy forced a laugh out. High-pitched and wobbly, it sounded beyond fake. Though hopefully Ben was laughing too hard to notice.

'Well, of course I wasn't suggesting that. I mean, that would be ridiculous. It was fine for us to have mutual lie downs in the same bed when we were six, but now? Well... you're dating Milly, and that would be weird, and even if you weren't dating Milly the two of us having a mutual lie down would be...' Poppy trailed off, at a loss for words. The word 'inappropriate' refused to come forth. Even though that's what the little voice in her head kept telling her spending a night with Ben would be.

'Poppy? Your feet still sore?' Ben hooked his arm, and Poppy threaded hers through it.

'Yes. Turns out laughter can't ease pain.' Or embarrassment.

'Then come on.' Ben gave her a gentle tug and they weaved their way through the thinning throngs.

'Where are you taking me?' Poppy asked, although she had a feeling she knew where, the landmarks being ones she passed twice a day on her way to and from work.

'I'm taking you home to bed.' Ben flashed her a cheeky grin. When had Ben become such a flirt? With her?

Tonight the barrier between them had evaporated into almost thin air. Tension vibrated between them, tension that could either bring them together or keep them apart.

Don't screw this up. He means too much to you.

Common sense dowsed the curiosity, the desire, that had her heart beating as fast as the band's snare drum. No, she wouldn't be overstepping the boundary their long-running friendship had established. She loved Ben too much as a friend to cross the line. She didn't want to see their relationship turned upside down, again.

Years ago – the night she'd left Muswell Hill – she and Ben had arrived home from a night out to celebrate the end of school. The beginning of the rest of their lives. Hers was wishy washy at best. With no place at a university, she had vague plans to find a job in London, to move out of home and into a flat as soon as she had enough money saved – whereas Ben's life was all mapped out. University, career, marriage to someone appropriate. As he'd swayed backwards and forwards on the pavement outside their homes, holding onto her forearms to keep himself up, he'd confessed how he envied her ability to be who she wanted, to do what she wanted. He'd told her he wished he was brave like her, that he'd love to be able to throw caution to the wind and just see what happened, without fear of repercussions, of disappointing those he loved. She'd tried to make him see that all that

112

freedom meant nothing when she wasn't even sure who she was, or what she should be, but he didn't listen, Ben had had too many beers in him to be able to.

She'd gone to walk him to his door, to see him inside safely, but Ben had stopped her. Placed his hands on either side of her cheeks, then slurringly told her he loved her. That he'd give it all up to be with her. That she was what he wanted. Not a career. Not a mapped-out life. Not a Milly.

'I want you.'

Poppy touched her stomach as she remembered how the beer inside had begun to swirl, mixing with the shock of Ben's confession, causing her to feel off-balance. Tempting her to blow up his planned-out life. But then his front door had opened. His father had wrapped his arm around his son's shoulders and propelled him inside, shaking his head as he did so.

So she'd gone home. Found her mother at the kitchen table, tipsy after another one of her parties. Not only tipsy, but willing to talk to her daughter, for once. And talk her mother did. The wine loosening her tongue, letting words – and the truth – fly across the table. Words that led to Poppy taking flight.

Poppy drove that memory away. The tendrils of it alone threatened to swamp her, to drown the confidence she'd built, the sense of self she'd worked hard to attain while travelling the world, finding out who she was, where she belonged, and who she belonged with.

'Here we are. Home.'

The clarity in Ben's voice dragged Poppy from her reverie.

'Poppy.' He touched her forearm, concern shining in his eyes. 'We're home.'

We're home.

It sounded so right. Like her home should be his home. His home ought to be hers.

'Good. I must be more tired than I realised. Asleep on my feet.' She fished around in her bag for her keys, and scooped them up, but shaking fingers saw them fall to the ground. 'Whoops. Clumsy old me. I guess that mojito was stronger than I realised.'

She bent down to grab them, and promptly knocked her head against something hard.

Ben let out a groan.

'Oh, shit. Ben. Sorry.' Poppy snatched the keys and stood up to find Ben rubbing his forehead.

'I know I've said you're hard headed in the past, Pops, but tonight you proved it. What's that skull of yours made of? Steel?' Ben's eyes squinted in pain, as he gave his head a small shake. 'I might have to start wearing a helmet round you from now on.'

'Is it that bad? Let me look.' Poppy reached up and removed Ben's fisted hand and inspected the damage. 'You've got a small egg forming, but I think you'll survive. Take two aspirin and call me in the morning so I know you're still alive.'

'I'll be fine.' He waved her concern away. 'If I could handle our old yearly ritual of stargazing in the snow, then I can handle a bump on the head.' Ben's lips lifted at the corners, the lines of pain crossing his forehead smoothed out. 'Speaking of morning. It's time you tucked yourself up. A local mothers' group has booked a couple of tables, and you know how their kids love to frolic on your side of the shop. Joe might want to get that horrible unicorn onesie of his ready.'

Poppy faked a shudder. 'Children running amuck. Terrible. Can't have that. They'll beg their mothers to buy something and I'll make money. Or their mothers will say no and I'll have a hell of a mess to clean up. I know! I'll create a box of unicorn toys that you can keep on your side of the shop for kids to play with free of charge. It'll be their gateway drug to all things unicorn and you'll be left with the tidying up.'

Ben leaned forward, his nose inches from hers. His eyes sparkled under the streetlight that bathed the front of the terraced homes in a golden light. Tawny flecks were scattered through amongst the decadent chestnut colour. How had she never noticed them before?

'Not. Going. To. Happen. Miss Taylor.' Ben grinned. 'You may have convinced me a smattering of red edible glitter on Jammy Dodgers is a cute twist on the classic, but I will not have any more of your unicorn garb on my side of the shop. Try it and I'll have a T-shirt printed saying "only dreamers love unicorns".'

Poppy clapped her hands together. Ben was onto something. 'That's a brilliant idea! What a gorgeous slogan. They'd be snapped up. I could do them in different shades and styles. I can imagine some cool hipster dude wearing one.'

Ben slapped his hand to his forehead, then groaned as his palm landed smack bang on his bump. 'Ow. Instant karma.'

'Poor Ben.' Poppy held up her hand for a high five. 'Or should I say, Brilliant Ben. When I make my fortune from those T-shirts I'll be sure to send you a whole bunch for free.' She jiggled her hand, reminding him he had to hold up his end of the high five.

An unwilling huff escaped Ben's lips. Then his hand met hers. His fingers closed over the back of her hand, locking their palms in place, sending delectable zaps of pleasure straight to her heart, which then spilled through her body, warming it, fighting off the slight chill in the air. 'Only you could take my attempt at giving you grief and spin it into something wonderful.'

Poppy attempted a casual shrug, and half-wondered if Ben could feel the way her pulse had picked up through the skin of her palm. Could he hear her heart beating as rapidly as the tempo of the music had earlier?

'Thanks for a wonderful night, Poppy. And thank you again for being there for me. Making the tea tasting something special.'

Poppy attempted to swallow and discovered you couldn't swallow if your mouth was bone dry. 'Anything, for a friend.'

Ben released her hand. 'Right, for a friend.'

They stood staring at each other, Ben's face unreadable. Poppy willed herself to take the two steps into the house, but her feet wouldn't budge.

'Right, well I'll be off.' Ben turned to leave.

''Kay. Bye.' Poppy whispered and went to unlock the front door. The thumping in her heart slowed. She paused, searching for the relief that should have enveloped her with Ben and his sexy new stubble, lush yet firm lips, and kind but intense eyes, now well on his way home. There was none. Just a hollowness in her heart.

A firm hand clasped her arm and she went to scream thinking she was about to be mugged, but before she could she found herself twisted around to face Ben, his arm encircled her waist, brought her to him with no hesitation, as his lips descended upon hers. Fast. Furious. Like he was afraid if he didn't kiss her then and there then he never would.

His hand found the nape of her neck, his fingers curling around it, his thumb stroking her soft skin, over and over, sending lightning bolts down her spine. No tantalising tingles. No delectable heart-warming zaps. Pure, raw, electricity.

She went to lean into the kiss, but Ben broke away before she could. His chest heaved as he sucked in a breath. His eyes bore into hers. Daring her to say what had happened between them was something that shouldn't happen again. That it hadn't been good. Good? Try unforgettable.

Poppy inched closer and placed her hands on either side of his cheeks and brought him to her. Their lips met, touched, feather-light, as she breathed in his clean lemony scent. Relished the prickly hair that pierced her fingertips. The kiss intensified as Ben wrapped his arms around her waist, his hands dropping lower, cupping her bum, bringing her to him, melding her to him, as their mouths opened to each other, their tongues twisting and pushing, tasting and exploring.

The energy between them was so great Poppy could see stars despite her closed eyes.

This was what she'd hoped for all those years ago, but refused to believe she was worthy of having. This was what she'd dreamed of. And it was a thousand, million, trillion times better than any teenage fantasy she'd ever concocted.

She blindly reached for the key in the lock. If their kiss escalated things were about to get X-rated, and she didn't need to wake up with her face plastered on the local social media page, blasted as an inappropriate strumpet hell-bent on destroying the innocence of local children.

'Poppy. Stop,' Ben murmured into her mouth, kissing her one more time before pulling back. But not away. His arms were still wrapped around her, keeping her in place. Keeping them together. 'I hate to do this, but I've got to go. I've got work tomorrow, and my business partner's nose gets all bent out of shape if I'm late.'

'Well we couldn't have that. I hear she's got a very cute nose, and I wouldn't want to be the reason it becomes disfigured.' She rolled her eyes and grinned. Hoped it would hide the disappointment that sat heavy in her stomach, dowsing the heat, the tension that had built during their kiss.

'We should do this again, sometime?' Ben raised an eyebrow. Daring her to say no? As if she would. She wanted more of what had been on offer. She wanted the lot.

'Definitely.' She turned the key and stepped inside. 'See you at work. And don't be late.'

Ben doffed an imaginary cap, then turned and sauntered off down the street.

Shaking her head, a grin stretching her cheeks, Poppy stepped inside, shut the door, then leaned against it. She'd kissed Ben. Ben had kissed her. And it had been hot.

Who knew behind that conscientious, do-everything-by-the-rules exterior there was a passionate, forceful, hot-as-hell man who had made her knees all but disappear with a kiss?

Okay. Two kisses. Technically probably about eight, or ten, if you were to be picky about it.

Poppy touched her lips, still tingling. Still hot. Still wanting more.

This is a very bad idea.

The little voice was back. Clearer than ever. And right as always.

Kissing Ben may have felt amazing. Kissing Ben may have felt *right*. But was a moment with a man who would want the world – something she could not give – worth putting everything they'd worked for on the line? Their business? The rebuilding of their friendship?

Poppy crossed her arms as a shiver skittered through her. She wasn't a teenager anymore, she was a mature, responsible adult. And that meant doing the mature, responsible adult thing and shutting the situation down.

The sooner the better, for everyone.

Chapter 11

Ben smoothed his hair, flicked his tongue around his teeth, checking for loose debris from that morning's Marmite on toast, then glanced down to make sure his shirt was buttoned up correctly.

All was in place, as always… which was a surprise. He'd been as hyper as a kid on Christmas Eve since Poppy had returned his kiss. Not just returned it but built on it, her touch, curious at first, growing bolder as the kiss had gone on. Lingering, discovering, relishing.

Part of him was kicking himself for breaking it off, for not exploring what might have come next had he followed her upstairs. But he knew holding off was for the best. He wasn't after one night, he wanted all the nights. The only thing getting in the way of that was Poppy and her loveless beliefs. But he could find a way around that. He'd take a battering ram to that particular wall if he had to.

The door flew open setting the chime's off and Poppy burst into the shop.

'Hey, how are you?' Ben took a step towards Poppy, then paused as she hurried behind the counter, and dumped her furry unicorn backpack so its head slumped to the side like it had had one too many sparkly drinks the night before.

Opening her laptop, Poppy stared intently at the screen. 'No deliveries I take it? I'm waiting for an order, and I needed it yesterday. The rate things are selling my shelves are going to be bare.' She twisted round and began rearranging the bath and shower section, spreading out unicorn-shaped bath bombs and rainbow soaps.

This scene wasn't playing out how he thought it would. In the plan he'd conjured last night as he tossed and turned while waiting for sleep to come, they were going to have some friendly banter. Go about their day exchanging flirtatious smiles. He'd suggest dinner. She'd agree. And a romantic evening would see them enjoying another one, or seven, or more, of those everything-he'd-ever-imagined-and-more kisses.

Instead, despite her friendly greeting, Poppy was radiating Miss Business. And she was twitchier than usual. Like she didn't want him in her space. Like she… regretted the night before.

Shit.

A rock appeared in Ben's stomach, one he was sure was the shape of his heart, because that area of his chest felt numb. Empty. He'd read the situation wrong. Poppy's hand-holding, her comfortableness with his closeness, her dragging him up to dance, those hadn't been signs she was interested in him like *that*. It was Poppy being Poppy. Fun and flirtatious, but never serious.

As for that unforgettable, sexy, all-in kiss? He'd been stupid to think it meant something. Poppy was impulsive. Impetuous. An adventurer. She'd been caught up in the moment, revelling in the adrenaline of a new experience. Prepared to take it further until the cold light of day made her reassess her rashness.

She twisted round, their eyes met, locked. Silence stretched between them, to the point the room positively itched with awkwardness. Since he'd been the cause of it, the one to start it, he'd have to be the one to scratch it out.

'Poppy.' Her name came out crackly and croaky. He cleared his throat and tried again. 'Poppy, look, about last night…'

Poppy glanced over her shoulder, yet her eyes didn't meet his. Instead they focused on the tins of tea lined up on shelves behind him. 'Oh. It's... um. Yeah. Look. I'm sorry. I was out of line. Tipsy. Should have controlled myself. Should have engaged my brain.' Poppy returned to her rearranging. 'And you're dating Milly so I should have known better...'

So that was it? She felt guilty? Thought she was treading on Milly's toes? 'No, Poppy. Milly and I aren't ser—'

'It's *good* that you're dating her. She's perfect for you. Can you imagine you and I going out? Being a couple? We'd kill each other. Besides, you're already in your dad's bad books, if you and I became "us", well, you'd be there permanently, and I can't let that happen. I won't be the one to make your life harder.' Poppy's flattened lips and straight, stern nose told him she'd made her decision, and that was that. She was taking the blame and she didn't want to hear another word about it. Well, he wasn't going to let her carry that blame. It took two people to kiss, and neither of them had a reason to feel bad or awkward about it.

Ben's mobile broke the strained silence with a chirp as a text came through. He scanned the message and inwardly groaned.

'Ben, we talked about you and Poppy coming over for dinner. Your father is free tonight. We'll see you at seven.'

Talk about bad timing. The way Poppy was behaving there was no way she'd want to spend the evening at his parents' with him. He glanced over at Poppy whose face was all but buried in her laptop, so he could only see the top of her forehead. His fingers tingled with the temptation to lie to his mother, to say Poppy was busy.

He began to type a message, then deleted it. A white lie was still a lie, and the chances of him being caught out were high. All it would take would be for his mother to tell Poppy she'd missed her at dinner and then the two most important women in the world to him would both know they'd been lied to. He was just going to have to mention it to Poppy.

121

His mobile chirped again.

'And don't try to get out of it. It's time your father and yourself had a good chat. Poppy will make the perfect buffer. See you tonight x'

Ben's gut tightened. His mother had a point. He couldn't avoid his father forever. Not that he wanted to. He loved his father and had done everything he could his whole life to make him proud. He just needed to show him that quitting law wasn't a mistake. That he could be just as successful in the business of tea as he had been in the business of law. His father was too proud to take the first step to reconciliation, so he would have to be the one to do it. But first he had to make things right, normal, with Poppy, and maybe this invitation was the way to do it.

'So…' He cleared his throat, unsure how to proceed. 'How about dinner?'

Poppy's head snapped up, her skin paling before his eyes.

Oh, God. He'd said that wrong. 'I mean, Mum has invited you for dinner tonight. With me.'

Poppy picked up a pen and began to twirl it between her fingers, its glitter-encrusted casing catching the sunshine beaming into the shop, creating a sprinkling of light that skittered around the floor with every twist and turn. 'Oh, that's kind of her, but I should probably work late. Get ahead of things.'

Poppy startled as her mobile let off a series of drum beats.

'What is that noise?'

Poppy shrugged. 'My text message alert. I never hear a single beep.' She turned her attention to her phone, her brows drawing together. 'Looks like I'm coming to dinner. I've been given the "no is not an answer" command from your mum.'

She made it sound like dinner with them, with *him*, was a death sentence.

'Look, if you really don't want to that's fine. I can say you've come down sick or something.' Ben's gut twisted. One kiss and his relationship with Poppy, his friendship, was buggered. What had he been thinking?

122

'Ben, shit, I'm sorry. Me not wanting to go to dinner has nothing to do with you.' Poppy left the safety of her counter and made her way to stand in front of Ben. 'You're going to think I'm an idiot.' Poppy's face flushed bright red. 'More so than you probably already think I am.'

Ben automatically went to reach for Poppy, to soothe her, to give her strength, but stopped himself. Poppy was embarrassed enough about last night, and by her behaviour this morning it was obvious she needed to keep her distance, and his hands on hers wouldn't help with that. 'I don't think you're an idiot, Poppy. I've never thought that. Frustrating? Sometimes. Complicated? Just a bit. A little crazy? Oh yes, absolutely.'

The heat faded from Poppy's face as her indignation grew. 'I'm going to believe that you're joking about most of it. I can accept "complicated" though.'

'"Complicated"? Really? I'd have thought you'd be more okay with the "crazy".' Ben grinned as Poppy lightly punched him on the arm. *Welcome back, solid ground.* 'So, what's stopping you from coming to dinner?'

Poppy paused, her chest rose and fell, and her shoulders sagged like the weight of the world had landed upon them. 'My mother still doesn't know I'm home, and I was hoping to keep it that way for as long as possible.'

Ben knew Poppy and her mother weren't tight, but he had no idea things were this bad. 'She hasn't seen you? You haven't been to visit? Or called?'

Poppy shook her head, her teeth sinking into her bottom lip.

'Oh, Poppy.' His heart went out to her. Complicated to the core. On the surface everyone saw smiley, happy-go-lucky, devil-may-care Poppy. Inside though, she was a mess of insecurity, indecision, and a whole lot of hurt. If he could take her into his arms and whisper those feelings away with truthful words – telling her she was loved, she was worthy, she was as brilliant as the shiniest star in the universe – he would. But she wouldn't have believed him. Poppy had to come to that conclusion herself. But that wouldn't stop him from helping her get there. 'Well, if we're going to smuggle you into my parents' house we're going to need a game plan. And a cup of tea. Also, a slice of ginger loaf, freshly baked this morning.'

'Two slices.' Poppy's stomach rumbled its agreement. 'Okay, maybe three.'

'But no more – you know how my mum likes to cook.'

'Enough for an army.' Poppy rolled her eyes then plopped herself down at the nearest table and began to fiddle with the tea menu propped between the honey and sugar jars. 'What's a soothing tea? Chamomile, yeah?'

Ben went to the window, where he'd set up a miniature herb garden, and snipped a few leaves off the peppermint herb. 'I wouldn't go chamomile at this time of day, you might find yourself curling up in that pile of soft unicorn toys over there and having a nap. Peppermint tea will do the trick. It's great for taking the edge off and, in my experience, it doesn't send me off to the land of nod quite the way chamomile does.' Ben walked the peppermint over to the kitchen door. 'Be back in a second, I'll just rinse these leaves.'

Poppy slumped back in her chair, glad for the moment alone so she could organise her thoughts… and try and detangle the hot mess that was her feelings. She closed her eyes and massaged her temples.

Damn it, she only had herself to blame for the warring that was going on between her heart and her head.

One moment's clarity combined with a split-second of home-sickness – not for home itself, but for Ben – had seen her book the first one-way flight she could find home, intent on setting up the business she'd longed to create, while reconnecting with the one person in the world who'd accepted her for *her*.

And now she'd gone and kissed that person, muddied the waters, and things were awkward. If she'd just left Ben alone – if she'd just kept her hands to herself – she wouldn't be sitting here facing her fears. Wouldn't be facing the one person who had the potential to hurt her every bit as much as her mother had. More.

'You okay, Poppy?' Ben returned with the freshly washed leaves. Placing them in one of his chic double-walled cups, he poured hot water over them and brought the cup to the table, along with two chunky slices of ginger loaf with a pat of butter on the side. 'You look like a woman who's about to meet a death squad. It's only peppermint tea, I promise it won't kill you.'

Poppy attempted a smile. Typical Ben, trying to cheer her up as always. 'I'm fine.' She wrapped her hands around the glass and breathed in the fresh, minty aroma. 'You know when I was living in New Zealand I went to this fancy café, and they had peppermint tea on the menu. Said it was their special "house-made tea". I ordered it thinking it would be something special. But guess what? Their house-made tea was exactly this. Fresh leaves with hot water dumped on top. And it cost the same as a coffee.' Poppy grinned ruefully to herself. That experience pretty much summed up life. You choose something thinking it's going to be special, then you get it and it's not quite what you thought it was.

'Something amusing?' Ben slipped into the chair opposite, a cup of his customary green tea in hand.

Poppy shrivelled her nose and shook her head. 'Not really. I was just thinking about how often you expect something to be a certain way, and it's so often nothing like your expectation.'

'Like family.' Ben's head angled to the side, his eyebrows drawn together in quiet concern. 'How come you haven't told your mum you're home, Poppy? Surely she'd want to know.'

Poppy thought back to the few emails her mother had sent after she'd upped and left. There'd been nothing for almost two years. Then one had appeared on her birthday. Then sporadically after that. Never filled with declarations of love, or asking when she'd return, they simply asked where she was and what amazing things she'd seen. Why she'd sent them Poppy didn't know.

Probably an attack of the guilts. Yet the part of her that had wanted to make her mother happy, had yearned to please her, to see the smile she gave others so easily turned in her direction, made her reply. Nothing deep and meaningful. She just told her mum where she was, what she'd seen, and left it at that. If her mother wanted a closer relationship to her she was going to have to be the one to make all the effort. Poppy wasn't putting her heart on the line, again.

Poppy tapped the side of the glass, watched the leaf release its colour, its flavour, into the water. Perhaps the only way she could truly move on was to confide in Ben. Explain the fear. The pain. Explain what kept her away for so long. 'We couldn't have grown up in more opposite kinds of families, could we, Ben?'

Ben nodded. 'Understatement of the year. It was just your mum and you. An artist and her freedom-loving daughter. The absolute opposite of a lawyer, a housewife and their goody-two-shoed son.'

'And the rest.' Poppy twirled the glass round. 'Did you know any other kids who didn't have to go to bed at a set time? That got to eat chocolate for breakfast if that was all they could find? That could go for walks at any time of the day or night without getting into trouble because their mother didn't so much not care to check on what they were up to, as didn't care full stop?'

'Oh, Poppy, don't say that. Don't say your mother didn't care. Of course she did. How could she not?'

Poppy nearly laughed. To someone like Ben, whose life had been cocooned by a mother who adored him and a father who was proud of him, hearing that would be beyond shocking. 'You know, despite the lack of parental laws I grew up with, I do wonder how I became the sort of, somewhat, kind of well-adjusted person I am today.' Poppy took a sip of her tea, hoping its calming effect would work its magic. 'Although, I think your influence had a lot to do with it. You and your rules. "We must go to school,

Poppy, or we'll get detention." If I had a pound for every time you said that to me...'

'If I didn't you'd have dragged me along with you to who knows where to do God knows what. The rules were my only defence against your persuasiveness. And even then, my rules only worked with you half the time.'

Cute that Ben thought she'd backed down because of 'rules'. She'd backed down because what she'd wanted to do was live like Ben. Go to school. Follow the rules. But she'd acted out, tried to do things that might capture her mother's attention, in the hope she'd also capture her affection, and the love, the acknowledgement she craved.

'If only my powers of persuasion still existed – your side of the shop would be looking a little more colourful right about now,' Poppy half-joked as she noticed a space in one of Ben's shelves where a tea trio gift set had sat before being sold. She had a unicorn teacup that would fit in perfectly. Maybe she'd sneak it up there later on when Ben wasn't looking. But first she had to get back on track. She could distract herself all she wanted, but Ben needed answers and it was time she gave them to him. 'Where was I? Oh, how could I forget? My mother.' She took another sip of the tea and forced herself to swallow it despite the lump that was building, blocking her throat. 'The thing is, she didn't love me. I wasn't a blessing like you were to your parents, I was a hindrance. And she made sure I knew it. Why do you think my clothing was always so old? It wasn't because I wore it out, it was because I had to steal it from bags left outside the charity shop. And all that "freedom" I had? I was running from an empty, cold home. Mum was always out partying, and being out in the world was less scary than being home, alone. And nothing I did to try and make her love me made a difference. I was a mistake she couldn't take back.'

Ben pushed his chair back, planted his elbows on his knees, knotted his hands together and leaned forward. A deep line ran down between his brows. His eyes narrowed, like he was trying to put the pieces of what Poppy was telling him together. Like he was trying to understand. 'How can you say that, Poppy? Of course your mother loved you. How could she not? You were funny, sweet, and so full of heart.'

Poppy closed her eyes and breathed the tears that threatened to build away. She'd cried enough over her mother's disregard for her. She wouldn't shed another tear. 'Easily. I can easily say she didn't love me, because I experienced that lack of love daily – ignored, treated like wallpaper, yelled at when I tried to get her attention, when I interrupted her work, berated for asking for clothing, food, for a stupid bloody birthday present. I was even stupid enough to try and get her attention when her friends were around, thinking she wouldn't treat me terribly in front of them, but it only made her worse. Telling me to go away, that my chattering only bored and annoyed her friends. That the saying "children should be seen and not heard" didn't apply to me, that in my case I should neither be seen nor heard. And then she'd laugh her light, brittle, cut-crystal laugh and her friends – all too busy pandering to her rising stardom as an artist – would laugh along too. It took me a while to learn her rules, but I got there. I learnt not to be seen. Not to be heard. I learnt it was safer, less hurtful, than facing her disgust at her "good-for-nothing daughter". And those were her words, not mine.'

Ben rocked back in his chair, like her words had given him a violent shove. 'Oh, Poppy. I'm so sorry. I had no idea.' He steepled his hands and gazed at the tips. 'I mean, I knew you and she would fight. I heard the odd argument. Saw the next day that you'd been crying. But I thought it was just the usual teenage stuff that my parents and I would fight about. Not being allowed to go somewhere or do something. Not having the latest fad bought for you because everyone else had one. God, to think all this time I thought your home must have been like a wonderland to live in. No rules. No pressure. Parties galore. Freedom to be who you wanted to be…'

Poppy caught a wistfulness in Ben's tone. He sounded like he'd been forced to walk the line, rather than been born to stick to the straight and narrow. 'Freedom isn't all it's cracked up to be. Sure, I made my own rules. I could go where I wanted, whenever I wanted, but I did it alone. It got lonely. Freedom's not so wonderful when you don't have anyone to share it with. Sure, I had friends while travelling, but they moved on as travellers do.' Poppy mustered a smile and a half-shrug, but it fell away quickly. 'The thing is I yearned for the kind of life you had, but then I guess when you face constant expectation the way you did, well, that isn't ideal either.'

'What I can't wrap my head around is that you lived there like that for so long, that you put up with it for so long, and not once did you mention any of it to me.' A shadow of hurt flickered through his eyes. 'But then, I shouldn't be surprised. You never mentioned your plans to leave. You just upped and disappeared.'

Poppy's stomach, already tight with tension, flick-flacked over and over, sending a wave of nausea through her. Ben sounded bereft. Like he was reliving that day. She should've told him she was leaving Muswell Hill. Going as far away as the money her grandma had left her when she'd passed could take her. But she couldn't have. Not after what he'd said the night she decided to leave. To face the person who said he loved her after being told by the one person who *should* love her that she wasn't wanted… it would have driven her to push Ben away. To make him hate her in order to save him from his feelings. 'I couldn't tell you I was going. It would have been too hard. You'd have tried to make me stay. And I couldn't. Not under that roof. Not for one second longer.'

'But what tipped the scales? What could possibly have been so much worse than what was already going on around you that you'd pack a bag and scarper like that?'

Poppy closed her eyes. She could see the moment, clear as she could see Ben in front of her. Her mother sitting at the kitchen table wearing a silver sequin party dress. A glass of red wine in front of her. Her ever-present sketchbook open on the table, a graphite pencil poised over the paper. She was so beautiful and brilliant, imaginative and intelligent, amazing and artistic. And charismatic. Their house had an open-door policy, and her mother had entertained with wild abandon.

To find her mother alone was rare, so she'd stopped by the kitchen and sat at the table, hoping for kind words, for a sign her mother cared. She was a fool to have even tried.

Poppy sucked in a steadying breath and released it. 'That night, we'd gone out, remember? To celebrate the end of school?'

Ben nodded. 'Kind of. I was off my face. Don't remember much about the end of it, to be honest.'

'Yeah, I thought that might have been the case.' The knots in Poppy's gut loosened a little. She'd suspected Ben had no recollection of professing his love for her. Was glad for it. It was one less thing to complicate their lives. 'After we got home I thought I'd get some water in me before bed, so I went to the kitchen, which is where I found Mum. She was sitting at the kitchen table, drawing as always, and I thought…' Poppy shook her head, folded her arms over herself. 'I thought maybe now that I'd finished school she might see me as an "adult", an equal, that maybe we could just chat. Like mums and daughters were meant to do. But of course, I was an idiot to think that.'

'Not an idiot, Poppy. Just expecting what every kid should expect. To be treated well.'

'Well, that expectation got me nowhere. Actually, I lie. It gave me another emotional kick to the gut. Because the moment I sat down she began to talk. To draw out my future for me. And to explain my past.' Poppy held on tightly to her teacup, resisted the urge to put her hands over her ears, knowing doing so couldn't silence the echo of her past. 'She told me she'd fulfilled her end of the bargain. That now I had finished school she was free of me.' Poppy scraped her chair back. She couldn't sit still for a second longer, not with her blood roiling as hot and violent now as the day she'd faced rejection one time too many. She paced back and forth, crossing from one side of the shop to the other – from stark and austere to magical and merry. God, their shop was a physical metaphor of her life. The life she'd left, with its lack of emotional connection, to the one she'd tried to create, full of life and love. But no matter how hard she tried she never felt like she belonged in either world. She was as disconnected now as she was then. 'She must've seen my confusion because she began to laugh. Told me I was naïve. Told me I expected too much from life. Told me she was forced to keep me, that my grandmother had given her free use of the house and the money to send me to a good school, in exchange for her keeping me. And how could she say no? She was young. Unmarried. My supposed father had taken off the moment he found out my mother was pregnant. And all she wanted to do was draw. To work on the portraits that she eventually became renowned for.' Poppy sank her top teeth into her bottom lip, grazed the soft skin. Allowed the pain to bring the now into focus. 'Just when I thought she was done, that she'd said her bit, she stilled, then took hold of my hand, held it tight. Gave me a reason to believe we had a chance. Then she said the words I'll never forget. "I should have turned my mother down. I should have had a termination."'

'God, Poppy, no. Surely not.' Ben reached out and clasped her wrist. Loose enough she could pull away. Strong enough she was forced to stop her pacing. 'I wish you'd told me. If I'd known I'd have…'

Poppy sank back into her chair. 'You'd have what, Ben? Asked your parents to take me in? You know that would never have flown. And I wouldn't have wanted to live with you. No offence. It's just…'

'What you wanted was for your mother to love you the way you loved her.' Ben finished her sentence.

'Exactly. And when I realised that night that it was never going to happen, I made a decision that it was time to put myself first. So, I packed a bag, grabbed my passport, my savings and told her I was leaving as I walked out the door. I told her that I was going abroad, off to discover the world and all it had to offer. Some stupid part of me thought she might try and stop me. That my leaving would shake her out of her self-absorption. But it didn't. She didn't…' Poppy mashed her lips together, breathed in the calming scent of peppermint, exhaled the pain she'd buried deep in her heart, that was now threatening to choke her. 'She didn't care. "Good. Have fun." That's what she said, then she dismissed me with a flick of her hand. And that was that. I was no longer her daughter.' Poppy gripped the edge of the table, fighting for control, her knuckles bulging, whitening against her skin. 'And you ask me why, Ben. Why I don't believe in love? Well that's your reason why right there. Because what I grew up surrounded by was not love. It was selfishness. It was intolerance. It was heartache. And pain. I don't believe in love because I never saw it. Never experienced it. Because I wasn't worth loving.' Poppy clutched the now-warm cup and brought it to her lips, held it tight so Ben wouldn't see the way her hands shook.

'You don't truly believe that, Poppy. Surely.' Ben's eyes were fixed on the table, as if he were afraid to see that she did mean what she said.

'I do. The evidence speaks for itself.' A rogue tear slipped down her cheek. She swiped it away. Refused to let the memory consume her, drag her down. 'But, I can't hide from my past any longer. I'm going to march up to your parents' front door tonight, and if my mother sees me, then she sees me. And she can decide what, if any, steps she wants to take. I'm done with this pity party, Ben. Life is too short.'

Ben's lips parted like he was about to say something, then shut again. Instead he gave a curt nod. 'Okay. Well, I'll text Mum and let her know we'll be there.'

Poppy knew Ben saw through her brave face. Her tough talk. He'd always had an impeccable radar like that. Knowing when she wasn't being straight up. But he also knew not to call her on it. That it would only cause her to dig her heels in deeper.

And Poppy knew, deep down, if she truly were as brave and tough as she made out she wouldn't be hiding from love. Ruling it out. But she had to. She couldn't put her heart on the line like she had that night with her mother ever again. Because that night had carved a crack in her heart. One more rejection from someone she loved, someone like Ben, would break it.

Chapter 12

Ben couldn't miss the way Poppy's gaze kept flicking up to the left. To her home. She'd done it every few seconds or so since they'd turned into the road they'd grown up on. Her steps quickened the closer they got.

'Hey.' He grabbed her hand and gave it a reassuring squeeze, releasing it before she thought he was looking for a repeat of the previous night. 'It's okay. Whatever happens you'll be fine. I'll make sure of it.'

She let out a shaky breath. 'What would I do without you? You're such a good friend. Always have been.'

Friend. The word that once lit up his world now dimmed it. He was tired of being friend-zoned. That, and he no longer accepted that was his place in Poppy's world. Not after the night before. She may be willing to put those hot-as-hell kisses behind them, make out like the whole thing was a mojito-made mistake, say that they were better off as friends, that he was better off with Milly or someone like her, but he'd been there. He knew what he'd felt. And it hadn't been him who'd gone in for the second kiss.

The way he saw it, there were two things holding them back. One was Poppy's refusal to entertain the idea that love could be

134

something wonderful. Something where people compromised, cheered each other on, and cherished each other.

The other thing holding them back? Himself. He needed to talk to Milly. Sure, they weren't serious, and they weren't exclusively dating each other, but she deserved more than a text, or an email, saying things weren't working out. She deserved a clean break. A proper explanation. Because as nice as she was, and as much as he enjoyed her company, he only saw her as a friend.

Once he'd sorted things with Milly, he'd set about proving to Poppy that what they had was worth giving a chance.

'Shit.' Poppy clutched his bicep and brought them to a halt. 'I just saw a very human-looking shape pass by the window upstairs. In the art studio.' She scanned the road. 'I can't see her car. Maybe she's moved?'

'I'm pretty sure my parents would have mentioned if she'd moved. Maybe she's just got a new car?'

'Right. Yes. Absolutely.' Poppy released her grip. 'You go ahead. I'll just…' She ducked behind Ben.

'Hide behind me?' Ben couldn't stop the smirk appearing on his face. It was the first time he'd ever seen Poppy unsure of herself. Nervous. Skittish, even. And she was all the cuter for it.

'Fine. Yes. I'm hiding. Kind of. If she's upstairs then I'll still be in full view if she happens to look down and see me, but if we do it this way then I feel like you're my bodyguard. You'll protect me against anything awful.' She gave him a meaningful look. 'What are you waiting for? Start walking. The longer I'm out here the larger the danger grows. And if you give me grief later about my talk of marching up to the house I'll find out where you live and stuff your bed full of unicorns.'

Ben held back a laugh as they proceeded to half-walk, half-scuttle the last few metres to their semi-detached homes. Ben paused when they reached the top of his parents' stairs. Should he knock? He didn't usually, but usually it was just him. No guest. No Poppy. And even Poppy had knocked when she'd come over to hang out when they were younger. There was a solemnity about the property that told you decorum was of the utmost importance. But it was his home… so surely he could barge in with Poppy in tow…

'Stop dithering,' Poppy hissed, while casting a furtive eye upwards. 'It's your home. Get in there!'

Poppy nudged him forward just as the door opened. The tip of his toe caught on the threshold and he found himself falling forwards. He braced himself for impact – the hard floorboards being merciless on bare knees – but instead two arms hooked under his armpits and pulled him backwards.

He regained his balance, righted himself and spun round. 'Poppy. When did you get so strong? And quick?'

Poppy shrugged. 'I did a little voluntary surf lifesaving when I lived on the Gold Coast in Aussie. I guess the training came in handy. Would've been a little easier on the arms if you'd tripped over in water though. Can you do that the next time you need saving?'

'If it pleases you, of course. Although you did push me so I'm not sure why my falling is my fault.'

'My fault?' Poppy released him, her hands flying upward in indignation. 'All I did was give you a nudge. I can't believe you would put this on me. It's no different from the time you and I decided to bunk school and—'

'Are you two going to fight all night? Will I have to seat you at opposite ends of the table like I did when you were younger?'

Ben looked round to see his mum holding the door open for them, eyebrows raised, an amused glint in her eyes. 'Sorry, Mum. No need to separate us. We're fine. Same as always.'

'That's good, dear. Now what was the rush?' Pam's gaze flicked between the two of them.

'Just excited to eat, Mrs Evans. I mean, Pam.' Poppy side-stepped past Ben and leaned in to give Pam a kiss on the cheek. 'I haven't had a good meal since I've been back and I've missed your cooking. I'm half-hoping for that delicious slow-roasted pork belly you used to make.'

'Sorry, Poppy. Not today, I'm afraid. It's a bit hot for slow-roasting anything. We were thinking of making use of the barbecue since it's such a nice evening. I picked up some beautiful eye fillet steaks from the butcher, and I've prepared a garden salad, and a potato salad to go with it.' Pam crooked her finger and indicated to Poppy to move closer. 'And for dessert I've made that tropical cheesecake I know you like so much,' she said in a stage whisper.

Ben waited for Poppy to jump up and down, clap her hands in joy, spin around. Something. Instead her face had paled, and she looked a touch unsteady on her feet.

'Poppy, are you okay?'

It seemed his mother had noticed as well.

Poppy managed a weak smile, but it didn't reach her eyes. 'I'm fine, Pam. Honestly. Must be hotter out there than I realised. A barbecue sounds great. Steaks, perfect. And I can't believe you still remember that my favourite dessert is tropical cheesecake.'

Pam patted Poppy on the cheek. 'You're not an easy person to forget, Poppy. That and you used to beg me to make it at least once a week. Even in the depths of winter. Why don't you two head out back? I'll have Robert bring out some drinks and I'll grab the steaks from the fridge.'

Ben grasped Poppy's forearm as she was about to follow her mother. 'Are you okay? You look like you're about to pass out.'

'I didn't expect to be sitting outside. We used to always eat inside. And outside *she* might see me.'

Ben turned to face Poppy and took her hands in his. 'You'll

137

be fine, Poppy. You always are. Ask yourself, what's the worst that can happen?'

Poppy fixed her stare on the cream wall behind him that held a portrait of him, his mother and his father. His father and mother with their shoulders back, eyes filled with pride, huge smiles on their faces. Ben sat between them wearing graduation garb, his future a solid and smooth path in front of him. Until he'd upended it by following his dream of opening a gourmet tea shop. Would his father ever forgive him? Would a new family portrait one day grace that spot? One of them all standing outside the shop, looking every bit as happy to be there as they had been at his graduation? He gave himself a mental shake. There was no point in worrying about that which he could not control, just as there was no point in Poppy worrying about her mother seeing her. She could no more control her reaction to Poppy being back home than he could control his father's reaction to his new path.

'The worst that could happen is that she sees me. I see that she sees me. And she then does nothing about it. She doesn't come to say "hello". She doesn't acknowledge my presence.' Poppy's gaze left the portrait and returned to him. 'And that I can handle. I handled it long enough growing up.'

'There you go. See? You'll be fine. Now let's head outside before my father takes over the barbecue and turns the steaks to rubber.'

Poppy tugged at her braid, fresh creases of worry appearing on her forehead. 'Another thing to fret about. Your father. He used to disapprove of me when I was young; now that I'm in business with you I'll have levelled up to career-ending son-stealer. On the plus side, he'll be too busy despising me to give you any grief.'

'We'll see. We'll just have to have each other's backs.' Ben offered his arm to Poppy.

'Just like always.' She hooked her arm though his without

hesitation, and they made their way down the hall, through the kitchen and into the backyard, where long shadows had begun to form as the sun began its descent towards the horizon.

Ben settled into the dark grey wicker dining chair and grabbed a crisp from the bowl his mother had set out.

'New outdoor dining set. Very nice.' Poppy sat beside Ben, her back turned to the two houses. 'I won't miss the wooden one. The amount of splinters I got from it.' She grimaced at the memory.

'You only got splinters because you used to wiggle your bum back and forth like an excited puppy whenever Mum brought us out glasses of lemonade as a treat instead of the usual milk or water. If you'd sat still you'd have been fine.' Ben grinned, remembering the chaos that would ensue post-splinter-in-bum. 'But then we'd never have been treated to the Poppy-arse-dance.'

'The what?' Poppy frowned. 'I've no idea what you're talking about.'

'You know… You used to leap up, hop from foot to foot, twist your head as far as it would go and then rush inside to the bathroom to try and get the splinter out. Then you'd call for Mum and she'd help you.'

'God. I'd forgotten. Actually, more like I'd blocked it out.' Poppy crossed one leg over the other and clasped her hands on her lap. 'Well, I promise to keep my happy lemonade wriggling to myself tonight.'

'Whose bum is wriggling? Not Poppy's? I'd hoped she'd have grown out of that.'

Ben stood to help his father as he attempted to juggle a bucket filled with ice and a bottle of wine, and a handful of glasses. 'Evening, Dad. How are you?'

'Fine, thank you.' Robert set the wine down on the table and settled into a chair opposite Ben. No handshake. No pat on the back. Nothing. 'How are you?'

Ben forced a smile to his face, hoping it hid the stranglehold of hurt on his heart. So much for not worrying about his father's behaviour. Still, he could be the bigger person so when, or *if*, this time passed there would still be a relationship to repair. 'I'm good, Dad. Busy. The shop's doing well. Better than projected.'

His father stood without comment, like he'd not heard a word Ben had said. Or hadn't wanted to. 'Good weather for a barbecue. It's nice to see summer living up to its name.' Robert turned to the barbecue, pulled up the hood and grabbed the tongs hanging off the hook.

Poppy nudged Ben's ankle under the table to get his attention. 'Is he for real?' she mouthed.

Ben shrugged. His stomach coiled with tension. His appetite was shrinking by the second. Why did he have a feeling dinner was going to be a long and dismal affair – for both of them.

'Robert, get your hands off those tongs.' Pam mock-growled as she stepped outside, a plate of steaks in hand.

Robert dropped the tongs on the barbecue's side-table and backed away with a flourish. 'I was just trying to be of help.'

'Your idea of helping is taking a good cut of meat and ensuring it's inedible. Stay away.' Pam wagged a finger of warning. 'Go sit with your son. Be sociable.' There was no mistaking her tone. *Be nice to your son, or else…*

Robert settled himself back in his chair, grabbed the wine bottle, busied himself opening it, then poured himself a glass without offering either one of them a drink.

His father was the epitome of manners, of doing things 'the right way'. If he wasn't offering them a glass of wine, he wasn't just mad, he was fuming. And Ben would put good money on the fact the anger came from a place of deep hurt. And it was all his fault.

His old job had been a grind. One he'd stuck with because he wanted to please his parents, and to be fair the money allowed him a certain lifestyle. But ultimately he didn't want to let them down. Growing up he'd been acutely aware of the ideals drummed into him by his parents: work hard; behave; be the best. And he'd done exactly that. Even the times Poppy had led him astray hadn't caused his father to react like this.

For the first time since he'd opened Steep, Ben wasn't sure his passion was worth the pain of losing the relationship he had with his dad. Perhaps there was a way he could make both work? It wouldn't be hard to go back into property law, to find someone to run Steep…

The coils circling his gut contracted further, reminding him that by making things right with his father he'd be making his life wrong, again.

So this is what the great 'they' meant by being stuck between a rock and a hard place.

'Don't mind if I do.' Poppy grabbed the wine bottle and two glasses, poured the pale-gold sauvignon blanc, then passed Ben a glass. 'You must be thirsty too, Ben. Bottoms up.' She lifted her glass towards him, pointedly ignoring his father, making it clear she found his behaviour rude.

Ben clinked glasses with Poppy and sent her a silent thank you. She was on his side. They were a team. And if she hadn't swept him up in her dream of opening her unicorn gift shop he'd never have discovered how happy he could be.

If only his father could see that. Be good with it.

'So, Mr Evans. How's the law life going?' Poppy ran her finger through the condensation that had settled on the glass. Her tone was polite, but Ben caught a certain sharpness, one that told him she was up to something.

Don't make things worse, Pops, he prayed.

'Fine, thank you. Busy. There's no lack of security in law. Always work to do.'

Ben gritted his teeth. Could his dad be any more pointed?

'And how are things with you, Poppy?'

'Well, Mr Evans. Like Ben said, things are busy at the shop.'

Ben hid a grin behind a cough. He knew what Poppy was up

to. She was going to run defence. Make things good. Show his father that their business wasn't a daft idea. And she knew that by asking him how he was that he would automatically do the polite thing and return the question.

Poppy took a sip of the wine. 'Really busy, actually. When Ben and I opened Sparkle & Steep we thought it would take a few months to get things going. Maybe even years before we turned a profit, but from the looks of the books we're already not only breaking even, but there's extra. Not enough for a first-class ticket to the other side of the world, granted, but enough that I won't have to curb my chocolate habit anytime soon.'

Robert crossed his legs, his arms falling on either side of the chair, his grip on the ends loose. Light. Ben knew that stance. That look. While appearing casual to the average eye, Ben knew it meant his father had found an angle that could be exploited to his own ends. 'And how were your travels, Poppy? Do you miss traipsing around the world? Any plans to take off again?'

Light and amused laughter spilled from Poppy. 'Mr Evans, you are a card. I'm not going anywhere. Who would run my side of the business? Not Ben. With the way Steep has taken off he doesn't have the time. And as much as my worker, Joe, is good at his job, I'm not ready to entrust him with my livelihood. Besides, I love what I'm doing. There's nowhere else I'd rather be.'

'Indeed.' Robert's jaw shifted to the left, to the right, then settled in the middle. Tight. Unforgiving. 'Though you say there's nowhere else you'd rather be, you've left abruptly before. Who's to say you wouldn't do it again?'

'She wouldn't.' Ben jumped in, tiring of his father's rudeness. He knew Poppy could easily defend herself, but it was time his father saw that his son wasn't a carbon copy of him, that he was his own man. 'If you'd bothered to visit, Dad, you'd have seen the work Poppy's put into her business. This isn't some school project. Or some flight of fancy. This is her life. She's not just going to abandon it. And neither am I.'

Uncomfortable silence, thick and tense, enveloped the table. Ben caught the worried glance his mother threw in his direction. So much for a nice family dinner. He'd all but declared war by going up against his father. Still, he wasn't going to say sorry. He'd spent his life doing what was right, trying to please. It was time he stood up for the things – the people – he believed in. It was time he stood up for himself.

He met his father's steely gaze across the table. Refused to flinch. An apology was needed, but it wasn't coming from him.

Poppy shifted in her seat, then made to get up. 'Look, I feel like things might need to be said… you lot need to chat… so… I'll just… um… go?'

'Stay, Poppy.' He placed his hand on hers. 'We're here to have dinner. Mum's put in a massive effort, and I refuse to let it go to waste.'

Poppy sank back into the chair, her eyes fixed on the back door and her bag that she'd grabbed as she'd made to leave still in hand.

'The thing is, Dad, Steep satisfies me on a level that law never did. When I was at the practice I always felt people came to me grudgingly. No one wants to see a lawyer, it's just something you have to do – whether you like it or not. But people love seeing me now. They enjoy discovering new tea, trying new flavours. Branching out. And I'd like to think my baking rivals Mum's and is, in some way, a way of continuing on the legacy of our family.'

'Until you give me grandchildren…' Pam shot Ben a warm smile, which Ben returned, grateful she wasn't backing his father as she always had done in the past. It wasn't in his mum's nature to rock the boat, but by keeping out of this conversation she was staging her own protest.

'I know you wanted that legacy continued through law, and who knows, maybe Mum's imaginary grandkids might take a shine to it, but I'm done with that part of my life, and you don't

143

have to like it, but I need you to accept it.' From the corner of his eye Ben saw Poppy settle back into her chair. Her gaze zeroed in on his father, her eyebrow was raised, and her hand gripped the stem of her wine glass. Her expression was all but screaming 'If you don't apologise to your son I will drench you with this wine, then tip the bottle over your head.'

Poppy's fierce demeanour settled the pounding crash of his heart against his chest. He wasn't in this alone. No matter what happened next, as long as he had Poppy by his side he'd be fine.

Robert's shoulders slumped, and resignation deepened the lines on his face. 'It would appear that I owe you an apology, son. And you too, Poppy.'

Ben kept his face impassive, not wanting to show the shock that had his breath caught in his throat.

'Don't look so shocked. I'm a big enough person to be able to say when I'm in the wrong.'

So much for not showing his feelings.

Robert looked up at Pam, who'd come to stand behind him, her hand on his shoulder. 'The thing is, when you left the practice I was angry and confused. I couldn't understand why you'd throw away everything you'd built. I couldn't understand why you'd throw away what I'd believed was your dream.' Robert paused. His broad chest lifted and fell, as if he were trying to keep his composure. 'I was also concerned what those in the law community would say. It's not every day someone leaves a successful practice to set up a combined tea shop and mad unicorn gift shop business…'

'I'm going to pretend I didn't hear the "mad" part.' Poppy rolled her eyes and topped up her glass. 'Unicorns might not float your boat, but they're rocking a lot of people's worlds right now, and they're making me a pretty penny.'

'Apologies again, Poppy. I guess you're right, they don't, er… float my boat. It seems I'm immune to their attraction.'

'Don't say that to her, Dad. She'll shower you in them, whether you like it or not. Poppy doesn't know the meaning of "no, thank you".' Ben laughed as Poppy blew a raspberry in his direction. 'Poppy's right though, Dad. The business is working. Both sides.' Ben nudged Poppy with his knee. 'For some reason Poppy's mad unicorn merchandise, with all its fluff and sparkle, complements my serious and grown-up gourmet tea shop. Although she has managed to get some glitter going on – you should see my Jammy Dodgers.'

A secretive grin crossed Poppy's face, stirring suspicion in Ben's stomach. Why did he have a feeling his shop may be more infused with Poppy's unicorns than he realised?

'I'm glad, Ben. Surprised, if I'm honest, but glad.' Robert's eyes misted up. 'And may I just say, I know I haven't shown it, but despite my bad behaviour I am proud of you. You followed your dreams. You embraced your passion. You didn't hold yourself back. You didn't let what I wanted for you get in the way of doing something that would bring you satisfaction. Ultimately that's what any parent wants for their child.'

Ben and his father had never been the hugging types, but then again, Robert had never been the type to say he was wrong, or to get wet in the eyes. Perhaps it was time to change that. Ben stood and moved round the table. His father stood to meet him.

'Thanks, Dad. Making you and Mum proud has been what's driven me my entire life, and I plan to keep on doing that. Mum, put the tongs down for a sec and come over here, please.' Ben held his arms wide and the three embraced.

Ben glanced over at Poppy. Her eyes were averted, her hands twisting round each other, and if he wasn't mistaken there was a single tear glistening on her cheek.

***

Poppy helped herself to a steak, then a big spoonful of potato salad.

'Garden salad, dear?' Pam passed the bowl Poppy's way and she accepted it with a small smile. One she hoped hit her eyes. One that hid the ache that had pulsed in her chest the moment Ben's family hugged.

This was the kind of family she'd yearned to be part of. This family stuck together and had a solid foundation that could weather the ups and down, that wouldn't let disagreements get in the way. Not for long anyway.

This family loved each other. Their in-jokes flew across the table, their smiles were wide and bright. Their laughter was as warm as the summer air. Once she'd thought their family was ruled by regulations and expectations, but now she knew it was ruled by love.

Knots intertwined in Poppy's gut, growing larger, tighter, and more twisted with every passing moment. She picked up her fork and pushed the potato salad around her plate, trying to ignore the little voice that came not from her head, but from her gut. The harsh whisper that would wake her at night, reminding her she wasn't good enough. She wasn't worth loving. That if her mother couldn't love her, then no one could. That anyone who thought they might would eventually change their mind.

'Poppy? Are you sure you're okay, dear? You've barely touched your food.' Pam reached out and placed the back of her hand on Poppy's forehead. 'You're not warm, but you're looking a touch peaky.'

Sadness weaved its way through the knots. Poppy sucked in air, sure she was about to throw up. 'I just… may I please use your—?' Poppy clutched her stomach, pushed the chair back – she didn't wait for an answer, figuring they'd know where she was going – and raced into the house, through the kitchen, to the second door on the left.

Slamming it shut, she crumpled to the floor, pushed her back against the wall, brought her knees to her chest and tipped her head up to the plain white ceiling. So different to the ceiling next door which her mother had painted a mural of a sky on, the walls a jungle of tropical flowers.

Just breathe, Poppy. Breathe.

She inhaled, counted to ten. Exhaled. Counted to ten. Over and over, until her heart's furious beat retreated to a steady thump, and the knots in her stomach loosened.

To think her biggest fear about coming to dinner was that her mother would see her, would know she was home… and would what? Try and make contact with her? Would see her and ignore her? Things she should never have feared because deep down she knew her mother didn't care enough to make meaningful contact. And if she'd seen and ignored her then it wouldn't have been any different from when she was younger.

Instead she'd been forced to face the one thing she'd run from for all these years.

A family that loved each other. A family that had their differences but didn't let them get in the way of how they felt. They were a team. They had each other's backs. They were the living embodiment of the thing she refused to believe in. Love.

Seeing them together earlier, toe-to-toe, arm-round-arm, their adoration for each other obvious, the strength they gave each other, had brought a tear to her eye.

And a surge of realisation.

Ben had the love he deserved because he didn't run from it. Because he opened himself to it and wasn't afraid to ask to be loved.

Whereas she had no kind of love at all. No chance of it, because she kept people at arm's length, too afraid to let anyone in, in case they got too close – in case they took a chisel and hammer to the crack in her heart.

A soft knock on the door jerked Poppy out of her head.

'Poppy? It's Ben. Just checking you're okay? Is there anything

I can do? I've brought your bag in case there's something in there you need.'

Poppy pushed herself up off the ground and opened the door. 'Thanks, Ben, and sorry.' She took her bag out of his hands. 'I must've eaten something earlier that didn't agree with me. My stomach's been set to a spin cycle, so I think I might have to head home. Could you thank your parents for me? And tell them I'm so sorry.'

Ben's eyes, dark with concern, searched her face. 'Sure thing, Poppy. Are you sure you're okay? You don't want me to walk you home?' His brow furrowed in worry.

How she wanted to smooth those wrinkles away. To soften their grooves. But she couldn't. She wouldn't. She'd led Ben on with that kiss last night; she'd led herself on, given herself an inch of hope, of which she would not take a mile. It wouldn't be fair on either of them.

'I'm fine, Ben. I'm sure an early night and a good sleep will sort out whatever this is...' She prodded her stomach and lifted her lips in what she hoped was a convincing smile.

'I'll walk you out then.'

Poppy trailed behind Ben, keeping her eyes on the ground, afraid if he turned around he'd see the relief in her eyes and know that there was more to her leaving than a dodgy tummy – then question it.

Ben opened the door and held it for her. 'You sure you'll be okay?'

Poppy nodded. 'Of course. I always am. Now get back in there and enjoy your family dinner. And enjoy your day off tomorrow, okay? The shop's closed and we've both earned some rest.'

Ben paused, his lips pursed, his eyes narrowing. Disbelief radiated off him, but Poppy wasn't backing down.

'Okay, well, you know my number if you need me.' Ben cast one more assessing look, then shut the door.

Poppy glanced up at the place she'd once called home. A lone figure stood in the window. Did it see her? Did it recognise her? She wasn't about to stick around to find out.

Poppy bustled down the steps and strode up the road, not once looking back. There was no point. There was nothing there for her.

Not then. Not now. Not ever.

Chapter 13

Bing bong. Bing Bong. Bing Bong.

Poppy pulled the pillow over her bare ear and squeezed her eyes shut even tighter than they already were. It was her day off. Her one day off a week. Who in their right mind would wake her up so damn early? Who would be brave enough to disturb her peace?

Bing bong. Bing Bong. Bing Bong.

The only person who knew where she lived, aside from her landlady, that's who.

'Beeeeeen.' She peeled open one eye, scrabbled for her mobile and checked the time.

10.30.

A respectable time to come calling. Especially on a Monday morning when most people already had a couple hours' work tucked under their belts, or had been up since the crack with little ones. But this was her day off, and after last night she didn't want to move. Didn't want to leave the cosy haven of her bed. Not for love or money.

Another echoing rap at the door met her ears.

How the hell did he get up here? Bloody neighbours. Must've decided he looked like a trustworthy type and let him in.

'Poppy. You in? The lady who lives on the ground floor said she hadn't seen you leave.'

Poppy stifled a groan. Of course it was Mrs Biddle. She kept an eagle eye on the comings and goings of the people of the house. She would have seen Ben come up with Poppy the day she moved in, then noted that he left at an appropriate time with his clothing unwrinkled and his hair unruffled, and deemed him an acceptable visitor.

'Poppy. Let me in. I'm carrying coffee and pastries and they're getting heavy and I'm in danger of dropping them. Think of the pastries, Poppy, think of the hours that went into making the pastries. Don't break the heart of some poor pâtissier by allowing their creations to be destroyed.'

Poppy tossed aside her sheet with a sigh, the mock-desperation pulling her out of her morning funk.

'Fine, I'm coming.' She shrugged on her robe, padded to the door, unlocked it and swung it open with a dramatic sigh. 'What are you doing here at this hour of the morning? And why are you here on our day off? Surely you'd be sick of the sight of me by now?'

Ben breezed past her, not even remotely concerned by the derision in her tone.

'Sick of you? Never. Besides, I wanted to check on you, make sure you were all right. You looked a right sight last night. I was worried.' Ben set the coffees on the kitchen bench and passed one to Poppy. 'Flat white, no sugar.'

Poppy accepted the cup and took a sip. 'Perfect. And needed.' She rubbed her eyes, still bleary from her sleep-in. 'Thank you.'

Ben shrugged. 'Least I can do. Hungry?' He opened the box of pastries and pulled out petit pains au chocolat, mille-feuille, and friands. 'I wasn't sure what you'd be in the mood for, so I got a few things.'

'They all look good. Really good.' Poppy picked up a pain au chocolat and bit into the buttery, sweet, flaky goodness.

'Ah-mazing.' She swiped her hand across her mouth, letting the crumbs fall to the floor. Poppy watched as Ben's eyes followed the journey of the crumbs, his eyes widening and brows raising as the flakes hit the floor. 'Don't freak out, Ben. I own a dustpan and brush.'

'No, it's not…' Rosy colour hit Ben's cheeks. 'It's, er…' He indicated to her robe.

Poppy glanced down to see it was gaping about the upper thigh area, showing off her bright pink knickers. 'Oh my God. I'm so sorry.' She pulled the robe tighter. 'Thank God I was wearing a pair of pants. Thank God I'm up-to-date with my washing! Imagine if I was knickerless… and now I'm prattling, and I'll just shut up. Bloody hell, I'm such a dork.' Poppy rolled her eyes and re-tied the robe, double knotting it.

'It's fine. Really. Um…' Ben's cheeks flamed from pink to red as he averted his eyes and turned towards the kitchenette, hoping she hadn't noticed the way his pants had perked up. 'How about I get you a plate? Save you spending all day cleaning up after yourself.'

Ben opened the cupboard above the sink and pulled out two plates. Without asking, and to Poppy's amusement, he took the pain au chocolat out of her hand and placed it on the plate along with a friand and the mille-feuille.

'You knew where the plates were without being told. I'm impressed.' Poppy followed Ben to the small dining table, took a seat opposite, then pushed aside the curtains, allowing the sun to stream in, brightening the room… and her outlook.

The veil of doom and gloom that had surrounded her since the previous evening retreated, as if it had realised it was no match for a day where the sky was a brilliant blue, with not a cloud to be seen. A day where the London cityscape rose up to greet her, reminding her there was more to life than brooding about the past and fearing for her future. More wonderful than the day that greeted her from her window, was that the person she cared most about had cared enough to make sure she was okay. And he'd brought her favourite treats *and* remembered exactly what kind of coffee she liked and how she liked it.

'What can I say?' Ben picked up a friand and inspected it. 'I'm housebroken. I know where things should go in kitchens – which I'm pretty sure makes me the perfect man.' He took a bite and chewed, a gleam in his eye. 'You know what also makes me pretty perfect? I never forget an important date.'

Poppy closed her eyes. She knew what was coming next but wanted no part of it. Perhaps ignoring the situation would make it go away. 'I think the perfect man knows when to let something go. When not to aggravate a situation. And this is a rather pleasant situation we're enjoying right now. Coffee and pastries while being bathed in sunlight? Best you eat up then go before things go downhill.' She turned her attention to the street below, where a mother was pushing her squawking baby along the footpath in a space-age style pushchair with one hand, while the other hand was gripping onto a toddler who was trying to make its escape. *You and me both, kiddo.* She had a feeling neither of them were getting away from their situations anytime soon. 'Eat up, Ben. Chop chop.'

'"*Chop chop*"?' A short, sharp guffaw filled the room. 'Who even says that these days? You've turned thirty-one, Poppy, not ninety-one.'

Poppy's lips twitched. Damn it. She could try and be pissy but it wasn't going to work. Not when Ben was determined to celebrate her birthday, whether she wanted to or not.

'So, you're going to force me to celebrate the one day of the year I couldn't care less about.' Poppy cupped her chin in the palm of her hand and drummed her fingertips on her cheek.

'You don't have to sound so excited about it, Pops, but yes, I am. And do I have something fantastic planned…' Ben smacked the table with the flat of his fingers in a rhythmless drumroll, then stood and jogged to the studio's door where a black backpack was hanging on the doorknob.

How did she miss that? Poppy pondered. And why was Ben oozing excitement? What did he have up his sleeve?

'Today is a grand day, Poppy Taylor. For today, thirty-one years ago, you chose to grace this world with your presence.' Ben reached into his backpack and pulled out a gold plastic crown covered in fake gemstones in blue, green, pink, red and purple. 'Frankly I can't believe there wasn't a bank holiday created in your honour. Clearly an oversight. I'm sure it will be rectified one of these days.' He crossed the room and placed the crown on her head, wiggling it a little to the left and a touch to the right, before giving a nod of satisfaction and stepping back. 'Perfect.'

Poppy touched the crown, and the grin she'd been holding back stretched her lips. 'I can't believe you bought a crown for me. What did the person at the store say when you rocked up to the till with it?'

'Nothing. I bought it online and had it addressed to Benjalina,' Ben smirked.

'Bollocks you did.' Poppy tore at a piece of her pain au chocolat and popped it in her mouth.

'You're right, bollocks I did. Bought it at a store. The teenage girl behind the counter didn't blink twice. Frankly I think I could have been dressed in a princess costume while buying it and she'd not have noticed. Now, what's next?' Ben tapped his chin, then raised his index finger. 'Oh, that's right. You need to go get dressed. We're heading out.'

'Head out, you say?' Poppy touched her crown. 'If I'm wearing a crown does that mean I'm the ruler of all that I survey for the day? Does it mean I can make the rules?'

Ben took hold of Poppy's hands, sending a frisson of excitement up her arms and down her spine. 'Cute, your highness. Good try. But no, you can't make all the rules, just the ones that won't interfere with what I have planned.'

'Damn it. You know me too well. In that case, I'd better go wash this filthy bod of mine.' She swivelled on her heel, then glanced over her shoulder. Ben's eyes snapped up, having clearly been focused on something a little lower and rounder than the back of her head. 'You. Sit. Eat. And leave my coffee alone. The queen commands it.'

Ben pressed his palms together and nodded a silent oath, then made his way back to the dining table. 'Why do I have a feeling giving you a little bit of power for one day was a bad idea?'

'I'd like to promise that I won't take things too far... but then, where would the fun be in that?' She winked, then sauntered towards the bathroom. Maybe the one day of the year she avoided thinking about at all costs wasn't going to be so horrid after all.

***

Ben checked his watch. Again. How long did it take Poppy to get ready? What was she doing in that bathroom? It had been twenty minutes already, and it wasn't like she was the kind of girl to spend half an hour on her makeup. Or at least he didn't think she was. She always looked fresh and natural to him.

He eyed the last of his mille-feuille. As tempting as it was with its rich custard, flaky puff pastry, and shiny glazed icing, if he ate it he'd struggle to get through the lunch he'd organised. Poppy was going to die of happiness when she saw what he'd pulled together. If that didn't make her realise how special she was to him, then nothing would.

He stood and stretched his arms above his head, then strolled around the small living area. Maybe a few steps would make some extra room in his stomach. At the very least it would help pass the time. Picking up the plates, he dumped temptation into the rubbish bin, then rinsed the cutlery and set it in the dishwasher.

Glancing around he noticed the walls were dotted with black and white photographs that hadn't been there the last time.

He moved to the closest one. A picture of Poppy in a string bikini on the beach, her arm slung round the shoulder of some guy. Some tall, curly-headed, too-handsome-to-not-notice guy. Their smiles were wide, laughter in their eyes, and they were both doing the peace sign to the camera. In the background a young fellow, swimming in the water, had photobombed the picture, sticking out his tongue and crossing his eyes. An act that would usually have seen Ben laugh, but instead jealousy snaked around his heart, squeezing it tight. His temples pounded as he focused on the happy couple.

If they were that happy they'd still be together, he reminded himself. *And you don't know that they were a couple.*

Ben forced his leaden feet to move to the next photo. Another shot of Poppy and the mystery man. Except this time he had his arms thrown around her and another woman, and they were standing on one of what looked like a million steps. Machu Picchu, Ben realised. Was there anywhere Poppy hadn't travelled?

God, what did she think of him and his homely ways? Sure, he'd left England, but only to go where so many others went. Boozy stag weekends with the boys in Dublin. The odd summer holiday in Malaga. Skiing in the Swiss Alps. More often than not his mother would join him. His father, too, if he could be forced out of the office.

Poppy must think him the most boring sod she'd ever met. In Ben's eyes opening his shop had been a big deal. An adventure. Yet she'd travelled to the ends of the earth, seen sights he could only imagine, experienced all the world had to offer...

After everything she'd done she'd find his birthday plans for her positively pedestrian. Doubt gnawed at his insides. What had he been thinking trying to surprise Poppy? The plan had been to spoil her, entertain her, sprinkle some Poppy-style magic into her life. To try and transform that attitude of hers that romantic love didn't exist. To show her how much he cared for her. To show her what love felt like. What love made people do. But were his plans enough to impress someone as worldly as Poppy?

Ben walked over to the next photo. A profile of Poppy sitting on a jagged rock, looking out towards a stormy sea. White caps dotting the turbulent waters. Tendrils of hair flew back in the stiff wind. Her face solemn. Bereft.

The previous photos were of the Poppy that she chose to show the world. Happy go lucky, smiley, easy to laugh. But this photo? It was the Poppy only he knew.

He, and whoever took the photo. The guy? Or someone else? A friend she'd made along the way? The jealousy that had eased off returned, slamming into his gut.

He'd always thought of Poppy as being *his*. Not a possession, but… his soulmate. The one person he could tell anything too, and vice versa. But someone else had seen the real Poppy, and it ripped him up inside.

'You like that?'

Ben spun round to see Poppy dressed in faded denim shorts that hugged her thighs and hips in a way that was going to drive him mad, and a plain olive scoop-necked T-shirt that skimmed over her curve of her breasts. She'd accessorised with big gold hoop earrings, and that was that. Simply stylish. That was his Poppy.

'What? No unicorn onesie just to spite me?' He swallowed the jealousy. There was no point in indulging that emotion. If anyone had meant anything to her then Poppy would have brought them home. Or stayed where they were.

Or would she? She'd run from home. Run from him. Who was to say that she wouldn't do that to another?

'No onesie. As much as I have an affection for unicorns I'm not quite as mad for them as Joe. He can get away with it being the bright, shiny young thing he is. But me? It's better I sell them than wear them.' Poppy stood beside him, so close he could feel the residual heat from the shower emanating off her. 'Anyway, I wouldn't want this horrid charade of a day ruining unicorns for me.' That easy smile he knew so well shaved the sharp edge off the words.

'You're mad, Poppy. Did anyone ever tell you that?'

Poppy flashed him a toothy grin. 'A million times. And you didn't answer my question. Do you like that photo?'

'I do. It's... you. The private you.' Ben glanced out of the corner of his eye, wanting to catch Poppy's reaction. Her face remained impassive.

'I think that's why I like it. It was taken on this blustery day in this tiny town called Kaikoura – it's in the South Island of New Zealand. I'd gone for a ramble and finished up in South Bay, a small settlement just outside of town with a gorgeous pebbled beach that frames the land. The beach has these amazing clay-coloured rock formations, all jagged and random, and – this will sound mad – but that day they called to me. So I ambled over them, nearly breaking my ankle half a dozen times, sat down as close to the sea as I could get, and just... let myself be.' Poppy's eyes shut, her chest rose and fell evenly. An aura of peace surrounded her. It was like she was there again. 'I allowed the wind to push me round as it saw fit. Let the sea spray from the waves crashing onto the rocks settle on my face, my clothes, my hair. I breathed in the briny air. Let my mind wander. And eventually I asked the universe some pretty big life questions.'

'And did the universe answer?'

'It did.' Poppy opened her eyes, clear and bright, the corners of her lips lifting in a small smile. 'The universe told me it was time to go home. So I went back to the backpackers' hostel I was staying in and booked my ticket home, then called you.'

Ben looked at the picture with renewed interest. This wasn't Poppy being Poppy, this was the moment something changed inside of Poppy. 'If you were alone, who took the picture?'

'A local photographer. They were roaming round and saw me,

snapped this shot, then waited for me to come to my senses and asked me if I'd like to be sent a copy.' Poppy touched the frame of the photo. 'It's one of my favourite memories from my travels. One of the most special. Maybe even *the* most special. That moment changed my life. My destiny.'

Hope swelled hot and heavy in Ben's heart. *That moment brought you home. Back to me. Where you belong.*

Resolve beat away any lingering doubt. He was going to make today the best birthday Poppy had ever had. He was going to give her every reason to never leave home, ever again.

Chapter 14

Poppy yearned to tug off the blindfold hiding the world from her, but knew to do so would earn her a stern word from Ben. And ruin all of the hard work he had clearly put into today. He had also made some very strong threats…

The glitter would disappear from the Jammy Dodgers.

He'd stop baking her favourite lemon drizzle cake.

And the unicorn-printed sugar bowl she'd sneakily placed on the table closest to the window would be removed.

Poppy couldn't help but laugh when that last threat had come out. Ben had been so po-faced, but she hadn't missed the way he'd attempted to secretly suck in his cheeks to stop himself from laughing.

It seemed her plan to infuse unicorn magic into his life was working. His strait-laced fashion sense had given way to shirt buttons no longer done right up to the neck. And instead of ignoring the world as it passed them by he'd taken the time to laugh and joke with strangers who'd been amused to see a man leading a woman wearing a crown down the street to… well, wherever it was he was taking her.

'Are we there yet?' She sniffed the air. An earthy scent surrounded them, and the temperature had dropped. The rustle of leaves met her ears. 'I know that smell.'

'I should hope so. I feel like we spent most of our childhood roaming about in here.'

Ben's grip tightened as he guided her up a flight of stairs. 'Nearly there, Pops. Take three steps forward.'

Poppy obeyed. The air changed around her, from moist and cool to warm and dry. A tug at the back of her head saw the blindfold fall from her eyes.

She blinked, trying to accustom herself to the light after the gloom of the blindfold. Blinked again, this time in surprise. What was she seeing?

Fairy lights were draped around the perimeter of the small cabin, and criss-crossed back and forth across the room, giving the space a magical golden glow. Dotted round the room were potted plants – yuccas, mop-topped Elephant's Foot, ficus, and palms – giving the ambience of a tropical jungle.

Poppy looked down to see faux grass had been rolled out the length of the cabin's floor and, in the middle of the room surrounded by flickering LED candles, was a giant mushroom. Red with white spots, and flat on top. On either side of it were two smaller flat-topped mushrooms, one painted green with white spots, the other pink with white spots. Sitting beside the mushrooms was a wicker picnic basket, so full she could see a bottle of champagne poking out of one its lids, and the tip of a baguette from the other.

'Happy birthday, Poppy.' Ben's voice was low, taut with tension, his skin a few shades paler than usual.

Did he think she wouldn't like this? That she hated her birthday so much that she wouldn't *love* the effort he'd made to make the one day a year that she'd rather didn't exist special?

'You did this.' It wasn't a question. And Ben didn't answer. 'You did it for me.'

Ben touched the small of her back, an intimate gesture that sent a delightful shiver up her spine. 'Please, sit, Queen Poppy Taylor, Ruler of the World, the Galaxy and the Universe beyond.'

Poppy giggled. 'Please tell me you're not going to call me that for the rest of today? Your tongue will drop off from exhaustion.'

'Is that a royal ruling?' Ben tapped the top of her crown.

'I command you to call me Poppy.' She gave what she hoped was a regal nod.

'Good, thank you. I must admit I was fearing for my tongue's longevity.' Unshouldering his backpack, Ben rifled through its mysterious contents and drew out a glittering glass flute. 'For you.'

'Wow.' Poppy held her gift up to the light, and admired the shimmering colours of gold and silver, pink and purple, orange and red. 'I need to get these for the shop.'

'But they're not unicorn themed.' Ben grabbed the champagne bottle and placed it on the table.

'We need to open a second store then. You can do what you do, as you do, if that's what you want to do, and I'll branch out. One of my stores can be unicorn-themed, the other can be rainbow-themed. It'd be amazing. I'd swan between the two, soaking up equal amounts of unicorn-induced happiness and rainbow-made magic.'

Ben set the baguette on the table, along with a cheese knife, and a platter on which he piled cheeses, meats, olives and grapes. 'I knew I should have rethought that crown. More trouble than it's worth. At this rate you'll have us going global.'

'We could, you know.' Poppy picked up the baguette and ripped off a chunk. 'Can you imagine it? I could travel the world setting up the stores, hiring people, organising fit outs, training people up. You could stay here, do all the business stuff, which you're great at, and, let's be honest, I'm not. We'd be bazillionaires by the time we're forty.' Poppy sliced off a hunk of gooey Brie, slathered it on the bread and popped it in her mouth. 'God, this is good. You've spoilt me, Ben.'

'Least I could do, Poppy.'

The words were kind but there was no enthusiasm backing

them up. Poppy ignored the danger of swallowing half-chewed bread and did it anyway. 'Are you okay? You've gone quiet all of a sudden. Did I say something daft?'

'No. Nothing. Really. It's... nothing.' Ben dismissed her query with a wave and smiled brightly. Too brightly.

'Is it the talk of expanding? Too much, too fast? Sorry, you know me. Give me an inch and all that.' Poppy pulled a grape off the bunch, popped it in her mouth and used the excuse to chew as a reason to think. Was it the talk of branching out that had upset Ben... or the talk of her leaving him behind while she travelled the world setting up stores? The half-eaten wodge of bread and cheese felt like a rock in her gullet. How insensitive was she? It sounded like she was abandoning Ben. Leaving him to run everything and do the hard yards, while she went gallivanting about the place. No wonder he looked like a dog who'd had his favourite toy taken away. 'When I said I'd travel the world setting up shops I didn't mean I wouldn't come back. I would. All the time. This would be our base. I wouldn't leave you, Ben. I promise.'

Ben shook his head as he opened the champagne, releasing the pressure with a hint of a pfft, then poured it elegantly into the flutes. 'I said it's nothing, Poppy. Just forget about it.' He picked up his glass and took a long sip.

'No, I won't forget about it. Look at what you've done, Ben.' She opened her arms wide and glanced around at the fantastical décor, seeing things she'd not noticed before. Delicate fairy lights hung off the branches of the bushes. A unicorn cake, complete with cascading mane and golden horn was set to the side on its own table. Vases filled with daisies and gerberas were placed in every corner of the room. 'You've given me something I never expected to have. Something I didn't even know I wanted.' She dragged her stool round to be nearer to Ben, took his hands in hers, and stroked his knuckles, white with tension, hoping to ease out whatever worries, whatever tension he was holding tight inside.

'I couldn't let this day go by without at least trying. It's been far too long since we've had one of our birthdays in the same country, Poppy.' Ben's gaze didn't leave his glass, his eyes following the strands of bubbles that made their way to the top before breaking on the surface.

Poppy ducked her head, forced him to focus on her. 'I'm glad you didn't. Coming home – coming home to *you* – was the best decision I've ever made.'

'Better than travelling the world? Seeing the sights I've only ever read about in books? Hanging out with… exotic-looking men.'

Ben's cheeks flushed red, and Poppy suspected it had nothing to do with the alcohol.

'You saw the picture of Diego?' Poppy couldn't help but grin. Ben was jealous? Because she'd made another man-friend? Or, jealous in another way? In a *romantic* way? 'Ben, Diego is a friend. He's now married to Martine. The girl in the photo at Machu Picchu. And they've made the most adorable baby you've ever seen.'

'Oh.' Ben straightened up, the colour returned to his knuckles. 'How did you meet them?'

'The usual way. At a backpackers' hostel. We got on, so travelled together. It was good fun. We did Thailand, Vietnam, Cambodia. A good chunk of South America, as you saw. Got each other into scrapes, got each other out of scrapes. But we always had each other's backs, which was nice after travelling solo for so long. And you know, it was really quite wonderful watching those two fall in love.' Poppy grinned. The attraction had been obvious from the start. The way the two after a few beers would sit a little closer. Find excuses to touch each other. Gravitated to each other, without even realising it most of the time.

Kind of like she did with Ben.

Shit.

The realisation whipped her breath away.

164

She was serious when she said she'd never leave Ben. Not again. Not for any great length of time. But it had nothing to do with the business. Or their friendship. It was because, despite the blocks she'd set up around herself to stop it from happening, from the feelings she'd tried to hide away in the deepest darkest mental-closet she had, she was falling for him. Again.

'I thought you didn't believe in love?'

Ben's knees were touching hers. Bare skin on bare skin. Tingles sparked up her thighs, to areas more covered. *When did knees get so erotic*, Poppy half-wondered as she noticed at some point their fingers had intertwined.

'I don't. I mean. I don't think I do. Shit, maybe I'm beginning to? Just a little?' Poppy squeezed her eyes shut, tight as they could go. How had she let this happen? It was the kiss. The kisses. First his. Then hers. Then all this sweetness… this caring… directed at her. *For* her. It had all combined to not so much chisel away at her wall so much as drive a sledgehammer through it.

She opened her eyes to see Ben's lips mashed together, his eyes damp with unshed tears. 'If you are planning on laughing at me, Ben Evans, then you'd better be prepared to find out what it feels like to have Brie smushed into your face.'

Ben's lips thinned even more. His broad chest shuddered as he tried to keep it together.

Deep down a tickle of humour unfurled in Poppy's stomach. It swirled its way through her belly, and started to grow until she couldn't control it anymore. The next thing she knew her laughter was filling the room, and soon joined by Ben's.

They collapsed into each other, arms wrapped round each other in mutual support as their shoulders heaved and their chests vibrated.

'Damn it, I'm getting soft in my old age.' Poppy sucked in a lungful of air. Then another. 'I guess it's one thing to say I don't believe in love for *me*, but even I can't deny it doesn't exist for others. I mean, look at your parents. They still love each other, even after all these years.'

Ben pulled away, a trail where tears had been still damp on his face. 'You should have seen them after you left and a couple of wines in. They were as bad as a couple of teenagers. I swear they've gotten more and more touchy feely the older they've got. I left early because if I didn't I feared I'd witness something no child ever should.'

'Stop. Stop now.' Poppy threw her hands up. 'Don't say another word. I don't need the images. My childhood scarred me enough as it is, I don't need your parents buggering up my adulthood.'

Ben's thumb and forefinger pinched together and mimicked zipping his lips.

'Good, thank you. I appreciate it. But...' Poppy leaned forward and unzipped his lips. 'We can't have you unable to eat, not when you've put together this feast. Here...' She ran a cheese knife through the pungent blue and placed it on another hunk of bread. 'Eat this and tell me if it's as smelly tasting as it is aromatically challenged.'

Ben chewed, his eyes drawn to the ceiling in thought. 'Creamy. Tangy. A hint of earthiness. Not nearly as smelly tasting as it is smelly. I think it'll pass the Poppy test. I wouldn't have bought it if it didn't.'

'Good. Thank you.' Poppy spread a little blue on the bread and took a dainty bite.

'Really? You're not going all in? You don't trust me?' Ben helped himself to another slab.

Poppy shook her head. 'It's not a matter of trust, it's a matter of taste. Sure, you think it's fine for me, but I can't trust a man who doesn't understand the joy of unicorns.'

Ben topped up their glasses. 'I don't know. I'm coming around to the idea. That unicorn teacup sitting on my shelf looks rather fetching. A nice pink and golden addition. I'd say it's the perfect contrast to my double-walled glasses. Also, just so you know, it's not there anymore – and before you get all huffy, I haven't taken it down and tossed it away. Someone came in just on closing while you were out the back and bought it. I'm almost unicorn-free once again, soon as I deal with that sugar bowl of yours…'

Poppy held her hand out. 'Money please.'

'Sure thing.' Ben patted his pockets, then fished about in them. 'So sorry. No money here. It went to my therapist. He's helping me deal with the overload of glitter and pink and purple fluff that's entered my life.'

'You're a nutter.' Poppy took a sip of her champagne, letting the fizz bubble away on her tongue, as she soaked in the easy atmosphere, all the stress and strain between them a thing of the past.

'That's what my therapist said.' Ben's face stilled, his eyes wide. Solemn.

Shock mixed with guilt seized Poppy's heart. 'Oh, God, I'm sorry. I didn't know you really were seeing someone… I'm so thoughtless. Ridiculous of me to assume you wouldn't. I mean, everyone does these days, right? I really should too.'

'Poppy.' Ben took hold of her hand and gave it a gentle squeeze. 'I'm joking.'

A wave of hot embarrassment hit Poppy square in the cheeks. 'Such a tosser.' Poppy rolled her eyes.

'Is that as insulting as you can get?' Ben raised his brows in a silent dare.

'Cockwomble.'

'Weak. Try again.'

'Knobhead.' She reached out and tickled his waist.

'I'm beginning to think you're obsessed with my appendage.' Ben grinned as he moved out of her reach, revealing a hint of flat, tanned, stomach, and one half of a V-line that led to the place she was definitely, totally, completely, most absolutely not obsessed with.

Just a tiny bit curious about.

Get your head out of Ben's pants, Poppy, she growled at herself. 'So, now that we've dined, what's next?'

'Come back to mine?' Ben began picking up the leftover food and putting it in the basket.

Poppy clamped down on the 'yes' that threatened to escape unchecked. She touched her lips, remembering the heat of Ben's lips. Could she trust herself alone with him in his house?

'Poppy?' Ben was staring at her with a mix of curiosity and concern. 'Just in case you were wondering… just in case it matters to you… Milly and I aren't together. We never really were.'

'Oh.' Poppy allowed Ben to remove her hand from her lips, to hold her hand in his. 'But you were going out. A lot.'

'We were.' Ben's thumb stroked the top of her hand, sending pleasurable tickles dancing along her skin. 'But it never went anywhere. Milly wanted it to, but aside from one awkward hand-hold while watching a movie, nothing happened because I couldn't muster those kinds of feelings for her.'

'Oh.' Relief rushed through Poppy. The guilt that had engulfed her stomach since she'd kissed Ben disappeared. She hadn't stepped on toes. She hadn't gotten in the way of their relationship once again. 'So… what was that you were saying about me going back to yours? And since when did you become the forward type?' Poppy stuck her tongue out so Ben knew she was joking, that she didn't really think he was inviting her back to his for romantic reasons, but that didn't stop her heart from accelerating in a pitter-patter of anticipation, or a bunch of butterflies appearing low in her stomach.

'What can I say?' Ben shrugged on his backpack then grabbed the half-full champagne bottle. 'Perhaps you don't know me as well as you think you do?' Ben opened the door of the cabin. 'Poppies first.'

Poppy stepped out into the dappled clearing, closed her eyes and breathed in the herbaceous, earthy air. Allowed the shush of the wind in the trees to settle the racing of her heart. Embraced the spots of sun that filtered down onto her bare skin.

'You okay, Pops?' Ben touched her elbow, bringing her back to the here and now.

'I'm okay.' She flashed a smile at him. And she was. She really, truly was.

She was where she was meant to be. She was with who she was meant to be.

And for the first time in a long time, it didn't scare her.

Chapter 15

'So, this is home.' Ben stopped outside his house, an attack of nerves gluing his feet to the pavement. It wasn't like he hadn't had visitors before, or a girl round, but this was Poppy. Her opinion mattered more than anyone else's. What if she hated his place? What if she thought it dull as dishwater? What if once she found out he wasn't exactly as skint as he'd made out, and that if he'd been willing to take the risk he could've paid the entire rent for the shop, she got the pip with him and took off?

Poppy's head was tipped as she took in the red-bricked Edwardian terraced house. 'Please tell me you're not renting the top floor. I ate so much I don't think I can heave myself up the stairs.'

'Er, not quite.' Heat prickled the back of his neck. He hadn't been joking when he'd suggested Poppy didn't know him as well as she thought she did. Yes, she knew his likes and dislikes as well as he knew hers. But she'd missed twelve years of his life, and he'd achieved a lot in that time.

'Well, are you going to just stand there or are you going to invite me in? I don't want to be left out here to freeze to death on my birthday.' Poppy hugged herself and faked a shiver.

'It's summer, Poppy. A beautiful one at that. I think you're in no danger of freezing to death.'

'Thirsty then. It's been a good ten minutes since I last had a sip of champagne.' Poppy's feet shifted from side to side in an impatient shuffle.

'Fine, I'll just get my keys.' Ben pulled his keys out of his pocket, unlocked the door, and pushed it open. 'My house is your house. Make yourself at home.'

Poppy stepped over the threshold, her head craned a little as she took in the simple entranceway, with its polished oak floors, partially covered by a plain, soft grey carpet runner. Ben joined her, placing his keys on the simple black banquet table, and hung his backpack on one of the wall hooks to the right of it.

'Gosh, it's very clean. Your landlord must be a tidy freak.' Poppy ran her hand over the banquet, then lifted her finger to inspect it. 'So, which floor's yours? And I was serious when I said I hoped it wasn't the top floor. Unless of course you want to carry me up?' Poppy shot him a winning smile that should've eased his nerves but served only to stretch them further.

Poppy would find out sooner or later. Sooner had to be better than later. So now was the time to just put the truth out there. 'Actually, Pops. This whole place is mine. I'm my own landlord. But not a tidy freak, like you said.' Ben rushed on. 'That was the cleaner. He came round this morning and went over the place. You see I wanted it to be nice for you. Not that I planned for you to come over. I mean, I didn't. Part of me expected you to chuck me out of your flat this morning, but you didn't, and well, the last part of your birthday surprise is here and I wanted you to enjoy it without seeing a stray sock or...'

Poppy's index finger pressed upon his lips cutting him off. 'Breathe, Ben. At the rate you're talking you'll lose all air and pass out. Now if I take my finger away do you promise to take in a great gulp of oxygen and let me just look around your pad?'

Ben nodded.

'Good.' Poppy turned away from him and pointed to the door to the right. I'm going in there first.'

'Go ahead. It's the sitting room.' The muscle-aching tension in Ben's shoulders faded as he followed Poppy into his second favourite spot in the house.

Two three-seater black vintage-style leather sofas stood at right angles to each other, with a matching high-backed chair and ottoman sitting opposite them. One wall was filled with a sixty-five-inch television, a soundbar placed discreetly below it. He'd spent hours in this room relaxing on the sofa with a good thriller on his e-reader or kicking back and binging on television shows.

Yet seeing it through Poppy's eyes it looked cold. Austere. Nothing like her studio, with its cosy cushions and snuggly throws.

'Okay, where to next?' Poppy turned to face him, her eyebrows high, questioning. Like she was trying to figure something out but didn't have all the pieces of the puzzle.

'How about the kitchen?' Ben led the way down the hall, pointing out the toilet should she need it. He pushed open the door and stepped inside the stark monochromatic space. God, it was as bad as the sitting room.

'You're not one for colour, are you, Ben?' Poppy pulled out one of the white dining chairs that he'd chosen because they matched the white high gloss dining table. 'Are your wine glasses white as well?' She lifted the bottle of champagne that she'd taken off his hands as they'd walked home.

'No, they're... well, clear.' Ben opened a cupboard – painted high gloss white to keep the kitchen's theme going – and pulled out two glasses. 'There you go. One for me too. I think I'm going to need it the way this house critique is going. I'm rather glad there's a second bottle in the fridge.'

'Your stainless-steel fridge. Silver. Like that space age coffee machine you've got sitting over there. Nice to see you injected some personality into the place.' The tip of Poppy's tongue peeked out between her lips. A sure sign she was having him on.

'So, you don't hate the place then?' Ben sat opposite Poppy and pulled his glass towards him.

Poppy ran her finger round the rim of the glass. 'Not at all. It's kind of what I expected.'

'Only kind of?' Ben set his elbows on the table and rested his chin on his fists. 'What does that mean?'

'Well I didn't expect it to be so big. Or so... expensive-looking. Those are fancy sofas you've got back there, Ben. And that television in the lounge did not look cheap.' Poppy took a sip of her champagne then set it down again. Her fingers drummed the tabletop. 'And this whole place is yours?'

'Mine. All of it.' Ben could see the pieces of the puzzle coming together. Things were about to go terribly wrong, or, well, not as wrong as he suspected, but there would be questions, and he'd have some explaining to do.

Poppy nudged back the chair, pushed herself up and moved to the kitchen window, which looked over the neatly manicured garden. 'I suppose you have a gardener too? I can't imagine you having the patience to tend to the lavender out there, or the roses. And that box hedging is clipped to perfection.' She twisted round and leaned against the kitchen bench, her arms folded over her chest, one ankle hooked over the other. 'What am I missing, Ben? You made out you couldn't afford the bumped-up rent on the shop, yet you own a whole house. What gives?'

'Is it hot in here?' Ben flapped the neck of his polo shirt. 'Shall we head outside? I'll open that fresh bottle of champagne.'

'Ben.' Poppy's tone stopped him mid-flight. 'What aren't you telling me?'

Ben sank back into his chair. 'I have money. A decent amount. I'm not crazy rich, but I have enough to keep myself comfortable and to ensure the business has time to build without worrying about it going under.'

Poppy's nostrils flared as a heavy whoosh of air filled the space between them. 'And how did you get all this money? I know you were well paid, I've seen your car, but this is… well, this house is beyond impressive.'

'I wasn't just a solicitor, I was a partner at my practice. A rather successful one.'

A tiny vein in Poppy's temple twitched. 'So, if you have money, if you're comfortable, then why did you lie to me? Why didn't you tell me the truth from the outset? You could have opened Steep without me. Easily.' Her head dipped towards her chest, rising and falling with emotion. The back of her hand swiped angrily at her cheek before disappearing under her arm once again.

Ben's heart shrunk. A pang of guilt sent the chair backwards as he rushed to Poppy's side. She knew the truth now. She could walk out if she wanted. Treat him from now on as a colleague, and nothing more. Or he could be honest, explain why he kept things from her, and see how the tea leaves fell.

***

Poppy shrunk away as Ben approached, cursing the bench between herself and the window. She didn't want him anywhere near her. She needed to think. Needed to rage. Needed to run.

'Poppy, don't.' Ben came to a halt a foot away from her, leaving room enough that she could duck to the left, make a break for the back door, and then what? Scramble over the neighbours' fences until she got to the road?

'I can see you're checking out, Poppy. And I don't blame you. You could slap me right now and I'd let you. I deserve it.'

Poppy shook her head, unable to speak. Afraid to in case the words unleashed a torrent of hurt upon them both.

'Fine. If you're not going to let me have it, then I'm going to explain things.'

Poppy ducked her head. Ben's feet, bare from when he'd taken his flip-flops off at the door, flexed. His toes lifted then fell to the ground, like he was rooting himself to it.

'The thing is, Poppy. I could afford to open the shop by myself, but at the same time there's no way I would have. You know me, I'm not a risk taker. I needed to know if my shop failed I wouldn't lose my house. Lose everything I've worked for. That's why I had a budget, one I wasn't budging from. It was my safety net. I'm not like you, Poppy. I can't just throw myself headfirst into something. I have to have a plan. I have to be sure it will work, or that if it doesn't I will still be comfortable. It's what my father taught me to do, it's how he taught me how to live. And, if I'd lost all the money I'd worked for by investing in Steep and having it fail, he'd have never looked at me the same. I couldn't disappoint him, not when I knew I already would be.' He fisted his hands and shoved them in his pockets. 'When the landlord said the rent had doubled and you jumped in and bargained the rent down in exchange for taking on Joe and Sophie, how could I say no? You were so excited, so happy, and…'

'And what?' Poppy dragged her eyes up to meet Ben's. 'You saw it as a chance to take pity on poor old Poppy, the way you always have? Bringing me home for dinners. Sitting with me at school when no one else would because they'd been told to ignore the girl with the sweets in her lunch box instead of sandwiches and fruit, and the clothing that never quite fit right? Was that what it was? You didn't want to hurt my feelings by saying no because you didn't think I could handle it? I could handle it, Ben. I could handle hearing no. I would have made my shop happen with or without you. God, all this time I thought we were on an even footing, but once again you were just there for me out of the goodness of your heart.'

'Stop it, Poppy. Now.' The sharpness in Ben's voice sliced the edge off her anger, and told her she'd overstepped. She'd gone too far, and was in danger of pushing Ben away. 'You're not a

175

charity case. You never were. Not to me. You were my friend and I wanted to be with you. And it wasn't like you came into this business with nothing. We've gone halves, fair and square the entire way. That business isn't mine, it's ours. And I don't for a second think it would be as successful if I'd gone into it by myself.'

'Bollocks.' Poppy tightened her grip on herself. 'You'd have been fine. More than fine. You knew how to run a business. You had all the practical stuff down. The ordering. Inventory. Stupid spread-bloody-sheets and fancy arse computer programs. You had it sorted.'

'Which one of us is the people person, Poppy? Which one of us has a way of brightening up the room with a smile? Gets people chatting? Makes them want to stick around and browse? Has them feeling no pressure to buy, so that when they do they're happy with their purchase? And comfortable enough that they'll come back again?' Ben angled his head, eyebrows raised high, daring her to deny her place in Sparkle & Steep.

'Anyone can chat, Ben. It's not that hard.' Poppy bit down on her lower lip, hoping the dull pain would fire up the fury that Ben had slowly but surely put out with his argument. 'You should have been a courtroom lawyer. You're good at arguing your point.'

'I get stage fright. You saw that when I held the tasting. You stepped in, made me comfortable, and gave me the courage to go on.' Ben looked past Poppy, his gaze settling on the garden beyond, as an aura of calm, or if not calm, then resignation surrounded him. His eyes met hers once again. 'Anyway, it was more than my keeping the budget under control that had me go into business with you, it was because I wanted you in my life.'

Poppy's breath caught in her throat. What was Ben saying? She'd have been in his life whether they'd had a business together or not. 'Ben, you didn't have to let me hog half the shop in order for me to be in your life. Of course I'd be part of your life. It doesn't matter where I am, where I live, what I'm doing, that's a given. Why do you think I kept emailing you all these years? Why do you think you were the first person I told about coming home to Muswell Hill? You're my friend, Ben. Always.'

'I'm not talking about that. Why can't I just make things clear to you? Why is it always so hard?' Ben took a small step forward, closing the gap. He took her hands, still tucked safely under her armpits, and released them, one by one, so he was holding them, and brought them up between them.

A barrier? Or a connection? Poppy wondered. And what was he trying to make clear to her?

'I don't want you as a friend Poppy. I mean, I do. But I want you as more than a friend. And I didn't want to risk you running away in the middle of the night again. By going halves in the shop – despite how nervous I was doing that – I made sure you had a reason to stay, because I didn't know that *I* would be good enough a reason, because I wasn't the last time.' Ben's chin ducked down, his gaze fixed on the floor. His cheeks flushed, like he was embarrassed, like he couldn't believe he'd just been so honest about his thoughts, his feelings.

Poppy blinked hard, once, twice, three times. Had the world gone a little hazy? She glanced over at the gas cooktop. It wasn't on, was it? The knobs looked to be in the right position, so no. Not on. No gas leak then. So why was everything feeling so off-centre? Off-balance? This wasn't the way her life went. She wasn't the wanted one. The one people wanted to have around. The one people cared for.

Except Ben did want her to stick around, and he'd taken a risk by joining businesses with her to do it. And he didn't do it out of friendship… which meant, just maybe, that he did it out of lo—Nope. She wasn't saying the word. Admitting the word. It was too big. Too scary. Too. Permanent.

Ben released one hand to smooth a stray hair back from her

face. He tucked it behind her ear, his fingertips grazing the soft skin, lingering on her lobe, sending a heady tornado of desire spiralling low in her stomach.

'I'm sorry, Poppy. I shouldn't have said anything. Should have kept my mouth shut.'

Poppy caught the bereft look in his eyes, the warmth that had been there, doused. Because he didn't believe she felt the same.

'Don't you say that, Ben. Never keep your mouth shut. That beautiful, wonderful, and sexy as all get out mouth needs to keep talking. Who else pulls me up and sorts me out like you do? Who else cares enough about me to force me into loving having a birthday. And I have, you know? Loved today. Every moment of it. Because of you. And I'm sorry for before, it's hard for me to believe that someone wants me, wants me around. It's instinct for me to push back, push away. It makes it easier to leave, should I need to.'

'But you don't need to. I won't let you.' Ben's eyes darkened. Glinted in the sunlight. 'Also, I need to clarify something. Did you just call my mouth sexy? Sexy as all get out?'

'Ben,' Poppy interrupted.

'No, don't "Ben" me. I want to make sure I didn't mishear that.'

'Ben.'

'Because if I did I'm taking myself to the ear spec—'

'Ben, stop talking.' Before he could say another word, Poppy pressed her lips to his. Sealed his silence with a kiss.

Her lips brushed against his. Slow, soft. Marking him, as she inhaled his clean, fresh scent. Uncomplicated, good, decent, yet strong and firm. Pure Ben.

His arms encircled her waist, pulled her closer, fusing their bodies together as Ben took her kiss and intensified it, his lips hard against her softness. His hand snaked up her back, tugging at the hair tie keeping her braid together, loosening it, then untwisting, pulling, until her hair was free. Untethered. Like the beat of her heart. Wild. Uncontrolled.

She opened her mouth and their tongues met, twisting, tasting. The pace slower than their kiss two nights ago, but no less potent.

Poppy found the hem of Ben's polo and edged her hands under it, laid her palms flat on his stomach, relishing its flatness, its tautness, as she caressed the ridges of his abdominal muscles. Pushing Ben back she made to lift the top. 'May I?'

Ben nodded, holding his arms up as she whipped the top off and tossed it on the ground.

'That'll give the cleaner something to tidy,' she murmured as firm hands gripped her hips, lifted her up onto the bench.

Lips, hot and wet, kissed down one side of her neck, nibbling the edges of her collarbone, before taking her mouth once more.

Heaven. This was heaven. Or what heaven would feel like. Her eyes flew open as a croaky, yet almost girlish, giggle pierced the air.

'Ben.' She pushed him away as heat flamed on her cheeks. She placed her hands on his bare chest, loving that she could do that. That it wasn't awkward. That his chest was hers for the touching. 'I hate to throw a wet tea towel on this, but there's a pair of eyes attached to a curly blond head peering over the wall.'

Ben swore under his breath. 'That'll be the Whittaker boy. Good kid. Just turned twelve. We're probably sending his hormones into overdrive.'

'Well, we can't have that.' Poppy slid off the bench, hooked her finger into Ben's shorts and dragged him out of the kitchen and into the hall. 'And we can't have his parents complaining that we've set a bad example. More importantly, though, we can't have the boy putting a halt to what I think is about to become one unforgettable way to spend an afternoon.'

Ben's eyes lit up as he caught wind of what she was suggesting. 'You know, I know a very comfortable spot… private too.' He caught her hand, pulling her to him for another kiss. With a nibble on her lower lip he released her but kept his hand in hers. 'I don't believe I've shown you the second floor.'

Poppy laughed as Ben invited her to ascend his stairs with a dramatic flourish and a roguish wink. 'You know, I think I could get used to liking my birthdays.'

Chapter 16

Ben pulled up the sheet that had been kicked to the end of the bed, tucked it around his waist, and went to tuck the rest around Poppy.

'Really?' She grinned, letting the sheet fall between them. 'You've just seen everything you could possibly want to see. I'm hardly about to get all prudish on it.'

'Are you saying I'm prudish? Would a prudish person do this?' Ben flapped the sheet up and down, with a wink.

'Idiot.' Poppy leant over and kissed him, long, lingering. Soft and sweet. 'And keep going, I don't recall asking you to stop the impromptu peepshow.'

'Sorry.' Ben twisted his finger round a length of her hair. 'Got distracted.' He bunched the pillow under his head and took in the sight before him.

A goddess. That's how Poppy looked. Reclining on his bed, her arm tucked under her head, propping her up a little. A lust-lazy smile stretching her lips wide. Her eyes dozy, yet dancing. And that hair, long, glossy, luxurious, spread about her. 'You know, this is the first time I've ever seen you with your hair out.'

'No? Really?' Poppy picked up a length and inspected its ends. 'Are you sure?'

'Totally sure. The day we met, you had it in a braid. You wouldn't let Mum take it out during sleepovers. You were adamant about that. You went to school with it up in a braid every day. Sometimes you twisted it up into a low bun on really hot days, or when we went for a swim. But you never wore it out.'

'You paid way too much attention to my hair.' Poppy's hand reached for his waist.

He wriggled closer.

'Thank you. I didn't want to strain my neck every time I wanted to kiss you. This bed is huge. All your old girlfriends must have loved it.' Poppy's brow creased as her lips turned down.

Disquiet stirred low in Ben's gut. Was Poppy already regretting what had happened?

'Pops, you're not freaking out on me, are you?' Ben itched to reach out, to touch her, to stroke away whatever had caused her to frown, but kept his distance. Too much, too fast, could destroy the tenuous, silk-fine thread of whatever it was that was happening between them.

Poppy shook her head. 'No. Just… processing. I mean, it's not every single day that you make lo—that you jump into the sack with your best friend. I guess I don't want to screw it up.'

'It? As in…' Ben probed.

'As in. Our friendship. Our business partnership. As in… whatever this is.' She waved her hand airily between them. 'It's new. It's…'

'A little scary?' Ben took her hand and kissed each knuckle.

'A lot scary. But not in a bad way, you know?' Poppy snuggled closer to Ben. Her soft curves pressed against him, stirring that which was hidden by the sheet.

He cupped her cheek and brought her to him, wanting to feel her soft, lush lips on his, then paused as a rumble filled the room.

'Pretend its thunder,' Poppy whispered as she found his lips.

A gurgle followed the rumble.

182

'Poppy, your stomach is crying out for food.' Ben hovered over Poppy, daring her to deny it.

'It's no—' Another gurgling grumble stopped her denial in its tracks. 'Okay, maybe just a little bit.'

'Well, I can't have the birthday girl starving to death.' Ben scooped up his underwear that had been tossed carelessly onto the floor and pulled them on. 'Also, I did say I had the rest of your present here, and now seems like the perfect time to get it. I'll be back in a bit.'

**

Poppy pushed herself up into a sitting position and pulled the sheet around her. She'd been comfortable enough lying in the nude while Ben was in bed with her, but without him it seemed… strange. Like when he was with her in the room she felt like she belonged, but with him gone the starkness of the room made her feel like a stranger. An intruder.

She took in the space, tried to make sense of it.

Ben's humongous bed was dressed in white linen, in direct contrast to the black headboard, and matching bedside tables. The walls were free from art or photos. And the wooden floors could have done with a big rug to keep feet from freezing when getting out of bed in the colder months. There was no personality here. No hint of the Ben she knew. The funny Ben. The kind Ben. The sexy Ben who had branded every part of her body with kisses. Who'd made love to her with such tenderness, yet had been firm, strong, commanding and demanding when it was time. Who knew almost instinctively what she needed, what she wanted.

It was like the room was waiting for someone to come and give it a lease of life. Like Ben was waiting for that person…

Could that person be her?

She sucked in her bottom lip and gnawed on the soft flesh, as self-doubt threatened to strangle the cautious joy and hope she held in her heart.

Was she the kind of woman Ben wanted? Someone fun and funny, he'd said. With fire in their belly, and a good heart.

On paper she read as his ideal woman, but would it be enough? Was she enough? The self-doubt she'd spent her life fighting began to unfurl. Would the humour and happiness she showed the world only take her so far before he realised she wasn't anything special? The way her mother had figured out all those years ago.

Poppy pushed the thoughts away. She wasn't going to allow her past to pop her bliss bubble. There was only one thing for it. She swung her legs out of bed and padded over to Ben's wardrobe. Pulling it open she smiled as she noted the perfectly coordinated clothing. Shirts were lined up, followed by pants hooked over hangers, then a row of T-shirts. She picked a navy-blue shirt and shrugged it on, buttoning it up as she padded down the stairs.

'Hey.' She hung about the kitchen door, suddenly feeling shy.

Ben glanced over his shoulder. 'Hey back. What are you doing hanging around by the door, come in and give me a hand. Love the shirt. It looks better on you than me.'

'You've excellent taste, Ben Evans.' Poppy sidled up to him and watched as he removed a pot of yellow batter from the stove then began to beat in eggs bit by bit. 'What's that?'

'Éclair mix. I remembered how much you enjoyed them and thought I'd whip us up a batch for...' He checked the time on the microwave. 'For dinner.'

'Perfect. And will they be filled with cream, with chocolate icing on top?' Poppy snuggled into Ben's back and wrapped her arms around his waist, held him tight, never wanting to let him go again.

'You know it. I've also sent texts to Joe and Sophie to let them know we'll be late tomorrow.' He began spooning dollops of the mixture onto a tray covered in baking paper. 'And don't worry, I made sure to say that we were having a big night out so that they don't come to the conclusion that we're spending the night together.'

'Which we're *so* going to.' Poppy kissed the nape of Ben's neck, pulled back and laughed as the fine hairs stood to attention.

'Yes, which we're going to. But they don't need to know that.' Ben shuffled them back, then placed the éclairs in the oven. 'Now, you go get the yoghurt from the fridge. First course is coming up.'

'First course?' Poppy opened the fridge door, located the yoghurt and turned around to find Ben had placed two dessert bowls on the table.

'Mum's cheesecake. She made sure I took it home with me last night and told me to wish you a happy birthday. On behalf of her and Dad.'

Poppy sat down next to Ben, pulled the bowl closer, picked up the spoon and dug into the silken pudding. 'I bet your dad has no idea it's my birthday.' She took a mouthful of the dessert, and let the savoury sweetness coat her tongue. 'So good. Every bit as good as I remember.'

'It really is.' Ben mumbled, his mouth full. 'And you're right. Dad would have no idea that it's your birthday. Probably doesn't know mine either.'

'Can we not talk about your dad while I'm kind of in the nude?' Poppy nudged Ben as she scooped up another spoonful of the dessert. 'It's putting me off my dessert.'

'Agreed.' He dropped a creamy kiss on her exposed shoulder, then licked it up, sending a delicious shiver down her spine, through her body. He set the bowl down and turned to her, his eyes heavy with intent. 'Oh, one more thing, birthday girl.'

'One more thing?' Poppy looked around the room. What else could he give her?

'You thought your surprise birthday had finished?' Ben turned

185

around, grabbed something from under a tea towel, the presented her with an upturned fisted hand. 'Open it.'

Poppy took Ben's hand and gently prised open each finger, one by one, until his palm revealed a shining silver unicorn charm, the horn plated in gold. 'Oh. Oh, wow. Ben. It's beautiful. Beyond beautiful. It's so… elegant.'

'I know. Who knew? I was beginning to think unicorns only came fluffy or covered in holographic material or different shades of glitter.' Ben oophed as she elbowed him lightly in the waist. 'Teasing. Mostly.' He grinned. 'You can touch it, Pops. It won't bite.'

'No one's ever given me anything like this before.' She glanced at the charms adorning her bracelet. Each a reminder of the places she'd been. She didn't want Ben's charm on there. That bracelet was for the past, and she didn't want Ben to be part of that. Didn't want to jinx their future.

'Do you want me to put it on your wrist for you?' Ben reached for her, a wrinkle of hurt etching his brow as she shook her head and moved her wrist away.

'No. Not yet. I think I want to keep it separate. For now,' she added quickly. 'I don't want to share it with my other charms just yet.' She picked up the charm and turned it over in her fingers, admiring the fine craftsmanship. Poppy pressed a kiss on Ben's cheek. 'Thank you for the gift, Ben. I love it.'

'I thought you would. It had Poppy written all over it.' Ben sniffed the air. 'Éclairs are ready. I'll pull them out, then get started on the chocolate ganache. Don't suppose you can whip some cream?'

''Course I can. As long as you like your cream buttery.' Poppy's heart warmed as Ben rolled his eyes and shook his head, mouthing 'I'll do it.'

She clutched the charm tighter as happiness beat away her fear.

She had Ben.

Her business.
She had finally found her place in the world.
Nothing could go wrong. She wouldn't let it.

Chapter 17

'You good, Pops?' Ben wrapped his arms around Poppy's waist and watched her dust the lemon-iced banana cake he'd made earlier with golden glitter. 'I can't believe I'm agreeing to this. More glitter. On my grandmother's very serious banana cake recipe, no less. She'll be turning in her grave.' Ben pulled her braid to the side, kissed along the soft line of her neck, and allowed himself a moment to breathe in her apricot scent. His heart danced a happy rhythm against his chest, as it had done every morning, every night, every hour in the weeks since he and Poppy had begun seeing each other.

'Grandmother on whose side?' Poppy backed into him, so their bodies were fused together, the same way she had the night before when they'd briefly gone downstairs to make sandwiches before retiring back to the bedroom.

'Mum's side.' He nuzzled her neck once more, then forced himself to pull away. To give her space to work. To be. He was all too aware that their relationship was fresh, new, and for Poppy, a more intimidating proposition to enter into than any new and unknown country.

'If it were your dad's side I'd believe it, but your mum's nowhere near as strait-laced. I bet your grandmother would be fine with it.' She picked up the knife and deftly sliced a couple of angular slabs, ready to be plated up. 'There you go. Can't bake to save my life but I sure can spread the sparkle.'

'Yes, you can.' Ben picked up the plate Poppy had placed the cake on. 'Poppy. What is this plate?'

Poppy set the glitter down, a pretty blush hitting her cheeks as a cheeky smile brought a glint to her eyes. 'It's a plate. No more. No less.'

'Poppy. I gave you an inch. Not a mile.' Ben shook his head in mock-despair as he took in the golden unicorns surrounding the edge of the plate, their manes painted in pink and silver, flying in a make-believe wind. 'This is too much.'

'It's just enough. Trust me. They'll love it.' Poppy nudged him towards the tea shop. 'Go get 'em, unicorn boy.'

Ben glanced over her shoulder, catching her mid-smirk. 'I'm not a unicorn boy.'

'You will be. Once I'm done with you. Grab me when the guests start to arrive. I'll be in the office doing more of that ever-present bloomin' paperwork.' She blew him a kiss and disappeared through the office door, her bum looking extra hot in a pair of candy-pink skinny jeans.

Ben stepped into the tea shop and stopped in his tracks. Bloody hell. Poppy hadn't taken a mile. She'd taken all the miles. She had transformed his side of the shop into a dazzling den of glitz and garishness. No wonder she'd insisted he sit out the back in the office catching up on his own paperwork while she and Joe decorated for the baby shower that had been booked for that afternoon. If he'd known she was going to do this he'd have put a stop to it. A little glitter on the cake. A hint of unicorn on a plate. That he could live with, but this?

Silver, gold and pink bunting in the shape of unicorns hung from each corner of the room, joining in the middle where a piñata in the shape of a unicorn head hung. Clear balloons filled with blue and pink glitter and sequins were hung up in big bunches around the room. The tables had been arranged in a U-shape and were covered in holographic tablecloths that caught the light filtering in from outside. A smaller table had been placed in the middle of the 'U' – with enough room for a burgeoning belly to pass round, Ben noted – and on that the piles of party food he'd baked were arranged, except they looked different from how he remembered them. He crept forward, pushed aside a few plates to make way for the banana cake, put it down and tried to figure out what had changed.

The white-chocolate cake pops he'd created had little iced flower rosettes in pink and blue adorning the top, along with a liberal sprinkling of matching coloured glitter. The glitter was also atop the cupcakes he'd created, and instead of being separated into blue icing and pink icing – the mother having kept the baby's gender a secret – they'd been mixed up, creating a far more fun vibe. Dotted throughout the table were vases of fresh flowers in shades of pink and blue, with white breaking up the colour. He recognised delphiniums and sweet peas from his mother's garden, but the rest were a mystery.

A further table, set up by the front door, had a giant stuffed unicorn with a large purple ribbon around its neck taking pride of place. A present table. Something he'd not thought of. Not put on the list of must-dos. Along with the piñata. Or the glittering gold notebook that sat at the top end of the tables, along with a fluffy-unicorn-headed pen placed besides it, on which Poppy had written 'All the Advice You'll Ever Need – From People Who Aren't Your Parents' in elegant purple-penned script.

Ben leafed through the notebook, blank for now, waiting to be filled with pearls of wisdom. He set it back down, wandered over to the stuffed unicorn, and opened the small card attached to the ribbon.

'May your life be full of magic, happiness and, most important of all, love. Best wishes, Ben & Poppy'.

Poppy really had thought of everything. And, once again, she'd saved him from making a misstep with his business.

'You like it?' Poppy lounged against the doorway, a smirk lurking about her lips. 'Or am I going to have to put up with you telling my customers that unicorns are for the puerile and pathetic?'

Ben strode over to Poppy. Bugger keeping his distance. If he wanted to be close to Poppy, he was going to be. She needed to know how much he cared. She needed to feel it. To *know* it.

He wrapped his arms around her waist, lifted her off her feet and spun her round and round until her fists beat his chest and she begged him to put her down through breathless giggles.

'What would I do without you?' He dropped a kiss on her pert nose. One on each of her pink cheeks, then a long kiss, that tasted of tangy, sweet lemon icing. 'You licked the icing bowl?'

'How could I not? And what you'd do without me is have twice the space, twice the customers, and twice the profit.'

'None of the joy though. None of your flare. None of your ability to take something dull and make it positively brilliant. Those are just some of the many things I love about you, Pops. This baby shower would have been a flop without you.' Ben ran his hand down the length of her braid and gave it a tug. He leaned in to kiss her but found himself kissing air as she ducked under his arm and ran to the front door where a heavily pregnant woman, dressed in a royal blue maxi dress, was hovering.

'Come in. Welcome. Can I take your bag?' Poppy was the picture of politeness, but her smile was strained, and her cheeks devoid of colour. When she introduced the lady of the hour to Ben she didn't meet his eyes.

What had he done? What had he said? He ran over the moment just gone and closed his eyes as his stomach turned to stone. *Shit.* He'd said the forbidden word. Crossed the line she'd set for all relationships. Crossed it? Bounded over it. Cleared it by a mile.

He could fix this. Laugh it off. Tell her it was off the cuff.

Yeah, he could sort it. But the question was... did he want to?

***

Poppy leaned against the back wall and surreptitiously watched Ben greet each guest through lowered eyelashes. He had the event running like clockwork, taking their presents and placing them on the table she'd set up, showing them to their seats, offering them tea menus and taking their order. The women were charmed by his easy demeanour.

The guests saw Ben the way she did. Kind, gentlemanly, funny. Except they didn't get to hold him, hug him, kiss him... feel about him the way she had over the last three weeks. Three weeks of laughter, of teasing, of fun, of discovering Ben was everything teenage Poppy had thought he'd be, and more. The eighteen-year-old boy she'd run from all those years ago had aged into the kind of man any woman in the world would be lucky to have.

He was a keeper.

And, apparently, he loved her. Or at least, he loved aspects of her.

A shiver ripped down her spine. A rash of goose bumps spread over her arms. She folded her arms to stave off the cold, but she knew it was of no use. No amount of warmth could beat back this chill.

Sure, strictly he hadn't said he loved her, he said he loved 'things' about her. Either way. He'd said the word he knew she never wanted to hear. Wasn't ready to hear.

She chomped down on the inner corner of her cheek, but the sharp pain did nothing to ease her panicked, racing heart. She'd known this would end up happening, eventually. There was no way Ben would be okay with keeping things light and easy forever.

But now what? Should she pretend he hadn't said he loved things about her? Keep things going as they were? Or try and

192

back off? Take things back to the way they were? Bury their relationship, pretend to forget it ever happened, and attempt to renew their friendship?

She sucked in her lower lip. She couldn't do that. It wouldn't be right. Ben would only end up hurt, or worse, resenting her. Hating her for messing with him.

Why couldn't she have just left well enough alone. If she'd just kept things simple. Stayed friends. Ignored her feelings. Pretended their chemistry didn't exist. Then surely, given time, he'd have met someone else. Someone simple, with no hang ups, someone... suitable.

Poppy's attention snapped towards the door as it flew open in a jingle of chimes, and giant helium balloons in the shapes of dummies, teddy bears, hearts and oversized baby feet bobbed through the entrance. 'I'm late. So late. I can't believe I'm late. Apologies, darlings. But I'm here. Ready to get things under way.'

Poppy knew that voice, and from the way Ben was smiling, he'd figured out who it was, too. Of course she'd turn up. The one person who was right for Ben. Who would fit into his world. Who always had. And who, more importantly, unlike Poppy, wasn't afraid to try.

'Milly, can I get those monstrosities for you? Where do you want me to put them? And please tell me you're taking them home with you. They're hardly my style.' Ben shoved the balloons aside to find Milly behind them. Her hair pulled back in a tasteful chignon. Lips blazing red. The rest of her makeup simple, yet chic. He planted a kiss on her cheek, as he took the balloons off her hands.

Was it Poppy's imagination or did that kiss linger? And what was up with her outfit? Where was the vampy Milly that had popped in and out of the shop during the time she'd been spending with Ben? This Milly was wearing a cream short-sleeved silk blouse, a burgundy pencil skirt, sensible black kitten heels, and... pearls. Of course she was wearing pearls.

As if sensing her appraising eyes, Milly shot a tight smile paired with an equally restrained nod in Poppy's direction, then straightened up and clapped her hands three times. 'Ladies, we're here today to celebrate Josie's impending arrival. The joyous bundle of adorability that I can't wait to get my hands on and snuggle. And breathe in.' She touched the expectant mother's shoulder. 'Lots. I promise I won't steal him… or her… but you may have to prise the wee darling from my poor, clucky hands.' Milly's gaze moved to Ben who shook his head with a grin.

God, could she be any more obvious? Milly was in full-on gimme-babies-now mode, and from the looks of it she had Ben in mind as the future daddy. Except he wouldn't be, couldn't be, because Ben was with Poppy.

Nausea swirled and tumbled in Poppy's stomach as she tried to sort out her feelings. How could she want to set Ben free, yet not want him to be with anyone else? Why did the idea of giving him up see bile burn its way up her gullet?

Because she felt something more for Ben? Felt the same?

No. She shunted the thought from her mind, from her heart. She wouldn't allow herself to go down that path. If she did, and Ben rejected her… she'd never recover from the hurt, the pain.

Poppy placed a hand to her mouth and swallowed the bile back. What a mess she'd gotten herself into.

She turned her attention to Ben, hoping to catch his eye, see a smile, a wink, an acknowledgement that he hadn't forgotten she was there, but his gaze was on Milly as he offered her a tea menu.

Poppy sidled into the kitchen and made her way to the office, catching her hip on the angular edge of the bench, barely registering the pain that zinged through her. She should have left well enough alone. Ought to have stuck to her rules. Don't get too close. Keep them at a distance. Don't give them a way in, an opportunity to hurt you. Be prepared to give it all up if things got complicated. And never, ever, no matter what, fall in love.

And that was the problem.

She'd broken all her rules.

Each and every one of them.

Especially that last one.

She sagged into the office chair and slumped onto the desk. Squeezing her eyes shut, she thumped her forehead repeatedly onto the hard wood, hoping to knock some sense into herself.

The problem wasn't with Ben, it was with *her*. She couldn't do relationships. Couldn't deal with the ups and downs, the insecurities. The only sure way to keep your heart safe was to keep it locked up, and that's what she was going to have to do… even if her heart screamed no at the thought.

Ben's head popped through the door. 'Poppy, could you give me a hand serving the tea please? Also, one of the guests is hoping to buy that unicorn costume for her husband. I don't even want to know why. Or for what.' Ben waggled his eyebrows suggestively, turned on his heel and took off back to the baby shower.

Funny. Cute. Sexy. Cheeky. Adorable. Handsome. Sweet. Intelligent. And far too good for her.

She dragged herself up and forced her feet to plod towards the sounds of laughter and happy chatter, mentally forming a list of things that had to be done.

Serve the tea.

Help clean up.

Make it clear to Ben things can't go further.

Go home and try not to cry.

She swiped a lone tear from her cheek.

Scratch that.

Go home and try not to cry too much.

Chapter 18

'Who knew fifteen adults could make such a mess?' Ben ran the broom over the floor for what would hopefully be the final time, amazed to see he'd still managed to miss a scattering of crumbs. He looked over his shoulder to see Poppy intently working on straightening her soft toy selection. 'Looks like they did a number on your stock too.'

'Yeah. They did.' Poppy moved onto the letter writing sets and pen selection that looked to have been pawed over by wild animals.

Ben raked his hand through his hair, grabbed a tuft and yanked it as he tried to keep his growing frustration from spilling over. Poppy had avoided giving him any answers that were more than one syllable for the greater part of the afternoon. Sure, she'd been polite to their guests. Serving tea when required. Tidying up the plates. Helping pack the presents into the mum-to-be's car. She'd smiled and said 'thank you' as she made sales, took money, packed things in her rainbow and unicorn printed paper bags.

To anyone who didn't know Poppy as he did, she was perfectly fine, pleasant without being overbearing, and accommodating to a fault – she'd even divvied up the boxed-up leftover treats for the party goers to take home, all without being asked. But Ben knew Poppy better than anyone, and he could see she was so far in her own head she was about to explode.

And there was only one thing that could cause her to go so far into herself… and that was fear. Of how close they'd become. Of what could happen next. Of being hurt. And it was all because of the innocent word he'd unleashed earlier.

He understood hearing that he loved things about her would upset Poppy. Scare her. But there was no way he was letting her use that fear as an excuse to back off from a chance of their having the kind of relationship he'd long believed they were destined to have. She may not like hearing the 'l' word, but if what was going on between them was going to continue, to grow, she was going to have to get used to it.

'Right.' Poppy straightened up and dusted her hands off on her dress. 'That's done. Home time.' She shouldered her bag and made for the front door.

That was it? She was leaving? Just like that? No 'goodbye'? No 'what are you up to later?' No… anything?

Pressure built in Ben's chest, growing tighter, heavier with every step Poppy took towards the door. Was this how things were going to play out? Like the time they'd spent together, entwined in each other, part of one another, meant nothing?

Like hell it did.

Every brush of her hand, every lingering glance from those beautiful eyes, every cup of tea she made him without even asking, every kiss she dropped on his lips, all of it proved one thing… Poppy insisted she didn't believe in love, but her actions proved she could love. Wonderfully. Deeply. Sweetly.

He wasn't letting Poppy run away from her feelings any longer. She'd dashed off without saying a word once. She wasn't getting away with it twice.

'Poppy, stop.' He hated how shaky the words came out. How weak. How her hand was still on the doorknob, turning it, like she'd not heard him. He swallowed hard. Lifted his chin. 'Poppy.

We need to talk.' Good. The words were firmer. Stronger. And her hand was no longer moving. But she wasn't stepping away either.

'What's to talk about?' Her tone was light, flippant. But an edgy undercurrent ran through her words. A warning. One he was going to ignore.

'What's to talk about? Really?' He crossed the room to stand beside her, close enough he could see the twitch in her jaw, and the vein at her temple pulsing. Too close for her liking? Tough. He'd done enough sitting, waiting and hoping. Patience had gotten him nowhere. It was time for action. 'Did I imagine the last few weeks? Hand-holding as we walked to work? Snuggling up together on the couch watching telly? Lots of really bloody amazing lovemaking? What about this morning? Feeding each other toast, chatting over tea, then… well, more of that amazing lovemaking. You were there. Or at least I thought you were, now I'm starting to think it was all some cruel, crazy dream. Will I go home tonight and not find crumbs in my bed because you can't eat without making a mess?'

Poppy's chin lifted. Her eyes focused on the steady stream of cars and people heading home after a day at work.

'Is this what happens now? You ignore me? Put me right back in the friend zone you've kept me in for as long as I can remember?' He curled his hands into fists and held them to his side, tried to stem the anger, the pain, the confusion, that had been packed away for years. 'No, I lie. For twelve years you didn't even have me in the friend zone. I may as well have been a ghost to you, for all you cared.'

Poppy's lips parted, determination turning her eyes flinty.

'Don't even go there, Poppy. Don't you dare go down the "I emailed you" route. You did. Sure. But it didn't make up for the way you left. Without a word. Under the cover of darkness. I guess I should count myself lucky that I'm at least conscious to see you go this time.' Self-loathing burned its way up the centre of his chest. 'I don't know why I still call you a friend. And part of me hates myself for hoping I could call you more.'

'Well, at least I was right to back off.' The words came out so soft Ben wondered if he'd heard them correctly. 'I knew this would happen. Eventually. And it's better it happens now than a year from now, or ten, or twenty.' Poppy's hand tightened on the doorknob. 'It's fairer, on both of us.'

'Fair? Fair on me?' Ben took a step back, then another, until his thighs hit the back of a chair. He gripped its rounded edges and rested against it as he tried to get his thoughts in order. 'How is this fair on me? How is it fair to dangle the one thing I've wanted for as long as I can remember in front of me, then snatch it away before I've had a chance to make my case, to prove how good we could be together, how good we *are* together?'

Poppy turned to face him, her eyes shining with unshed tears. 'As friends, Ben. That's how we're good together, but anything more than that? You'd tire of my indecisiveness. My chronic crumb dropping. The way I forget to clean the bowl of toothpaste foam after brushing my teeth. I'd only end up disappointing you, and I can't bear the idea of that.'

Ben couldn't believe what he was hearing. Did she really think so little of herself that she believed insignificant details like foam in a bowl and the odd crumb would see him one day no longer want her in his life? 'Poppy, are you listening to yourself? You're being too hard on yourself. Too hard on me. Crumbs don't bother me. Foam I could care less about. You're amazing to me. My God, you set up a whole business. You've got it running like clock-work…'

'Only because you showed me how. And…' Poppy paused, sucked her cheeks in, then released them. 'It's not like any of this is what I really wanted. Sure, I liked unicorns. I'd seen themed gift shops before, and… well… I had the money sitting there, and it gave me something to do until I figured out what I was going to do next.'

Ben clocked Poppy's hand gripping her braid. She was lying. Was this how she planned to disconnect herself from their situation? By pretending she'd never wanted to surround herself with unicorns, to share the happiness and magic they brought with others?

'I don't believe you, Poppy. You wanted to open this shop. You'd planned for it. The only thing you hadn't planned for was to open it with me. You'd planned to go it alone.' Ben clapped his hand to his forehead as the pieces of the Poppy puzzle fell into place. 'I'm an idiot. It all makes sense. How did I not realise it before? How did I miss what was staring me in the face? You're letting the relationship you have with your mother interfere with the relationship you have with me. You're treating me as if I were her.'

'I'm not. You're wrong.' Poppy folded her arms across her chest, putting an emotional and physical barrier in place.

'But you are.' Ben pushed himself away from the chair and began to pace the room. The movement helping him think. 'She hurt you. Terribly. And because of that you refuse to let anyone get close in case they hurt you. And you're afraid that I'll end up like her, that I'll push you away, ignore you, withhold my feelings.' Ben came to a stop in front of Poppy and placed his hands on her upper arms, waited for her eyes to lock on his. 'But I wouldn't hurt you, Poppy. I never could. I never have. I need you to see that. I need you to give us a chance. I need you to stop living with the shadow of your mother hanging over your head. I am not her. I won't ignore you. Toss you aside. Because I see that you're worth loving.'

Poppy shook his hands off, her eyes blazing with indignation. 'Thanks for the psychobabble analysis of my life, Ben. I appreciate it. Really.' She took a step back and swept her hand from the top of his head, downwards. 'Especially coming from you, a man who's spent his entire life trying to please his parents. You studied hard to make them happy. You learned to bake because it made your mum happy. You became a lawyer to please your father. You stuck around here when you could have gone anywhere. Why? Because it's what they would have wanted. This isn't your life you're living. This is theirs.'

Ben's heart stilled. Is that how Poppy saw him? As a daddy's boy? A mummy's boy? Someone who didn't have a life? Nausea tumbled and twirled in his gut. There was truth in her words. He knew this. He was their only son, their only child. The pressure to be perfect, to perform, to bring pride to their small family had been there from the get go. And yes, he'd let their expectations rule his life for a long time, but he'd changed. He had moved forward, forged his own path, even though it had put his relationship with his father at risk. Poppy knew this. So, what was she doing? Trying to push him away? Trying to make him hate her?

He pulled out a chair and sank into it. He was done with the fighting. Done with the persuading. It was time to put his feelings into words and let Poppy choose what she wanted to do with them. 'First of all, Poppy, I like living here. I didn't want to leave. Second of all, I may have done all I could to please my parents. I respect them. I love them. I wouldn't be who I was without them. And you know as well as I do opening this shop was a shock to my father, it wasn't what he wanted… but I did it anyway.'

'Only because I came along and made it happen.' Poppy thumbed her chest, then switched directions to point at him.

He held his hand up. 'That's not true and you know it. It may not have been *this* shop that I set up in, but it was going to be *a* shop. The reason it was you and me was because you just did what you've always done… pushed me to do something I might not have otherwise done.' He held his hands up at Poppy's sharp intake of breath. 'Don't take it the wrong way, Poppy. It's a good thing. Hell, I wouldn't know what sleeping under the stars felt like if it weren't for you. I wouldn't understand the thrill of taking risks. God, I probably wouldn't know what it was like to kiss a

201

girl had you not forced me to go out with Milly when we were teenagers.'

'I don't believe that. You'd have kissed someone, eventually.' Poppy's chest deflated, Ben had not so much argued as rationally talked her into a corner, and there was no getting out. 'And it probably would have been someone opposite to me. Someone your parents approved of. That's why I pushed you towards Milly. You two are well suited. Similar temperaments. Similar dress sense. You're perfect little peas in a pod.'

'But I don't want a perfect pea, Poppy. And Milly is not the person I want to kiss. I only want to kiss you. I want to hold your hand as we traipse through Queen's Wood in the middle of the night. I want to dance at summer festivals with you. Serve tea to people and look up to see you cuddling the latest batch of unicorn soft toys. Even when my father suggested perhaps your friendship wasn't the best for my scholarly ambitions I didn't listen, because you were better for me. You were back then. You are now. Don't you see, Poppy? I love you. I love you so much I've let you put glitter on my baking. Allowed unicorns onto my side of the shop. I might even be starting to like them. A little.'

Poppy's lips pursed together and twitched to one side. Her grip tightened on herself as her body angled to the door.

Ben waited for her to say something, anything. But no words came. The atmosphere between them hung thick and heavy, like rainclouds on a humid day, waiting to burst open, to cleanse the ground, to freshen the air.

'I love you.' He breathed the words out. One more time. Just to make sure she'd heard them. Just to be sure he'd said them. Good and proper. Not some 'things I love about you' kind of statement. Actual, proper, head over heels, now and forever love. He hung his head and closed his eyes. He'd done all he could do. The rest was up to Poppy.

Electronic chimes met his ears, the flood of the outside world invaded the shop. 'I believe you, Ben. But you can't guarantee love will last. That years from now you'll still love me. People change. Love changes.'

The door shut, muting the outside world, but not silencing the roaring pain of his heart.

His mobile vibrated in his pocket. Pulling it out, he saw it was Poppy.

'I'll pack up my store. You can expand. You'll be fine. I'm sorry.'

He'd be fine? His head felt like it was clamped in a vice, his throat like a giant marble was lodged in it, and every inch of his body may as well have been glued to the chair. Not only had the fight gone out of him, but so had all hope.

Poppy had left. Again. She may have left the glitter in the shop, in his life, but she'd taken the sparkle.

Chapter 19

Sandals. Trainers. Sandals. Heels.

Poppy kept her head down as she strode home.

Trainers. Espadrilles. Sandals. Trainers.

Her heart stuttered as a break in the crowd forced her to stop focusing on the footwear passing her by. No footwear meant facing the whirlwind of feelings that were trying to fill her head. Not happening. It was too hard. Too dangerous.

Too devastating.

Her steps faltered.

Ben was right. She was like her mother. Cut off. Emotionally stunted. Unable to show affection. Unable to change.

She picked up her pace again, then found herself being pulled backwards.

'What the—?' She twisted round to swat away the hand that gripped her shoulder. 'Milly? What the hell is going on? Get your hand off me!'

'Not going to. Sorry.' Milly didn't sound the least bit sorry as she slid her hand down to clutch Poppy's bicep and began guiding her towards a wine bar across the street. 'You need a good talking to, Poppy. And if you're not going to listen to Ben, you're going to listen to me.'

Poppy found herself pushed through a doorway into the gloomy bar, then marched to a chair in the farthest corner, the only light coming from a flickering LED candle. She contemplated getting up and making a run for it, but Milly's eyes didn't leave the table while she ordered drinks, and from the look of Milly's shapely calves she could outrun Poppy.

A large glass of white wine was plonked in front of her. 'There you go. I hope you like pinot.'

Poppy gave a non-committal shrug. 'As long as it's wet.' *As long as it wipes away the memory of today.* She picked it up and took a sip. Then a bigger sip. Followed by a slug.

'Steady on.' Milly eyed her over the rim of her glass. 'I want you to remember what I'm about to say.'

'If you're here to tell me to back away from Ben, then you can keep the words in your mouth. I'm not going anywhere near Ben. In fact, I think it's time I moved on. Places to go. People to meet. Ben's all yours. Go on dates. Get engaged. Married. Make a bunch of babies for you to breathe in.' Poppy reached for her bag only to find the chair she'd placed it on shoved out of reach.

'My God, Poppy. Could you be any more selfish?' Milly fingered her pearls, holding them away from her throat like she was afraid Poppy was going to use them to choke her to death. 'You're so busy over-thinking everyone else's lives, their motivations, you can't see what's right in front of you. What's been in front of you your whole life. Well, for as long as I've known you anyway.'

'Well, why don't you enlighten me then?' Poppy signalled to the barman to bring her another glass of wine, then drained the one in front of her. The way Milly was glaring at her she had a feeling she was going to need a little extra something to ease the barrage about to come her way.

'You know nothing is going on with Ben and I. And that's not a question. I know you know that's the case because Ben admitted his feelings for you to me, and then apologised profusely for wasting my time. I've never heard someone say sorry so much within a five-minute conversation. And quite frankly he was only confirming what I already knew.' Milly settled back into her chair, crossed her legs and placed her perfectly manicured hands in her lap.

Poppy glanced down at her legs stretched out in front of her, her dress creased, her nails lacking colour and ragged from ripping open boxes.

Milly was ladylike. Perfectly put together. And she had her life together.

Poppy was a mess. In all aspects of her life.

Ben may like that about her now, but time would see him lean towards the lifestyle he'd grown up in. The perfect, proper one. The kind Milly could offer.

Milly pursed her lips, her shoulders rising then lowering as she exhaled slowly with a small shake of her head. 'And the fact is, Poppy, if Ben and I were the type to stick it out through thick and thin, don't you think we would have gotten back together after you took off all those years ago'

'What do you mean? I don't understand? What does my leaving have to do with you two?'

'What doesn't it?' Milly picked up her glass by the stem and took a long drink. 'God, I was a fool to stick it out with Ben for as long as I did. Three years, wasted. He was only with me because it's what he thought was for the best. His parents liked me. I liked him. We got on. But he never felt about me the way he did about you. You know we broke up all those years ago because I felt you got in the way. After you left… well, I hoped he'd see sense. Come back to me. I imagined we could go through university together. Forge our careers with each other's support. Instead he moped after you.' White bloomed on Milly's knuckles as her grip on the glass tightened. 'It was like I never existed.'

Poppy's heart went out to Milly. She had always seemed so in control, yet behind that carefully constructed façade she carried her own emotional scars.

'Don't be like that, Milly. Ben liked you. So much.' Poppy caught the barman's eye and ordered another glass of wine, this time for Milly. 'You made him happy. You made his life easy.'

'I made his life boring.' The words were as flat as Milly's expression. 'He didn't want boring. He didn't want a ride-by-the-seat-of-your-pants life either. But he wanted the odd thrill. A touch of excitement. The things you gave him, but I couldn't.'

'You make it sound like he was with you out of convenience. That's not Ben. He's not the type of person to take advantage of someone like that.'

'You're right. He's not. Ben is the sweetest guy in the world. He's the whole package. He's the guy you root for in romance movies. The one who gets overlooked by the heroine in favour of the big-talking, brawny, alpha male type. Or, in this case, in *your* case, looked over for the safer option of the big, wide world.' Milly folded her arms over her chest and caught Poppy's eye. 'I saw you argue back at the store. I didn't mean to, but I left my bank card on Ben's counter when I paid and went back to get it. When you left I went in to check on Ben and he showed me your text.'

Poppy gritted her teeth. How dare Ben show Milly her text? This had nothing to do with Milly, this was between the two of them. 'He had no right to do that. It was a private text. Meant for his eyes only.'

Milly threw her hands up in the air with an exasperated sigh. 'Really, Poppy? You're about to throw away the best thing that ever happened to you and all you care about is that I've seen a text you sent?'

Poppy pushed herself back into her chair as Milly leaned forward, her eyes narrow with intent.

'Here's the thing, Poppy, and listen closely, because at this point I'm not even sure why I'm helping you when it's Ben who's hurting.' Milly took a sip of her wine then set it back down again, hard enough that the liquid sloshed back and forth, like a contained tsunami, in the glass. 'Ben loves you. He's always loved you. When we were going out I hoped he'd get over it. That it was just some teenage crush that would pass. But deep down I knew it wasn't. You'd enter the room and he'd visibly brighten. If I suggested we do something together and it clashed with something you and he had planned, he wouldn't rearrange his time to suit me. You came first. Always.' Milly focused on the wall behind Poppy, her lips in a thin line, her eyes glassy. 'And what grates is that you're about to leave him. Again. There I was, here I *am*, ready, willing to give things another go, but you're the one he wants and you're about to throw it all away. But here's the thing, Poppy.' Milly ran her manicured finger around the rim of the glass, eliciting a high-pitched squeak that set Poppy's teeth even more on edge. 'One of these days you'll come back and you'll find he's not going to be there waiting for you to see sense. Because even Ben has his limits.'

'And what sense would that be?' Poppy knew the answer, but there was no way she was going to say it aloud to Milly. Thinking it was hard enough. Her brain telling her she was wrong. Her heart telling her she was oh so right.

'That you love him. You love Ben as much as he loves you. The only difference is that you're too afraid to admit it. Or, maybe you're not. Maybe you don't love him at all and I've read things wrong. So, tell me, Poppy.' Milly leaned in, her head angled to the side. 'Do you *not* love Ben?'

Poppy went to nod her head. Stopped. Milly knew the truth. Knew any denial would be a lie. And she'd had enough of being called out by Milly for one day. It was time to face the truth. Time to figure out what to do with that truth. 'You're right. I love Ben. I've loved him since… well, forever. First as a friend, and that's where I thought the love would stay, but it changed. I blame teenage hormones.' Poppy attempted a laugh, but it came out sounding like a frog was being strangled. 'But, you're right, I was afraid then. I'm still afraid. What if…'

'I don't want to hear "what if". Wondering and pondering won't get you anywhere.' Milly slumped back in her chair. The tension that had kept her back ramrod straight gone. Like she'd given up fighting. Like she knew she'd lost. 'So, what are you going to do about it, Poppy?'

'I don't know.' Poppy shook her head. 'I really don't. Have you ever repeated the same mistake over and over? Like a bad loop you can't get out of?'

A harsh barking laugh filled the space between them. 'What do you think I was doing when I got back in touch with Ben? I hoped we could… rekindle our relationship. Even after all these years. Fool that I am. I even tried to dress up in a way I thought he might like. A little sassier. A little sexier. But I didn't know you were there, and soon as I saw you I knew I was fighting a losing battle.'

'But you still tried. You still went out on dates. You didn't just give up at the sight of me.'

'Well, maybe I should have. It would've meant not enduring the embarrassment of having him turn his cheek so my attempt to kiss his lips ended up with me kissing the collar of his shirt.' Milly shook her head. 'That must be the only time lipstick on a man's collar meant nothing happened.'

Poppy grinned. Who knew Milly had a sense of humour? And that she could bow out gracefully? More than gracefully… helpfully. 'God, you really are perfect.'

'Just on the outside. Underneath all this…' Milly pulled at her top, then tugged her pearls. 'I'm just as much a bundle of insecurities and angst as the next person.'

'You hide it well.' Poppy attempted a smile, but knew it fell flat. Milly didn't need her smiles, let alone want them.

'I do my best.' Milly unfolded herself from the chair, pulled out her bank card, then paused. 'One piece of advice? Don't screw it up. Ben deserves more than that.'

Poppy chewed on her lower lip as she watched Milly pay, then leave without looking back, without a goodbye wave. The most straight-up, to-the-point, take-no-prisoners fairy godmother, was Milly. No doubt about it.

Don't screw it up.

How did one unscrew what was already screwed?

Especially when it wasn't the last conversation she'd had with Ben that had screwed things up. Or the text she'd sent.

It had all started when one person hadn't shown her how to love.

Well, it was time to learn how.

Dread billowed, heavy and black, in Poppy's gut. If she wanted any kind of future she was going to have to come to terms with her past.

***

Just answer already. Poppy shuffled from side to side, waiting for the door to open. Hoping it would open. Praying it would open. The claustrophobia that had cloistered her heart on the walk to the street she'd grown up in had begun to lift as she realised for the first time in her life she wasn't running. She was taking action. Her leaden steps had lightened. Her chin, pressed to her chest, had angled higher. By the time she'd reached the front door she knew she was ready for change. Ready to be the woman Ben deserved.

She jumped as the door opened. 'Poppy? What are you doing here? Come in. Come in.' Pam held the door wider and waved her through. 'Is Ben okay? He never mentioned you were popping over?'

Pam brought her in for a hug, kissing her cheek. Poppy breathed in the pungent scent of Chanel. As elegant and timeless as the woman before her.

She broke the hug and took Pam by the hands. 'Ben doesn't

know I'm here, but I... well, I need to talk to someone, and I may even need a bit of advice, and I can't think of a better person to help me than you.'

Pam's head tilted to one side, her eyes enquiring. 'I'm not sure if I'll be much help in the advice area, but I've two ears that hear well enough.' She threaded her arm through Poppy's and they walked companionably towards the kitchen. 'Tea?' Pam turned the kettle on without waiting for Poppy's answer and pulled two mugs down from the cupboard. 'So, what's on your mind?'

Poppy pulled out a chair from the kitchen table and sank into it, glad to give her knees a reprieve from the trembling that had begun the moment Pam had greeted her at the door. Who knew change was so nerve-wracking? 'Tell me about love.'

Pam turned to face Poppy. The edges of her lips lifted in an amused smile, her warm brown eyes twinkling. 'I don't think I need to teach you about love, Poppy. You were born loving.'

'But I wasn't. I don't know how.' Poppy wrung her hands, hoping to disperse the nervous energy that was zipping through her body, making it hard to think. She pushed the chair back, stood up and began to pace the length of the kitchen. 'I can't seem to let myself love people. Or let people love me. I don't even know if I believe in love. How can I? It's not like I've experienced it.' She hit the wall at the end of the kitchen, twisted around, her breath hitching in surprise at the sight of the figure haunting the back door. 'Mum.'

Her mother's hands twisted around each other. Her shoulders stooped. She appeared... cowed, like she expected Poppy to turn on her. To yell. Scream. Throw insult after insult.

Except Poppy wouldn't. Couldn't. Because, despite everything, the woman standing before her was still her mother. And some small part of her still yearned for her approval, her love.

'I'm sorry to interrupt. But... I saw you at the front doorstep, and I saw you the other day. And I had to come. I'm sorry.' She directed a hesitant smile at Pam. 'I came through the hedge. Like Poppy used to do. I hope that's okay?'

'It's fine, Helena. Come in.'

Despite the invitation her mother's feet didn't move an inch, much like Poppy's feet, which appeared to be cemented to the floor.

What was she supposed to do? Hug the woman who'd become a stranger? Become a stranger? More like, had always been a stranger. Should she leave the room, run away, never look back? Sit and talk?

'Poppy. Here's your tea.' Pam pushed the cup into her hands and gave her a meaningful look. 'I told you I wouldn't be one for advice. I guess that's because the universe, or something, had a better person in mind. Go, sit.'

Poppy did as she was told, still unsure how she was expected to act, or react, to her mother's arrival. She'd have to wing it, like pretty much everything else she'd done in her life.

'Helena, you have my tea. I've got the bed to make and the bathroom to clean upstairs.' She passed her mug to Helena and pulled out a chair for her to sit in. 'Shout if you need anything.' And just like that Pam was gone.

Poppy lifted her eyes from the beige liquid, curious to see how time had treated her mother. She looked older than her fifty years. Her hair, once as black as Poppy's had grown out a steely grey, but it was still long. Still loose, the waves tumbling over her shoulders and down her back. Deep lines were etched into either side of her mouth. Horizontal versions ran along her forehead. Her eyes were almost wrinkle-free. No laughter lines framed her eyes. No laughter lines, no laughter?

Of course not. Her mother had rarely smiled or laughed in her presence. That was reserved for the parties she held, for the people she called friends. Not for the daughter she'd borne.

'When did you come home?' Helena's long, slim fingers, splayed around the mug, tightened. Daubs of paint, in red and blue, dotted her knuckles. 'I mean, when did you return to London?'

'Two months ago, give or take a few days.' Poppy stopped herself elaborating, afraid if she said too much she'd lose control, chase her mother away with hurtful words, when what they needed was to have a proper conversation. Perhaps not one that would heal all wounds all at once, but one that might start the process. 'How have you been?'

Helena closed her eyes and pinched the bridge of her nose. When her hazel eyes opened, Poppy saw resolute determination. 'Shall we skip the pleasantries, Poppy?'

Defences up, Poppy. Rejection ahoy. 'Sure, what's the point of pleasantries anyway? They just suck up time.' Poppy forced her lips to rise into a half-smile.

'And we've lost so much of that already.'

The wistful tone in Helena's voice caught Poppy off guard. What was her mother on about? Wasn't she here to tell Poppy she couldn't be moving into the house? Not that she wanted to. Or that family dinners were off the menu? Family anything? She didn't need to be told that, she'd assumed it. Never thought to think anything else.

A rhythmic clang and clank brought Poppy back to the room. She zeroed in on the source of the noise. Her mother's ring-filled fingers tapped on the mug of tea. Over and over. Her mother seemingly unaware she was making the racket. Was her mother *nervous*?

Helena shifted in her seat, a soft sigh escaping her lips. 'I don't know about you, Poppy, but I have a lot that needs to be said, and I feel the sooner the better.'

A large lump formed in Poppy's throat. She braced herself for the conversation ahead. She didn't know if she was ready for it, but she knew she couldn't move on with her life if it didn't happen.

'Sorry is a good place to start, I think,' her mother said, as

213

much to herself as to Poppy. 'And I am, Poppy. So sorry. For so much. My self-absorption. My lack of care with your heart. Your life. The way I let you do whatever you wanted whenever you wanted, because I was too busy thinking about my needs. My wants. I should never have…'

'Been a parent? Been a mother?' Poppy choked out. She gripped the edges of her chair, tried to stop the tears that were rising on the tide of emotion. 'Should never have gone through with the pregnancy? Because that's what you said to me. You only had me because if you didn't Grandma would never have given you the house. Left it to you. I was your meal ticket to artistic freedom, since my arrival stole away your freedom to do whatever you wanted, whenever you wanted, wherever you wanted…'

'Oh God, Poppy. No. Please don't…' Helena reached for Poppy.

Poppy shrank back instinctively. 'Don't what? Put the ugly truth on the table? You never wanted me. You were forced to have me. And you resented it. You resented me…'

Helena squeezed her eyes shut. Her nostrils retracted, then relaxed. When she opened her eyes they were hard, clear. Determined. 'I should never have said what I said to you. Never have behaved the way I did.'

'Well, that makes us in agreement over that. And the truth is, I didn't deserve the kind of life I had to live with you. More than that, you didn't deserve me.' Poppy clapped her hand over her mouth. Stopped the venom spewing. 'I'm sorry. That was uncalled for.'

'No. It wasn't.' Helena shook her head. 'I deserved it.' She folded her arms across herself, tucking her hands into her armpits. Into a hug.

It was like seeing a mirror-image of herself. How often had she hugged herself when she was nervous? Scared? Hurt? Worried? Alone? Had she learnt it from her mother? Were there similarities between them that she'd never considered?

'All I wanted was to live a life free of any trappings. To live the bohemian lifestyle of a "true" artist. At least the lifestyle I thought an artist should live. And then you came along, and I ran to my mother, who had the means to help. But those means came with restrictions. Raise you in the family home. Send you to a good school. Give you a stable life. It wasn't you I resented, it was the rules. But I was young. Stupid. Short-sighted. And I took my feeling of being trapped, being caged, out on you. Convinced myself that you were enough like me that you didn't need to be smothered in love, cossetted, reined in by rules. Except you weren't. You liked the rules. You liked school. You enjoyed a regime.'

'And yet you ignored that. Moved stubbornly forward with your belief that I was like you.' Much as she moved stubbornly forward with her belief that she couldn't love. Didn't know how. And that no one could love her in return, because she was unlovable.

Helena's eyes glittered. 'I screwed up. I let my own selfishness get in the way of being a good mother, and by the time I matured enough to realise it you'd been gone for years, and I didn't know how to tell you I was sorry. That I would do anything, give anything, to go back. To start again. To be the kind of mother a child as kind, and sweet, and filled with sunshine as you deserved.'

Abandoning any pretence of toughness, Poppy moved from her chair to the one closest to her mother, tugged her mother's hands away from her armpits and took them in her own. 'I never thought you saw me like that. I never thought you saw me at all.'

'I saw you. I just pretended not to. It made it easier to convince myself that by giving you freedom I was being the opposite of my own mother. That you would never come to resent me as I resented her.' Helena flipped her hands over and curled them into Poppy's. 'Please don't think I'm expecting you to feel sorry for me. To suddenly want to have anything to do with me. I don't. I don't know that I deserve that. That I even deserve your forgiveness… but I came over because, well, I just wanted to let you know that if you ever wanted to come by for a cup of tea, or if you wanted to see what I was working on…'

'I'll pop in.' The words flew out before she'd had time to consider them, but Poppy knew she meant it. Maybe the first step to learning that love was possible, to learning how to love, was giving it a chance. And Poppy couldn't think of anyone else she'd rather take that step with.

A warmth filled her heart, spread through her body.

Actually, she could.

Someone whose eyes lit up when he saw her.

Whose hair never fell out of place, even after the biggest mussing.

Who was thoughtful, and careful of others' feelings.

Someone who'd opened his heart to her. Who'd accepted her for who she was – unicorns and glitter and fluff galore.

Someone who she'd run from. Not once. But twice.

Someone who deserved an apology. An explanation.

And to know that she loved him back. With everything she had.

Poppy gave her mother's hands a small shake and a squeeze. 'You know, Mum, I'd love to see what you're working on. I always enjoyed watching you work. You had such a way of making the people you drew come to life. I'll come around after work one day this week – if that's okay with you?'

Helena's lips lifted in the smallest of smiles, like she couldn't quite believe her luck. 'It's more than okay. I think you'll like what – who – I'm working on. I think you'll even recognise her.' She lifted her hand to Poppy's face, traced her cheek with her thumb. 'Thank you, Poppy. Thank you for this chance.'

The kitchen blurred as Poppy leaned in to give her mother a kiss on the cheek. Even if she'd buggered things with Ben, at least she had the beginnings of a relationship with her mother. And that was worth sticking round for.

Poppy walked her mother to the front door and let her out with a quick hug goodbye.

'You all right, love?' Pam appeared beside Poppy and took a long appraising look at her. 'You are. I knew you would be. And you've got the answers you were looking for?'

Poppy nodded. 'I do. And you were right.' Now that she'd accepted the love that was innately within her – the love she'd shunned for so many years – her being, her soul, vibrated with it. Warming her, fulfilling her. And the urge she had to share it was even larger than the urge she'd felt to share the joy and magic of all things unicorn.

'Good. Now go take that love of yours and do what you should have done a very long time ago.' Pam winked, gave Poppy's hip an affectionate tap, and sent her off down the street.

Poppy felt for the unicorn charm she'd stashed in the pocket of her shorts, tipped her face to the sun-bleached sky, made a wish and promised herself she'd make it come true.

Chapter 20

Ben sighed as he tipped another batch of over-whipped meringue into the rubbish. He shouldn't be whipping, or beating, or whisking anything right now. At the rate he was stuffing up the baking he wouldn't be getting any profit out of anything he sold the next day. That was if he could convince himself to get out of bed and open up. The prospect of huddling under the covers and binge-watching the latest crime show on his tablet was far more appealing than spending the day working in a Poppy-less shop.

He tossed the bowl into the sink and flicked on the tap, letting it fill with water. Setting his elbows on the bench, he placed his head in his hands and massaged his temples. For the first time in a long time he didn't know what to do next. He had no plan.

Sure, he could go on with the shop, extend into the space Poppy occupied. His business could handle it, he knew it could. It wasn't like Poppy had been part of the plan all along, he'd come up with the plan to include her in the spur of the moment. But now he couldn't imagine her not being part of the shop. Or his life.

He squeezed his eyes shut and cursed out loud. If he'd only shut his mouth, not told her he loved her. If he only could have been satisfied with their friendship, not wanted more, she'd still be here. There wouldn't be a text on his phone telling him she was done. There wouldn't be half a shop that, as filled with colour as it was, felt dull without her. And his heart wouldn't feel like someone had taken a wrecking ball to it.

The chime of the doorbell brought him to his senses. He must've forgotten to lock the door when he'd shut, but who'd be coming in at this time? Flicking off the tap, he put on a customer-ready smile and entered the shop.

'Oh. It's you.' Ben abandoned the niceties. Poppy wasn't here to make amends. To say she'd made a mistake. To say she'd stay. That he was worth sticking round for.

Fool me once? He'd been fooled twice. No way was three times an option.

Poppy hung about the door. Her bottom lip had disappeared into her mouth, held in by her teeth, and her gaze didn't leave the floor.

'Have you come to pack up? Did you think I'd be gone? Because I can go, if it makes things easier.' Anger coiled low in his stomach. Damn it, he was being cordial. Making life easy for her. Why should her life be so simple? Why should Poppy be able to flit in and out of his life without consequences? No more. If she wanted to leave him she'd have to do it in his presence. He wasn't the one going anywhere. 'Actually, I can't.' He made a show of checking his watch. 'A mothers' group is booked in for tomorrow and I need to get the tables organised and get my lemon meringue tarts into the oven and cooled down before I finish up.' He nearly added a 'sorry' but stopped himself. He wasn't sorry for anything.

Poppy nodded and trudged to her side of the store, sat down and opened her laptop, then began to type.

His phone pinged in his pocket. He pulled it out and saw Poppy had sent him a message.

I'm a knob.

He shoved the phone in his pocket, went back to the kitchen

and turned on the kettle. She could be here for some time and a strong cup of black tea would keep his eyelids from drooping.

The phone pinged again.

Actually, I'm fond of knobs. I wouldn't want to insult them. I'm an idiot.

Ben rolled his eyes. Of course Poppy was going for the charm offensive. It had worked in the past, she'd naturally think it would work now. He flipped the phone onto its face. If he couldn't see her messages he wouldn't be tempted to look at them, to begin to empathise with her… to forgive her.

Ping.

Ping.

Ping.

He tipped the floating white detritus of the meringue down the sink, then turned on the hot tap, squirted washing up liquid into the bowl and began cleaning it, readying it for his third meringue attempt of the evening.

The scrubbing of plastic on metal combined with the rush of running water kept the pings from infiltrating his conscience. He turned off the water, picked up a tea towel and began drying the bowl.

Ping.

Ping.

How had she not given up by now? Ben reached over and muted the phone. Poppy was obviously too embarrassed to talk to him in person so he was safe to get back to the task at hand. Placing the clean mixing bowl on the bench he cracked open the first egg, tipping the runny mixture from egg-half to egg-half, letting the white drop into the bowl, praying the yolk wouldn't snag on a sharp edge and break.

Ben breathed a sigh of relief as the last of the white gave up its grip on the shell. One down. Two to go.

He cracked the second egg and began separating, watching in satisfaction as the white plopped cleanly into the bowl.

'You know there's a far easier way to do that.'

Ben glanced up to see Poppy hovering by the door.

'Your yolk's broken.'

Ben looked down. 'Shit.' The globular whites were strewn with bright orange yolk. Another batch ruined. God, it was like the meringue was a symbol for his day. One big mess. 'Couldn't you have waited until I was done?' He dropped down into a squat and hunted in the cupboard for a container. Unlike the over-whipped meringues, the eggs could be used in other baking.

'No. I couldn't wait. You're ignoring me.' Poppy's feet inched closer.

Finding a container, Ben straightened up, poured the eggs in, then sealed it up. Each action purposefully slow, knowing it would drive Poppy crazy. She didn't like being ignored? Well, it was time she got a taste of her own medicine. He'd been ignored by her for twelve years. She could survive thirty seconds.

He dropped the bowl back in the sink and made to grab the washing up liquid for the third time that evening, except Poppy whipped it away before he could take hold of it.

'No. Don't. I'll do it. It's the least I can do since I caused you to stuff up the eggs.' She shooed him away from the sink and began to wash the bowl. 'What you want to do is crack the egg, then open it into your cupped hand, let the white drip through then set the yolk aside. Or, if there's a spare plastic bottle around, you crack the egg into a ramekin then you take the bottle, squeeze it, pop the rim by the egg yolk then release the bottle and it sucks it up, like magic. Here you go.' She passed the bowl to Ben for drying. 'Takes a bit of practice to get it right, though. I prefer the hand method.'

She ran her damp hands over her shorts and stepped back, giving Ben space to start again.

Taking another egg, he cracked it and began separating it from shell to shell.

'Or you could ignore me and do it the way you want.' Poppy

folded her arms over her chest. The tap-tap-tap of her toe on the floor filled the air.

Eggs successfully separated, Ben attached the bowl to the mixer and set it beating. The mechanical whirring blocking any attempts at conversation. Ignoring Poppy's growing glare of impatience, he added sugar, bit by bit, to the eggs, until he had a perfect glossy meringue.

He flicked off the machine and began spooning the mixture into a piping bag.

'Thank God that's done. Honestly. How can we talk if there's all that noise going on?' Poppy pushed the portable kitchen island that held the prepared tarts towards Ben.

Bending over, avoiding eye contact, he began to pipe swirls of meringue onto the glistening, tangy lemon curd.

'If I didn't know you better, Ben, I'd think you were ignoring me on purpose. But I know you wouldn't do that. Even after… everything.'

Ben squeezed the piping bag in frustration, sending a misshapen splodge onto the tart. He set the bag down and faced Poppy. 'What do we have to talk about, Poppy? What's got you so impatient that I have to down tools and forget about my business? Because I don't see why I should. You accused me of being a people pleaser all my life, and you were right. I was, on the whole. Now I don't have to be, because the only person left to please is leaving. And, after the way she's behaved, I feel no need to do anything to make her happy anymore. And you know what? It's nice to have relief from that particular pressure.' Ben picked up the piping bag, finished off the tarts and placed them in the oven.

'Fine. If that's how you feel. Before I go though…'

His phone was thrust before his eyes. The screen lit up with message after message.

'Read your phone.'

Taking the phone from Poppy, he keyed in his password,

opened up his messages, slid left on Poppy's name and the many messages, then turning the mobile round he hit the delete button. 'Don't want to.'

Poppy's eyes narrowed as nostrils flared. 'It took me ages to think of those texts. They were important.'

'If they were that important you wouldn't have sent them. You'd have said them. To my face.' Ben's heart thumped against his chest in a drumbeat of irritation and frustration. He glanced over at the kettle, where steam drifted up towards the ceiling. Tea. He needed something nice and calming. Something that would soothe his stretched nerves. He strode past Poppy and into the shop to snip off some mint leaves. Footsteps echoing behind him telling him Poppy was on his tail.

'I just thought it would be easier if you read what I was thinking. What I was feeling. I was afraid if I tried to say what I want to say I'd make a mess of it. Make *more* of a mess.'

He turned to see Poppy was no longer following him, but was sitting cross-legged on the floor, looking up at him with those beautiful eyes. It was like being transported back in time. Seeing Poppy sitting on his bed, holding Mr Flumpkins, her face pale and tired, sad, refusing to answer his questions. Refusing to tell him why her eyes were rimmed in red. Why her shoulders were hunched. Why her sparkle had disappeared.

Bugger the tea. The only thing that was going to settle his nerves, the only way he was ever going to move forward with his life in a meaningful way, was to sort things out with Poppy once and for all.

***

Poppy's heart, her soul, wilted in relief as Ben settled himself on the floor, crossing his legs, mirroring her. The tension in his jaw had eased. The harsh light in his eyes had softened. And his shoulders no longer looked like they were permanently attached to the sides of his neck.

'You know the good thing about messes, Poppy?' Ben placed his hands on his knees, his back straight, proud. 'You can tidy them up.'

'Says the guy who keeps his side of the business pristine. Whose house would shake on its foundations if it saw a hint of dust.' Poppy gritted her teeth, tried to find the courage to say the words she'd been able to write in text form.

'There were crumbs in my bed this morning, remember? And my house seems stable as ever. So, what was in that string of messages you sent me?'

Poppy hugged herself tighter. No matter what happened next she had her unicorns. She had a shop. One that was showing all the signs of being successful. If things didn't work out with Ben, she could leave him be, and set up elsewhere. She would survive, as she had her entire life. She thought back to the tentative strands of reconnection she'd shared with her mother earlier. The jittery pit-pat of her heart settled. She wouldn't *just* survive. She would be fine. Maybe not better than fine anytime soon, but fine was a good starting place.

'I'm sorry feels like a good place to start.' Poppy locked eyes with Ben. He had to see what she was saying was coming from the heart. 'And I am. For so much. I shouldn't have left. Not just earlier today, but all those years ago. Not the way I did.'

'So, you're saying you still might have gone?' There was no censure in his words, just curiosity.

Poppy shrugged. 'Maybe. Maybe not. I couldn't have stayed at home for much longer. And when you said what you said the night I left, I panicked. Freaked. Felt I had to go.'

'What I said?' Ben's head angled in confusion, his forehead wrinkling into a frown. 'What do I have anything to do with it?'

Keep going, Poppy. You've got this. 'I didn't tell you the entire story about the night I left. I didn't tell you that...' Poppy's mouth

224

felt like it had been lined with moisture-sucking soft toy fur. 'I didn't tell you that before I saw my mother, you and I had a conversation. Except it wasn't really a conversation. It was three words. And you said them. And I wasn't ready to hear them. I was nowhere near ready to say them back, even if I knew deep down I felt them.' Poppy paused, waiting for the penny to drop. Waited some more. Ben's expression remained neutral, albeit with a narrowing of the eyes. How could he not say anything? She'd declared that she loved him. That she wanted to be with him. Except… she hadn't. And why would he care when loving her meant every chance that she'd up and leave if things got tough? 'I'm buggering this up,' she muttered to herself.

'No. You're not. I'm just…' Ben raked his hand through his hair, then cupped the back of his neck. 'I don't know that I understand what you're saying. I said something? Three words…' Recognition dawned in his widening eyes. 'Oh. Oh my God. I said… I don't remember. I mean, I was well toasted that night. I had no idea. I feel like I should say I'm sorry. I mean, things might have been so different if I hadn't said what I'd said. I can only imagine the pressure it put on you, especially on top of what your mother said…'

'Don't say you're sorry, Ben. You've nothing to be sorry for. As for things being different had you not said what you said… perhaps. But better?' Poppy slowly shook her head. 'I don't know about that. That space, that time away, was good for me. It gave me time to find out what I could do. What I was capable of. How strong I was. Maybe had I not gone away you'd have discovered I didn't fit into your very grown-up adult life.'

'Impossible. We were meant to be friends from the moment you poked your head through the hedge. I don't believe anything could have changed that.'

She dragged her gaze up from the floor to see Ben smiling, as wide and open and beautiful as his heart. 'There's one more thing I have to tell you. Something you need to know.' Poppy mashed her lips together, squeezed her eyes shut and willed herself to get the conversation over and done with. 'The thing is, the whole time I was away, I missed you. It didn't matter where I was, or who I was with, there was this Ben-shaped hole missing from my life. I'd hoped travelling to the ends of the earth, throwing myself into all sorts of new situations, would help me fill that space. Lord knows I used the distance to convince myself that had I stayed we'd have ended up hating each other. Resenting each other. That you'd one day see why my mother didn't love me, and then you too would push me away.' Poppy fiddled with the charms on her bracelet. Touchstones for the people, the places, she'd left. 'Time didn't fill the hole. Or space. Then one day – that day the picture was taken of me on the rocks in Kaikoura – I knew it was time to come home. Not just to start my business, but to return to you. And when I saw you at the airport in your fancy pants and shirt, I knew returning was the best thing I could have done. I may have been raised here in Muswell Hill, but you, Ben, are my home.'

'I see.' Ben's hand went to his chin, stroked it thoughtfully. 'I can wear that getup to work, if it means that much to you.'

So that was it. He was happy to keep her on as a business partner, but nothing more, and he was being light-hearted about it in order to let her down easy. After what she'd put him through she couldn't blame him.

Ben stretched his arms behind him and propped himself up on the palms of his hand. 'So, what was in those messages? You just told me a decent-sized story, those text notifications were coming far too thick and fast to be that.'

'Oh, you don't want to know what was in those messages.' Horror chilled Poppy's heart. It was one thing for Ben to read them if she thought there was a chance they would get back together. But to relay them to Ben the Friend? Ben the Colleague? Nope. No way were those words being spoken out loud.

'Actually, Poppy, I kind of do want to know what's in those

messages. I'm sure I could have one of my tech-savvy friends recover the texts for me if you're not comfortable sharing…'

God, either way she was doomed to die of embarrassment. Better to get it over and done.

'Earth, feel free to swallow me whole,' muttered Poppy as she reached up and grabbed her mobile from the counter behind her. 'Fine. But you need to know I wrote this in the heat of the moment, and I don't expect you to think anything or feel anything or even care. In fact…' She scrolled through the messages. 'Looking at these I wish I'd perhaps censored myself a little. Things are going to get awkward. Are you ready for that?'

Ben flicked her the thumbs up. 'Go for it.'

Poppy poked her tongue out, then cleared her throat. 'Here goes nothing.'

Ben, I'm sorry.

And I love you.

More than all the unicorns in my shop.

In the world.

I'm sorry.

I said that already, but it can't be said enough.

Because I really am sorry.

I ran because I was afraid.

Afraid you'd get bored of me.

Or that things would change between us.

And we wouldn't be 'us' anymore.

But I'm a dick.

Stop smiling.

Poppy glanced up to see Ben was indeed doing as she thought he'd do. It seemed she'd underestimated his reaction. His smile was a toothy grin, and his shoulders were shaking. She suppressed her own smile and returned her attention to the screen.

But I can't run anymore.

I can't let my fears stop me from finding out what might be.

Because what I know in here…

227

(I'm tapping my heart right now)
… Is that I love you.
I've always loved you.
And I don't think I'll ever stop.
And even if you don't love me back.
That's okay.
Because now I know I can love.
And that I want to love.
And if I love one person in my life.
I'm glad it's you.
Thank you for loving me, Ben.
Now stop ignoring me already.

Poppy set her phone down. Her heart rate had ratcheted up, but the roiling in her stomach had stilled. She swallowed hard, surprised to find no fear-filled lump was blocking the words. 'It's true, Ben. I love you. I love you more than anything.' She bum-shuffled her way towards Ben until their knees were touching.

'I don't know what to say.' Ben reached out and cupped Poppy's cheek. She leaned into his strong, sure touch.

'You don't have to say anything. I know I've been up and down like a yo-yo. I know that you might need time. I'm not going anywhere – if you don't want me to, that is. And if you decide I'm too much hard work then that's okay too. We had friendship first, and I'm happy with that. Mostly.' Poppy rolled her eyes. 'I mean I will be happy with that if I have to be. God, I really am useless at this love thing.'

'I think you're doing it rather wonderfully, actually.' Ben ran his thumb over her lips, across her cheek. 'I'm glad you want to stay on at the shop, but I feel we need to set up some new rules.'

'Ugh,' Poppy groaned. 'More rules. I'm so over rules.'

'You might like these ones. And there's only two. I think you can handle that.' Ben sat back, lifted his fist in the air and raised his thumb. 'First rule. You can't up and leave this shop. And I can't either. If for whatever reason one of us needs to exit the business we need to consult each other, chat it through, and if leaving is on the cards then it needs to be timely, not done in a rush.'

'No leaving in a hurry. Right.' Poppy nodded. 'What's the next rule?'

Ben raised his index finger. 'You'll let me love you. You see I think it's only fair that if you're going to be mooning around the shop loving me, that I can do the same.'

'Hmm.' Poppy placed her finger to her chin and cast her gaze to the ceiling. 'Tough rule. But I can live with it. I don't think we're going to need to worry about the first rule though.'

'Oh really? And why's that?'

Poppy took Ben's hands in hers. 'Because I'm going to be too busy loving you to ever think about leaving.'

'So, we have a deal?'

'Not quite. We need to make this love thing we've got going on official. A handshake won't do.' Poppy glanced round at the jewellery stand she had set up on the counter. She pushed herself up and sorted through the bracelets and necklaces, rings and earrings she had hanging off the stand. 'I'm sorry I didn't put your charm on with my others. Actually…' She stopped rummaging around and unhooked the heavy bracelet from her wrist, then placed it on the counter. 'That's better. You see that bracelet was filled with charms representing the past. Ah, here it is!' Poppy pulled a delicate silver link chain off the rack and fingered the tiny heart that linked the bracelet's ends together. She pulled the unicorn charm from her pocket. 'I didn't want your charm to be part of that. I don't want you to be the past. I want your charm, I want *you*, to represent the fu—' Poppy sniffed the air, an acrid waft filled her nose. 'Erm… what's burning?'

Ben slapped his forehead with an exasperated sigh. 'It's those bloody lemon meringue tarts. It's like they were cursed from the start.'

'Better them than us.' Poppy giggled. 'Although I did wonder…'

229

'I'd better go turn off the oven.'

Ben made to leave but Poppy pulled him back and wrapped her arms around his waist. 'Kiss first.'

Ben's lips found Poppy's. A quick peck and the embrace was broken.

Poppy stomped her foot. 'Really? Is this as romantic as our life's going to get?'

'Romance later. Stop the shop burning down now.' Ben winked as he jogged to the kitchen.

Poppy leaned against the counter, joy pumping through her veins, lighting up every atom in her body, as she fastened the unicorn charm onto the dainty chain. 'Love. I love you. I love you, Ben Evans. Love you, Ben. Hey Ben? I love you.' She turned the words over, liking how they rolled off the tongue. Natural. Like it was always meant to be.

'I like the way that sounds. All of it.'

She glanced up to see Ben in the doorway, a tray of blackened tarts in his mitted hands.

'And I also like that you know how to crack eggs. Come do some more for me while I get another batch of pastry ready.'

'Slave driver,' Poppy grumbled.

'Get used to it.' Ben laughed.

Poppy swatted his backside as she followed him into the kitchen, loving she could do that. Loving that she loved him. And that he loved her back.

Get used to it?

She fully intended to. For the rest of their lives.

Epilogue

What little light she could make out through the soft cloth of her eye mask darkened as the air transformed from clean, fresh and kissed by the sun, to earthy and damp.

'I know where you're taking me, Ben.' Poppy giggled as he tickled her waist, which he had firm hold of as he guided her towards her birthday surprise. 'You took me here last year remember? I'm going to have to knock points off for originality. I'm just waiting to feel the squish of dirt and grass under my feet.'

'Is that so?' Ben's voice was warm with good humour. 'We'll see about that.' He scooped her up in his arms and hugged her close. 'How do you know I'm not leading you astray? That it isn't all some big elaborate trick?'

'Because you're not a trickster, and the only person who's ever led us astray was me.' Poppy wrapped her arms around his neck and nuzzled into his shoulder, relishing the muscles she felt beneath his polo shirt. Every morning without fail he was up and at the gym for his swim and weights session. She was half-tempted to join him, if only to watch those muscles flex as he worked out. Tempted, but not enough that she was willing to give up the extra hour's sleep in his fancy giant bed. Correction. In *their* fancy giant bed.

The squeak of hinges as a door was pushed open told her they'd reached their destination.

'Are you ready?' Ben's voice was low, and Poppy was sure she caught a hint of nerves. What was beyond the blindfold?

Her pulse raced as the anticipation built. What might he have planned that could make Ben, the least-likely-to-be-rattled man in the world, sound this nervous?

A quick tug and the blindfold fell away. Poppy blinked once, twice, and again, accustoming herself to the golden glow of the room, while at the same time trying to figure out just what she was seeing.

They weren't at the cabin. They were at the shop. But their shop had been transformed into... well, she wasn't quite sure what.

Fairy lights hung in rows from the walls, criss-crossing the ceiling. Surrounding the walls were the tea shop's seats, each with a sequin cushion settled upon them. And in the corner that her plush unicorn toys usually occupied was a three-piece band.

With a tap-tap-tap of drumsticks, the band began to play. Swing music.

That's why they seemed familiar. They were the band that played the night she and Ben had kissed at the Summer's Night Festival.

'Champagne?' She spun round to see Joe, dressed in a pale-blue, Seventies-style suit, complete with ruffled shirt, holding a champagne flute in one hand and a bottle in the other.

'Where did you get that suit?' Poppy tugged on a ruffle as Joe poured. 'It's fabulous. Feel free to wear it to work.'

'Gladly. It cost me a small fortune from the vintage clothing store up the road. I need to get all the wear out of it I can.' Joe handed her the glass and bowed at the waist. 'Happy birthday, boss. I hope it's everything you've ever dreamed of, and more.' Setting the bottle in an ice-filled silver bucket, which was nested in an ornate metal stand, he backed away and disappeared out the door.

'Did you have to pay Joe to stay late?' Poppy turned to Ben who was sipping his own glass of champagne. Sipping? He'd taken a good swig from the looks of things.

'No, he was happy to do it free. He adores you. Adores the shop. And you know, if you did want to start spreading Sparkle & Steep's wings, he could well be the man to set up the next store. He and Sophie, both. Speaking of Sophie…' Ben coughed into his hand and Sophie emerged from the kitchen, dressed in an elegant black cocktail dress, a makeshift bowtie around her neck, a silver tray filled with delicious looking canapés in one hand.

'Hungry?' She set the tray on the counter. 'I can recommend the crab toast, and ceviche spoons.'

Ben rolled his eyes as Sophie backed away, a smirk on her lips. 'I told her she wasn't to sample the goods until all our guests had arrived.'

Poppy helped herself to a ceviche spoon. 'Can't say I blame her, these look delicious.' Looked and tasted. She involuntarily moaned as the mix of cream and zesty lemon, along with the freshness of the tuna, melted in her mouth. 'So good. And what do you mean by "guests"? Who are these guests you speak of?'

'You'll see.' Ben raised his eyebrows, then took her by the hand. The small act sent tingles of electricity, far more delicious and far more moreish than any canapé, up Poppy's arm, then down her spine. Would he ever stop having this effect on her? She hoped not.

With a fancy foot shuffle, he began to lead her about the room, their bodies in perfect time, just as they had been the night they'd first danced together. The night they'd first kissed.

'I really did think you were taking me to the cabin again.' Poppy pressed her cheek against Ben's, breathed in his heady fresh scent. 'I can't believe you managed to trick me.'

233

'It was surprisingly easy, actually. I had Joe shove a container of dirt under your nose as we walked closer to the shop. And Sophie held a piece of cardboard over your head in order to make it seem like trees were blocking out the sun. When I swooped you up I was able to dull the street noise when you leaned into me by cupping your other ear under the guise of stroking your hair.'

Poppy ducked her head back, hoping to catch a cheeky grin on Ben's face that would tell her he was having her on. But there was no cheeky grin. Just an innocent pair of eyes and an air of dead seriousness. 'You went to all that trouble to trick me?'

'I wouldn't want you getting bored, Poppy.' Ben kissed the tip of her nose, then spun her out, and brought her back in so she was pressed up against him, but not facing him, as they swayed back and forth.

Poppy leaned into his touch and counted her blessings for what must have been the gazillionth time in the last year that Ben was hers. She was his. They were each other's. 'I'd never be bored of you. If I were going to tire of you I would have that time you insisted we weren't to smuggle our way into the cinema because it was essentially stealing, and you wouldn't be party to that kind of behaviour. And those were your exact words.' She squealed in delight as Ben whirled her out unexpectedly, then brought her to a stop in front of him in perfect time with the end of the song.

She blinked when she realised he wasn't standing in front of her, instead he was kneeling, and looking up at her with adoration in his eyes. Adoration, and that hint of nerves that had confused her, but had now become perfectly explainable.

Her stomach flip-flopped, tumbled, twisted and turned as a herd of unicorns ran amuck in her stomach, trampling back and forth, dipping and diving. What was going on? What was she seeing? 'Ben.' The word came out a whisper. 'What are you doing?'

In the back of her mind she registered the change of tempo

234

in the music as the band began to play the song she and Ben had slow danced to. He really had planned everything out. As always.

'I'm hoping you're serious when you say you'll never tire of me,' Ben whispered back. He let go of her hand, dove into his pocket and pulled something out.

Something delicate. Something sparkly. Something… perfect.

An oval opal, shimmering with greens and blues, pinks and yellows, surrounded by a halo of diamonds.

Poppy pinched the skin on her inner forearm to make sure she wasn't dreaming. Was this really happening? Was Ben about to ask her to… 'Ben, I need to check on something. This fancy ring you've got there, is that what I think it is? I just don't want to find out I'm thinking something daft, and then when you realise what I'm thinking you'll freak out and run away, and then the shops will be in disarray, and it would be all to do with one ridiculous jump to a conclusion.'

'Geez, woman, can't you leave a tender moment alone?' Ben shook his head, then held out his free hand to Poppy. 'Help me up, my knee's gone stiff.'

'Romantic.' Poppy matched his head shake, then pulled him up.

'Romantic was what I was going for, although I'm not sure it's going to plan. I'll rectify that, shall I?' Ben cleared his throat and held the ring up so that it sat in the space between their hearts. 'Since that braided head of yours popped through the hedge to say hello you've had a place in my heart, Poppy Taylor. When you left, you left a hole that no amount of work or any other person could fill. When you returned, you filled that hole.'

'I'm human spackle,' Poppy muttered, then mimed zipping her lip when Ben gave her an exasperated glare. 'Sorry,' she mouthed.

'It's not just my heart you've filled, it's my life, it's my soul. It's my everything. Because, you Poppy Taylor, *are* my everything.

Which is why I'd love for you to do me the honour of becoming my wife.' Ben paused, his head dipped closer as he took hold of her hand and held it in his, his thumb stroking her skin, sending zaps of happiness mixed with love spilling through her. 'Will you marry me, Poppy?'

'Ye…' The word came out a croak. She turned her head and coughed into her shoulder. 'Sorry. Too happy. Can't talk.' She coughed again, straightened up and pulled herself together. 'Yes. Yes, I will. I would be honoured to marry you, Ben Evans.'

Ben took hold of Poppy's hand, ran his fingers over her knuckles, then slid the ring on her finger.

'Nice ring, by the way. It's really quite unicorn-esque' She grinned as he tugged her towards him, a delicious mix of desire and joy darkening his eyes as he leaned in and placed one of his spine-zapping, goose-bump-rippling kisses on her lips.

'It was my grandmother's. Mum had it tucked away for the day we came to our senses and found each other again.'

'And I'm so glad you did. And I'm even gladder, Poppy, that you've said "yes".' Pam made her way through the kitchen door, carrying a bottle of champagne, followed by Ben's father, flutes in hand. 'I'm one step closer to having grandchildren.'

'We both are.' Poppy's mum brought up the rear. 'Congratulations you two. May your life together be as happy as it is long.'

'Thanks, Mum.' Poppy kissed her mother's cheek.

How was it possible to have so much happiness bubbling inside and not pop? How was she lucky enough to be surrounded by people who loved her, treasured her, and who wished she and Ben the best?

'I can't believe this is happening.' She turned to Ben, wrapped her arms around his neck, and began to sway to the lilting tune filling the room. 'Mrs Poppy Evans.' She turned the words over, liking how her future name rolled off the tongue. Natural. Like it was always meant to be. 'I'm glad we found each other again.'

'Truth be told, Poppy, I don't think we ever left each other.'

His lips found hers, soft, tender, full of hope, full of the kind of future she'd never dared believe she could have.

Steeped in history. Sparkling with hope.

And built on the most solid of foundations – friendship, respect, acceptance, but most importantly... love.

And the magic of unicorns.

Acknowledgements

The first thank you has to go to the crew at my favourite eating spot, The Milk Bar. Carol, Shannon, Erin and Leigh – thank you for fueling me with your excellent coffee and nourishing me with your amazing food during the writing of this book. I don't know that it would have happened without you! I'm honoured to be considered a piece of your fabulous cafe's furniture.

To The Husband. Thank you for letting me bounce story and scene ideas off you, and for not minding when dinner is 'there's stuff in the fridge, help yourself'. Most of all, thanks for keeping me on and for believing in me.

A massive thank you to Rhys Watkinson and Sandra Pavic-Watkinson for answering all the questions about Muswell Hill that Google couldn't. I can't wait to visit one day and see your beautiful corner of the world.

Natalie Gillespie – I'm so grateful for the way you put me straight when I can't figure out the English equivalent of my crazy Kiwi-isms. You rock, girlfriend!

Thank you to HQ Digital for letting me write another book for your good selves. You've given me the chance to follow my dream and I'm eternally grateful.

Hannah Smith. You. Are. A. Legend. Your honesty, humour, insight and guidance have made working on this book with you an absolute pleasure. I count myself lucky to be one of your writers. Bring on the next one!

Dear Reader,

Thank you so much for taking the time to read this book – we hope you enjoyed it! If you did, we'd be so appreciative if you left a review.

Here at HQ Digital we are dedicated to publishing fiction that will keep you turning the pages into the early hours. We publish a variety of genres, from heartwarming romance, to thrilling crime and sweeping historical fiction.

To find out more about our books, enter competitions and discover exclusive content, please join our community of readers by following us at:

🐦 @HQDigitalUK

f facebook.com/HQDigitalUK

Are you a budding writer? We're also looking for authors to join the HQ Digital family! Please submit your manuscript to:

HQDigital@harpercollins.co.uk.

Hope to hear from you soon!

Read on for a sneak peek at *The Cosy Coffee Shop of Promises...*

Chapter 1

'Wine. Now. And don't get mouthy with me.'

Mel watched Tony's sea-blue eyes light up as his lips parted slightly...

'What's got your knick...'

'I'm serious,' she cut in, before he had a chance to be the second person to grind her gears that day. 'I'm in no mood for your cheek. And I can tell by that twitchy jaw of yours that you're contemplating still trying to give me some.' Mel took off her navy peacoat and shuddered as wintry air wrapped its way around her thin form. She promptly buttoned up again and tugged her scarf tighter around her neck. 'All I want from you is for you to do your job, pour me a glass of pinot gris and leave me to drink it, alone, and in peace. And why is it so cold in here? It's freezing out. It shouldn't be freezing in.' She shook her head. 'No matter. I don't care. The wine will warm me up.'

'Bu...'

'No. No buts. No whys. No questions.' She pointed to the glass-doored fridge. 'Just get the bottle, get a glass, and pour.' Mel gave Tony her best glare, hoping to get past his notoriously thick skin.

She watched the muscles in his jaw continue to work, as if

debating whether to ignore her order to be left in peace or do that clichéd 'had a bad day, tell me about it' barman patter. Sensibility must have won, because he turned and bent over to grab a bottle of pinot gris from the chiller, giving her a fantastic view of his toned and rounded rear. A view she'd usually take a moment to appreciate, but not right now, not after the unexpected, and not in a good way, phone call she'd just received from her mother.

Tony sloshed the wine into a tired-looking, age-speckled glass, pushed it in her direction, then punched at the card machine. 'Here you go,' he said, proffering the handset.

Mel squinted at the numbers on the screen. 'Tony, um, that's not right. You've overcharged me.'

'No, that's the price.' Tony nodded, but kept his eyes firmly on the bar. 'Since the beginning of this week.'

'Really? You can't tell me a bottle of wine rose in price by almost double in the space of seven days?'

'You're right, it hasn't.' He glanced up. 'But the hole in my muffler is yelling at me to put the prices up. And I haven't in years, so…'

'Oh. Okay. Sorry.' Mel handed over her bank card, embarrassed to have questioned the price rise. She'd heard the village gossip. Tony's business wasn't doing so well. Apparently hadn't been for years, but had got worse since his dad passed away the year before. Not that she knew much about that. She'd been new to town, and didn't want to get a reputation as a gossip, so had only heard the odd conversation here and there over the coffee cups in her café, nothing more.

'So, are you going to just stare into that glass of wine or are you going to drink it? Because I don't have a funnel to pour it back into the bottle. Although reselling it would make my mechanic happier faster. And if you buy two glasses I might even be able to afford to put the heating on.'

Mel shot Tony a grateful smile. Despite his infamous reputation as a ladies' man, he was also known about the small farming town of Rabbits Leap as being something of a gentleman and had quite the knack of making you feel at ease, which, considering her current heightened state of irritation, was quite a feat.

'You're still not taking a sip, or a slug. And, well, it sounds like you needed a slug.'

Mel narrowed her eyes at Tony, hoping to scare him into shutting up with a stern look. 'What did I say about getting mouthy? And teasing for that matter?'

'I'm not teasing. You look pale. Paler than usual, and you know you're pretty pale, so you're almost translucent right now. Even the bright streaks of pink in your hair are looking a little less hot.'

'You pay attention to my hair colour?' Mel's hand unconsciously went to her hair and tucked a stray lock behind her ears. Tony looked at her hair? Since when? She'd always assumed he'd seen her as nothing more than a regular customer, a friendly acquaintance, not someone to take notice of. Sure, they got along well enough, would chat for a moment or two if they passed each other on the street, or if it was quiet in the pub, but that was the extent of their relationship.

'Well, you're about the most exciting thing to happen in this place for the last ten years…'

'Me? Exciting?' A tingle of pleasure stirred within her.

Tony winked and turned that tingle into a zing. Since her last boyfriend, the local vet, had taken off to care for animals overseas, Mel hadn't had any action, let alone a compliment, from a man. And apparently, if that unexpected zing frenzy that had zipped through her body was anything to go by, she'd been craving it.

'Yeah, exciting.' Tony's glance lingered on her face, as if drinking her in. 'And pretty, too.'

She rolled her eyes, trying to ignore the way her body reacted

247

to the words of approval. She picked up her glass and took the suggested slug. She was being stupid. Tony wasn't calling *her* exciting, just her hair. And the only reason he was calling her pretty was because that's what he did; he called women pretty, he charmed them, he took them to bed, and that was that. And she'd had enough of her love life – heck, her life in general – ending with 'that was that' to be interested in someone who'd pretty much created the phrase.

'Feel better?' His eyes, usually dancing with humour, were crinkled at the corners with concern.

'Not really.'

'Have another slug.'

As she lifted the glass she glanced around the bar, taking in the bar leaners with their tired, ring-stained, laminated tops and obsolete ashtrays in their centres. The tall stools next to them looked rickety from decades of propping up farmers, the pool table needed a resurface, and as for the dartboard… it was covered in so many tiny pin holes it was amazing a dart could stay wedged in it. The village chatter was right, Tony was doing it tough…

Her eyes fell on a machine sitting at the far end of the bar. All shiny and silvery and gleaming with newness. That shouldn't be there.

Her blood heated up, and not in an 'oh swoon, a man just complimented me' kind of way.

'What is that?' Mel seethed through gritted teeth.

She couldn't believe what she was seeing. What was he thinking? Did he have it in for her, too? Was it 'Let's Piss Off Mel Day'? She'd moved to Rabbits Leap just over a year ago to try and create a sense of security for herself. A place she could settle down in, call home, maybe even meet a nice, normal guy she could fall in love with. And in one day what little security she'd carefully built was in danger of being blown apart. First her mother calling to tell her she was coming to town and bringing her special brand of crazy with her, and now this?

'What's what?' The crinkles of concern further deepened.

'That.' She pointed to the cause of her ire.

'The coffee machine?'

'Yeah, the coffee machine. The coffee machine that should not be in your bar, because I have a coffee machine. In my café. The only café in the village. You remember that? The one place a person can get a good cup of coffee? The place that just happens to be my livelihood, and you want to screw with it?'

Tony took a step back as if he'd been hit with a barrage of arrows. *Good.* His eyebrows gathered in a frown. But he didn't look sorry. Why didn't he look sorry? And why had he straightened up and stopped looking stricken?

'It's just business, Mel.'

'And it's just a small village, Tony.'

She looked at her wine and considered throwing the contents of it over him, then remembered how much it had cost. Taking the glass she brought it to her mouth and tipped it back, swallowing the lot in one long gulp.

She set the glass back on the bar, gently, so he wouldn't see how shaken she was. 'There's only enough room in this village for one coffee machine.' She mentally slapped herself as the words came out with a wobble, not as the threat she'd intended.

'And what does that mean?' Tony folded his arms and leant in towards her, his eyebrow raised.

Mel gulped. He wanted her to throw down the gauntlet? Fine then. 'It means you can try to make coffee. You can spend hours trying to get it right, make thousands of cups, whatever. But your coffee will never be as good as mine and all you'll have is a big hunk of expensive metal sitting unloved at the end of your bar.'

'Sounds like you're challenging me to a coffee-off.'

How could Tony be so cavalier? So unfazed by the truth? He'd spent a ton of money on something he'd only end up regretting.

249

Mel took a deep breath, picked up her wallet and walked to the door. She spun round to face her adversary.

'There's no challenge here. All you're good for is pulling a pint or three. Coffee? That's for the adults. You leave coffee to me.'

She leant into the old pub door, pushed it with all her might and lurched over the threshold into the watery, late-winter sun and shivered. Could today get any worse?

***

Had he done the wrong thing? Was buying that ridiculous monstrosity and installing it in the pub a stupid idea? He'd spent the last decent chunk of money he had to get it. What if it didn't fly? What would happen next? He couldn't keep the place open on the smell of a beer-soaked carpet, but he couldn't fail either. It was all he had left to remind him of his family. The Bullion had been his dad's baby. The one thing that had kept his dad sane after his mother had passed away. More than that, it was where what few solid memories he had of his mother were. Her smiling at him as he sat at the kitchen table munching on a biscuit while she cooked in the pub's kitchen. The violet scent of her perfume as she'd pulled his four-year-old self into a cuddle after he'd fallen from a bar stool while on an ambitious mountaineering expedition.

Then there was the promise he'd made to his father, the final words they'd shared as his father breathed his last. His vow to preserve The Bullion's history, to keep her alive. Dread tugged at his heart. What if he couldn't keep that promise?

God, why couldn't his father have been more open, more honest with him about their financial situation? Why couldn't he have put away his pride for one second and seen a bank manager, cap in hand, asked for a... Tony shoved the idea away. No. That wasn't an option. Not then. Not now. The McArthurs don't ask

250

for help. That was his dad's number-one rule. A rule his father had also drilled into him. No, he wasn't going cap in hand to a bank manager. He didn't even own a cap, anyway. He just had to come up with some new ideas to breathe life into the old girl. The coffee machine had been one of them, and he'd spent the last of his personal savings buying it.

But what if Mel was right? What if he couldn't make a good coffee? Heck, what if she stole into the pub in the middle of the night and tampered with it so he couldn't?

Tony shook his head. The potential for poverty was turning him paranoid. Besides, the coffee machine was a great idea. Lorry drivers were always stopping in looking for a late-night cup, and who knew? Maybe the locals would like a cup of herbal tea or something before heading home after a big night.

Buy herbal tea. He added the item to his mental grocery list, along with bread, bananas and milk. Maybe he'd see if there was any of that new-age herbal tea stuff that made you sleep. Normally he'd do what his dad had always done and have a cup of hot milk with a dash of malt to send him off. But lately it hadn't done the trick and he'd spent more hours tossing and turning than he had actually sleeping, his mind ticking over with mounting bills, mounting problems and not a hell of a lot of solutions. Heck, he was so bone-tired he wasn't even all that interested in girls. Maybe that was the problem? Maybe he needed to tire himself out …

'Hey, baby brother!'

'Might be. But I'm still taller than you.' Tony grinned at his sister and two nephews as they piled into the pub. 'How you doing, you little scallywags?'

'Scallywags?!'

Tony laughed as the boys feigned insult and horror in perfect unison.

'You heard me. Now come and give your old uncle a hug.'

The boys flew at him, nearly knocking him over as they hurled themselves into his outstretched arms. He drew them in and held them, breathing in the heady mix of mud and cinnamon scent that he was pretty sure they'd been born with.

'Have we cuddled you long enough? Can we have a lemonade now?' Tyler peered up at him with a hopeful eye.

'And a bag of crisps?' asked Jordan, his voice filled with anticipation, and just a hint of cheek.

'Each?' They pleaded in perfect unison.

Two peas in a pod those boys were. And the loves of Jody's life. Since the day she'd found out she'd fallen pregnant to a man she'd met during a shift at the pub, a random, a one-nighter, she'd sworn off all men until the boys were old enough to fend for themselves.

Tony watched as the boys grabbed a bag of crisps each and poured two glasses of lemonade and wondered at what point Jody would decide they were old enough, because at nine they looked pretty well sorted, and he was pretty sure he spotted flashes of loneliness in her eyes when she saw couples holding hands over the bar's leaners.

'So what's with the shiny new toy?' Jody jerked her head down towards the end of the bar.

'It's what's going to save this place.'

Jody snorted and took a sip of Tyler's lemonade, ignoring his wail of displeasure. 'It's going to take a whole lot more than coffee to save this dump.'

Tony bristled. Just because this place wasn't the love of her life it didn't mean it wasn't the love of his, and just as she wouldn't hear a bad word said about her boys, he didn't like a bad word said…

'And don't get all grumpy on me, Tony McArthur. I know you love this joint, but it needs more than one person running it. You need to …'

'If you say settle down, I'll turn the soda dispenser on you.'

'Oooh, soda water, colour me scared.'

'Not soda, dear sister. Raspberry fizzy. Sweet, sticky and staining.'

Jody stuck her tongue out. 'But you should, you know, settle down. It'll do you good having a partner in crime.'

'You're one to talk.'

'I'm well settled down and I've got two partners in crime, right, boys?'

Tony laughed again as the boys rolled their eyes, then took off upstairs to his quarters where his old gaming console lay gathering dust.

'Besides, you're only going to piss off the café girl with that machine in here. You're treading on her turf, and frankly it's not a particularly gentlemanly thing to do.'

Heat washed over Tony's face. Even though he had a reputation for liking the ladies he always tried to treat them well. But that was pleasure, and this was business. Not just business, it was life and death. Actually, it was livelihood or death. And he intended to keep on kicking for as long as possible. Without the bar he was nothing. No one.

'Well, I can see by the flaming shame on your face that she's seen it.'

'Yep,' he sighed. The more he looked at the hunk of metal the worse he felt about what he'd done. There was an unspoken rule among the business people of Rabbits Leap that they didn't poach customers. It was akin to stealing. Yet he'd done just that in a bid to save The Bullion. What was worse, he'd done it to a member of the community he actually respected and always had time for.

'Tony, you've got to apologise, and then take the machine back. Do something. It's a small town and the last thing you need is to be bad-mouthed or to lose customers. Find a way to make it work.'

***

Ting-a-ling.

Mel looked up from arranging a fresh batch of scones on a rose-printed vintage cake stand to see who'd walked in, her customer-ready smile fading as she saw her tall, broad-shouldered, blond, wavy-haired nemesis.

'Get out.' Her words were cool and calm, the opposite of the fire burning in her veins, in her heart. No one was taking away her café, her chance at a stable life, especially not a pretty boy who was used to getting what he wanted with a smile and a wink.

'Is that any way to treat a customer?'

'You're not a customer. You never have been. I've not seen you step foot in here since I opened up – not once.' Mel pointed to the door. 'So get out.'

'Well, maybe it's time I decided to change that. And besides…'

She watched Tony take in the quiet café. Empty, bar her two regulars, Mr Muir and Mrs Wellbelove, who were enjoying their cups of tea and crosswords in separate silence.

'…It looks like you need the business.'

Mel rankled at the words as they hit home. She'd hoped setting up in Rabbits Leap would be a good, solid investment, that it would give her security. But that 'security' was looking as tenuous as her bank balance. The locals weren't joking when they said it was 'the town that tourism forgot'. In summer the odd tourist ambled through, lost, on their way to Torquay. But, on seeing there was nothing more than farms and hills, they quickly ambled out again. As for winter? You could've lain down all day in the middle of the street without threat of being run over. And this winter had been worse, what with farmers shutting up shop due to milk prices falling even further.

'Really? I need the business?' She raised an eyebrow, hoping the small act of defiance would annoy him as much as he'd annoyed her. 'I'm not the one putting prices up. Unlike someone else standing before me…'

Tony threw his hands up in the air as if warding the words off.

Good, she'd got to him.

'Look, Mel, I'm not here to fight.'

'Then what are you here for?'

'Coffee. A flat white. And a scone. They look good.'

'They are good.'

'Then I'll take one.' Tony rubbed his chin. 'Actually, make that two.'

Mel faked ringing up the purchase on the vintage cash register she'd found after scouring auction sites for weeks and weeks. 'That'll be on the house.'

'That's a bit cheap, isn't it?' Tony's lips lifted in a half-smile.

'It's on me. A man desperate enough to install a coffee machine in a pub clearly needs a bit of charity.' Yes, Tony was trying to take business away from her, but really, how much of a threat would he be to her business anyway? It wasn't like he could actually make a decent cup of coffee.

'So, are you going to stand there staring at me like I'm God's gift or are you going to give me my free scones?'

Mel blushed.

'Sorry, I wasn't staring. Just…'

'Imagining me kissing you. Yeah, yeah, I know. Don't worry, you're not the first woman.'

'I wasn't.' Mel sputtered, horrified. 'I wouldn't.'

'I know. I'm teasing. Relax.'

The word had the opposite effect. Mel's body coiled up, ready to attack at the next thing he said that irritated her.

Why was he having this effect on her? Usually nothing ruffled her feathers, or her multicoloured hair. She'd weathered so much change in her life that something as small as someone making an attempt to kill off her coffee business should be laughable. But as she looked into his handsome and openly amused face she wanted to take up her tongs, grab his earlobe in its metal

255

claws, give it a good twist, then drag him to the door and shove him out of it. Instead she picked up the tongs, fished two scones out onto a plate, added a pat of butter and passed the plate to him.

'Can you just… sit. I'll bring your coffee to you.'

With a wink and a grin Tony did exactly as she asked, leaving her to make his coffee in peace. The familiar ritual of grinding the beans, tamping them down, smelling the rich aroma of the coffee as it dripped into a cup while she heated the milk relaxed her, so much more than a man telling her to relax ever would. Maybe the problem wasn't that he was trying to ruin her business; maybe it was that he was trying to take away the most stability she'd had in years.

After her café in Leeds had shown the first signs of bottoming out, Mel had sold while the going was better than worse and decided to search out a new spot to move to. She'd had two rules in mind. One, the place had to have little to no competition. Two, after moving around for so many years, she finally wanted to find a place she would come to call home. So she'd packed up her life, headed south, and stumbled across Rabbits Leap after getting lost and motoring about inland Devon with a perilously low tank of petrol.

The moment she'd seen the pretty village filled with blooming flower boxes, kids meandering down the main street licking ice creams without parents helicoptering about them, and a store smack bang in the middle with a 'for rent' sign stuck to the door, a little part of her heart had burst into song. The plan had been to settle down, set up shop and make enough to save and survive. But, as she watched Tony flick through a fashion magazine, she could see her plans to make Rabbits Leap her forever home go the way of coffee dregs, down the gurgler.

She picked up the coffee and walked it over to Tony's table where he was stuffing his face.

'Your coffee.'

'Thish shcone is amazhing.' Tony swallowed and brushed crumbs from his lips and chin.

Full lips, strong angular chin, Mel noted, before mentally swatting herself. She wasn't meant to be perving at the enemy. 'Well, it's my grandma's secret recipe, so it should be.'

'Can I have the recipe?'

'What part of secret do you not understand?' She set the cup down with a clank.

'Sit.' Tony pushed out the chair opposite him with his foot.

'I've things to do.'

'Sit.'

Mel huffed, then did as she was told.

'So how are things?' Tony picked up the cup and took a sip, giving a small grunt of appreciation.

'That's how good yours are going to have to be.' Mel folded her arms across her chest and tipped her head to the side. A small show of arrogance, but for all the things she wasn't great at, she knew she could cook and she could make a damn good cup of coffee.

'It's good to know the benchmark.' Tony's voice was strong but she was sure a hint of panic flashed through those blue sparklers of his. 'Anyway, this isn't about me. How are you? I haven't seen you in the pub with that vet of yours for a while now.'

Mel narrowed her eyes in suspicion. 'Have you been staking me out? Figuring all the ways you can try and horn in on my bit of business?'

'Rabbits Leap makes a habit of knowing Rabbits Leap. We keep an eye on our own. We take care of our own…' A tightening of those lush lips. A moment of regret? No matter. He'd given her ammunition.

'You take care of your own by taking over parts of their businesses? My, how civically minded you are.'

'I know you're annoyed about the machine, Mel, but you don't have to be sarcastic about it. Can't we deal with the situation like adults?'

Mel's grip around herself tightened as her irritation soared. 'I can be whatever I want in my café. And I can say whatever I want, however I want, especially when dealing with a coffee thief. What's next? You'll be calling my beans supplier? Good luck with that. They know what loyalty means.'

Tony's lips thinned out more. Good. She was getting to him. Giving him something to think about.

'As for the vet? Not that it's any of your business but we're over. He decided small-town veterinary work wasn't for him and headed over to Africa to work with wildebeest or something like that.'

'Thought he would.'

'Really?' Mel's chin lifted in surprise. She'd never thought Tony was the kind of guy who delved below the surface of anything. With that easy smile and light laugh, he seemed… well, about as shallow as one of the puddles that amassed on the main street after a spring shower.

'Yeah, he had that look about him, the "this place will do for now" look. I've seen it before. I knew it was only a matter of time before he left.' Tony picked up his coffee and took a sip. 'God, this really is good. Is everything you do this good?'

Mel's ears prickled hot. Was she imagining it or was that a double entendre? She met his blue eyes and saw not a hint of sparkle or tease. Nope, no double entendre; he wasn't trying to pick her up.

'I guess that means I was "this girl will do for now",' she said out loud, more to herself than to Tony.

'Then he was a fool. A man would be lucky to have a pink-haired barista and amazing cook loving him, cooking for him and making his morning coffee.'

'That sounds more like a slave-master relationship than a real, true-love one…'

'I'm sure the man would repay you in other ways.'

This time the sparkle was definitely in his eyes.

'I'd make sure he did.' The words came out before she could stop them, along with a wink. *Traitor*. She dipped her head to hide the flush creeping up over her cheeks. How dare her body flirt so easily with the enemy, even though, with his kind words, he was acting more like a friend. Or someone who might be angling for something more than that. Not that she'd ever sleep with the enemy. Uh-uh. No way.

Taking a long, slow, cooling breath she looked up into Tony's eyes. Something flashed through them. Something quick, hot, fierce. A heck of a lot like desire. Had he been thinking about her... with him? Mel shook the thought clear. Nope, that'd never happen. They were chalk and cheese. Besides, there was no way she was playing around with the local lothario. He didn't tick any of her boxes. Well, not all of them. Hot. Yes. Fun. Yes. But he couldn't commit. She'd heard the village gossip. He was a one-man band. No woman lasted more than a night. Anyway, he was hardly boyfriend material. He only loved himself, and he was obviously careless with money, which meant careless with security, and that was the one thing Mel was always careful about.

'So why did you come here, Tony?'

'I need to apologise and then we need to have a conversation.'

Mel sat up straighter in her chair. An apology? She hadn't seen that coming. 'So, apologise.'

'I'm sorry I bought the coffee machine. Actually, I'm not. But I'm sorry you had to find out about it like that.'

'Not much of an apologiser, are you?'

He at least had the good grace to look slightly ashamed.

'Well, I'm hoping we can come to an arrangement about it.'

'Really? How about I arrange for it to be removed and you go back to bartending?'

'How about you teach me how to use it... and maybe even teach me how to cook?'

259

Mel couldn't believe what she was hearing. Was Tony mentally deficient?

'Cook? What are you on?'

'That smell, what is it?'

Mel sniffed the air and remembered she had lamb shanks slow-cooking in a tomato balsamic jus in the back kitchen.

'That's my dinner.'

'It smells amazing.'

'Don't try and distract me.' She waved her hand in impatience. 'Why would I teach you my whole trade? Coffee and baking? I'd be out of business within weeks.'

'No, I don't want to know how to bake. I'm talking about learning to cook real food, like whatever it is you've got going back there.' Tony's eyes sparkled with excitement.

Mel could almost see the ideas forming in his head. His whole demeanour was changing in front of her eyes, energy fair sparking off his disturbingly muscular body.

'You've seen the food we do at The Bullion. It's all deep-fried and artery-clogging. I need to get with the times, update the menu, make it appealing, *maybe* even get entertainment in on special nights, see if I can't pull in a few more punters. Turn the place into a tourist attraction, or something. Which would be good for your business, too…'

Tony leaned forward and placed his hand over hers.

Pull away.

But she couldn't. Tony's fingers tightened around the outer edges of her fist, warm, strong, capable. Hands that knew how to work. Weren't afraid of getting dirty…

Did he work out, she mused, as her eyes travelled up the length of his legs and settled on his stomach. Was there a six-pack hiding beneath that grey T-shirt? Strongly defined, hard thighs underneath those denims? Biceps made for picking a woman up and pinning her to a wall…

Get it together, girl! She squeezed her eyes shut, hoping not seeing Tony would stop those unneeded images forming in her head. It didn't work. Was this the effect he had on women? Is that why he was known for having a string of them? Was he truly irresistible?

'So are you going to help me? Or are you too busy meditating over there?'

Mel tugged her hand out from under his and rubbed her face wearily. It had been a long day. Between her mother's announcement sending her stomach into free-fall and the revelation that the man sitting opposite her had decided to pit himself against her in the business stakes, she was ready to go to bed. Alone.

'What's in it for me?' Mel opened her eyes to see Tony giving her a charming smile.

'The pleasure of my company?'

'I'm not seeing anything pleasurable about your company.' The lie came quick and easy.

'Well, maybe it's time you did.' Tony's teasing tone was back. 'Look, how about this for a deal. You help me create a dinner menu, maybe show me how to make a decent coffee…'

Mel's eyebrows shot up, her hackles rising.

'…and I promise to not serve the java until your café closes at…'

'Three.'

'Three it is.'

'I still don't feel like it's a good enough deal for me to give you this much help…'

'Any wine you drink at the pub will be free for the duration of your help?'

The teasing tone was tinged with desperation. Tony had alluded to things not going great, things needing fixing, but maybe he was in deeper than he was willing to let on? And maybe – an idea flitted about her mind – he could help her with her latest drama, the drama that was about to blow into town any day now…

'Okay. I'm insane for doing this, I'll probably regret it with every fibre of my being, but okay. I'll help you… but you've got to do one more thing for me.'

'Anything. Just name it.'

Mel screwed up her courage and forced the words out before she could talk herself out of them. 'I need you to be my fiancé.'

DIGITAL HQ

If you enjoyed *The Little Unicorn Gift Shop*, then why not try
another feel-good romance from HQ Digital?